Dictates of the Servators: Book 1

LEVITICUS

Kallen Samuels

ISBN: 978-1-7779901-0-7
Imprint: Innov@t Publishing - https://www.innovat.org

DEDICATION

Thank you to my family and friends
for their feedback and support.

CONTENTS

ACKNOWLEDGMENTS

Cover design: Kallen Samuels
Editor: Theresa Rempel

Other books by Kallen Samuels

Levigator – Dictates of the Servators: Book 2
Leavening – Dictates of the Servators: Book 3

Prologue

Selica shivered in the cold chambers of the Third Anarch. An *escort* had dragged her from her work without explanation in the middle of a complicated writ weave. She shook her head at the thought. *You have bigger worries than writ weaves right now.*

She glanced at the man who'd brought her here. He'd stationed himself at the door and no longer seemed to have an interest in her. Selica knew better — the Sicari were notorious assassins, skilled in intrigue. She had no doubt he could sense her fear from across the room. If the Sicari were involved, then the Anarch either felt threatened or meant to threaten someone. Since she posed little threat at all, it had to be the latter, but she couldn't imagine why. She'd spent the last ten years dutifully serving, never causing trouble. She'd completed her tasks well, but not too well. Every action calculated to avoid unwanted attention — to be forgotten — to avoid this very meeting. *Why has he summoned me?*

Cruel looking knives adorned the walls, suiting the Anarch's character. She shivered again, but not from the cold. A long-forgotten memory surfaced. She was a child, clinging to her mother's leg — eyes squeezed shut to block out the angry bellowing of what must surely be a monster. Selica recalled her mother yelling back, but nothing beyond that. She didn't want to remember — she would rather be anywhere but here.

"It's been awhile."

Selica was startled. She hadn't noticed the Anarch's arrival. Somehow, his stealth made him seem that much worse. She held her tongue. One did not speak to an Anarch without permission.

Toller Villecrest bade her stand and gave her an assessing look. "You're not a little girl anymore, you've inherited your mother's — charm."

Rage threatened to loosen Selica's tongue. Oh, how she wanted to wipe that smile off his face and pay him back for all he had done.

The Third Anarch's feral grin receded. "And your mother's defiance as well, I see. Remember your place." The Anarch nodded, indicating that he expected a response.

"Of course, Anarch. How may I serve?"

"I've heard you are a talented writ weaver. Is this true?"

Selica knit her brows in consternation. "I don't know why anyone would say so. My work is passable — average."

Toller raised his voice in warning. "Don't lie to me. I'm aware that you like people to think so, but you can't hide true talent. Your coworkers all recognize it in you. You offer creative solutions and grasp matters quickly where others struggle. I'm told you picked up writ weaving on your own when you were very young — shortly after your mother died, I believe."

Selica made an effort to tamp down her anger. *He's toying with me, bringing up painful subjects to get a rise out of me. I won't give him the satisfaction.* Even so, her blood was boiling. Selica's eyes wandered to the Sicari. Some crazed part of her mind wondered — just for a moment — if she could get to Villecrest before the Sicari could interfere. The thought was quickly dismissed for the madness it represented. The Third Anarch was not helpless. He was familiar with the use of every blade adorning the surrounding walls. Her experience was limited to slicing vegetables with a kitchen knife. She lifted her head and looked him in the eye with an eyebrow raised in question.

Toller lifted his chin. "Ask your question."

"I don't understand why you've brought me here, Anarch."

"It's simple, I need a good writ weaver and you come highly recommended."

"You have weavers with far more experience."

"Perhaps, but none of them are attractive or young enough."

"Excuse me?"

"I need someone who can pass as a student. Someone who will blend in with the students at the Computational Engineering Department at Denmount Court of Learning."

Selica's eyes widened. Denmount was thousands of miles from this place. She might have an opportunity to escape.

Toller laughed as if reading her mind. "I know such a long journey can be daunting, but you won't be going alone. My assistant, Decar, will be joining you — as will Fogar." The Anarch gestured toward the Sicari leaning against the wall. It was the threat she had been anticipating. They would be watching her like a hawk. It was unlikely she could escape, and even if she tried, the Sicari would hunt her down. They had too many connections for her to remain hidden in a strange land.

"What would you have me do there, Anarch?"

"I've arranged for you to join the engineering program for the final term. One of your classmates is a young man named Leviticus Radix. My sources tell me he is a prodigy — an exceptionally talented writ weaver who just happens to be working on a project of particular interest to me. You will get close to Radix and bring him to me."

Raised as an orphan behind the walls of the compound, Selica had no idea how to act around people her age who lived free lives. She had fantasized about it, but felt inadequate now that it might actually happen. Selica looked down at her plain clothes and unconsciously stroked her hair.

Toller noticed her distraction. "Decar will take you shopping for appropriate clothes and a proper hairstyle so you'll fit in. You'll receive instruction in the local customs of Caralithica and a language coach will tutor you on the proper accent. I expect you to adapt quickly to your new role. I want Radix here within the month."

"What if I can't convince him to come?"

The Third Anarch glowered at her. "I haven't forgotten the debt your family owes me. You *will* bring him to me and you *will* do whatever it takes to convince him. Do you understand?"

Selica gnawed at the inside of her cheek and looked away.

"You know what will happen if you disappoint me."

"Yes — Anarch."

Toller laughed at her discomfort. "Take heart. If you succeed, you'll help change the world. Perhaps your name will be mentioned alongside mine in the history books."

Selica didn't want her name associated with Toller Villecrest or anything he stood for. She certainly didn't want to see his name written anywhere other than a grave marker.

Selica sighed — it wasn't like she had a choice. She'd managed to avoid the Anarch for years, but she'd always known it wouldn't last. She supposed she should be grateful he wasn't asking for something worse. Selica would do as she was told until an opportunity to escape presented itself.

"I'll do my best, Anarch."

Toller looked displeased. "If, for some reason, you can't bring Leviticus Radix to me, it will be your responsibility to identify another student well-versed in the technology I seek. I want Radix, but if you fail to acquire him, you will not return empty-handed or there will be consequences. I will not have my plans delayed beyond the deadline I have set."

Selica squirmed. Ugly rumours existed about the types of consequences Toller Villecrest liked to dispense. "Yes, Anarch!"

"Find Decar Tosh, he's expecting you. You will leave immediately."

Selica released a tension-filled breath as the door closed behind her. She made her way to Decar Tosh's office with her newly acquired Sicari shadow in tow. Toller's orders made her very uncomfortable. How could she lead an innocent person into captivity? On the other hand, she would get to pretend to have a normal life for a short time. It was a selfish and shallow consolation that did nothing to ease her conscience. This was her life, always forced to enact the will of others before her own. She would move forward in the only way that she could — one moment at a time.

Chapter 1

"Can anyone tell me what year the quantum revelations began?"

Leviticus Radix sank lower in his seat. He hadn't completed the required reading for this class. The last thing he needed was Archivist Gilad calling on him. She wasn't one for excuses.

I just need to get through the next ten minutes, and the lecture will be over. Before next week's class, I'll read the material for sure. Lev had promised the same for three consecutive weeks.

An uncomfortable few minutes of silence ensued before the instructor chose a student across the theatre.

Lev couldn't hear the answer given by his classmate, but he could certainly hear Archivist Gilad's brusque response.

"If you had finished the reading, you would know that it began in 3022 AG."

Right, Lev thought, *3022 After Genesis. I need to remember that for the exams.*

"It was the beginning of major advances in our world," she continued.

Lev found himself nodding in agreement. With the discovery of the Exotic Particle Reactor, it was possible to power all manner of equipment, automating many modern miracles of engineering. EPR's came in many shapes and sizes, powering everything from handheld lamps to vehicles for ground and sea.

The last one hundred years had seen the development of communications systems, electrical imaging devices and the new gas-filled Lighter-Than-Air vehicles. An age of excitement and opportunity, and he was living it.

The world seemed a smaller place as a result. With global access to information, cultures were becoming homogeneous.

Not everyone considered it a positive development, but it was difficult to dismiss the benefits.

People enjoyed a better quality of life than ever before. At least that's what the *experts* claimed. Some truth existed in the numbers, but it didn't quantify the damage from a social decline that seemed to run parallel to the benefits.

It was inevitable, Lev supposed. People were pushing aside tradition in a rush to embrace all things new.

Abundant energy, plentiful food, and self-indulgence prevailed. As humanity embraced self-empowerment, people felt less inclined to consider the wisdom of their ancestors — or anyone for that matter. The conservative practices and ethical standards of the past seemed irrelevant.

Lev found himself pulled from his thoughts by the sound of Archivist Gilad building up a head of steam. Her voice held a slight whistle and he snorted as he imagined her vibrating from some unseen internal pressure. Maybe her arms flailed about as she spoke for that reason.

"Since that time, we've made great strides in scientific and medical research. We've levelled mountains, diverted rivers, and built berms to reclaim vast tracts of fertile land once covered in water. Perhaps we can finally let lie that pernicious fear of flooding."

A smattering of laughter filtered through the auditorium, but not everyone was amused. Lev looked at his friend Nico who had a deep frown on his face. The Callan family believed in the prophecy of the coming deluge.

Most people knew the story. Shortly after the formation of the earth, a seer had prophesied a future where the world would be washed clean of wickedness so the earth could begin anew.

Lev wasn't sure how he felt about the prophecy. His parents hadn't raised him with that belief. However, they didn't speak negatively about those who adhered to it, either. He supposed they held a wait and see attitude.

Regardless of his uncertainty, the Callans were some of the finest people Lev had known. If one judged social peers using the truth of a philosophy as a standard, the Callan family's integrity and generous giving placed them high above others. If their attitudes and behaviour arose from those beliefs, he wasn't about to dismiss it out of hand.

Lev felt a sudden protective anger and shot a glare at the instructor. Her comments were petty and judgmental. If she had known Nico's family, she wouldn't find those flippant remarks so easy to voice.

Unfortunately, Nico's parents weren't alive any longer. The world was that much poorer for the loss.

A chime sounded, announcing the end of class and Lev's anger evaporated. "Finally," he sighed. "Now the interesting work begins."

If Lev had to point to one thing he appreciated most about the advances in technology, he'd choose computational engineering. He loved writ weaving and had committed to doing his best. It was important to him that he make a positive contribution in his chosen field.

Lev was convinced that he could change the world, even if only in a small way. With that aspirational thought, he headed off to his next class.

Chapter 2

"Remind me again Nico, how did you talk me into taking that Cerebral Therapy class?"

"Come on Lev, it's not that bad. It might even help you figure out your compulsion issues."

Lev shot him a glare. "I don't suffer from compulsion issues!"

"Ha! Leviticus Radix you are hands down the most obsessively compulsive person I know!"

"Being organized and intentional is a positive thing."

Nico rolled his eyes. "Oh, is that what you call it? Organized and intentional?"

"Case in point," Lev continued, hooking his thumb at a student walking away from his ground transport. The fellow had left the window open. "How many vehicles get stolen each year because people don't take a moment to check that it's secure before rushing off? Just because I make a habit of checking the door doesn't mean I'm obsessing. It's called *being intentionally proactive.*"

"Do you need to check it three times?" Nico grinned.

"Never you mind." Lev put on an affronted air.

It was true that Lev liked to keep things orderly in his life, but that's because he habitually worked to simplify the input from his surroundings. Reducing clutter and catalysts for drama made it easier to find detail in the patterns he saw everywhere. Patterns were kind of his thing. It didn't mean he was mentally unsound, just different.

Lev knew Nico was joking, but he shuddered at the thought of their Cerebral Therapy Sage analyzing him. He'd had enough of that as a child and the experience soured him on the whole mental health experience. If he didn't need the credit to graduate, he would have quit the class by now.

As far as he was concerned, it was best described as pseudo-science. A glut of practitioners voicing uneducated guesses. As a school of thought, it seemed to value a variety of theories over reliable empirical evidence.

The truth is that all humans seek patterns, Lev thought. *It's what places us above the animals and allows us to evaluate to our advantage.* Lev wasn't different in that sense. His ability set him apart in that he noticed and retained far more detail than others. He compartmentalized his mind in a unique manner. Or so he'd been told. By categorizing types of chaos or order, he could isolate them. Then he could compare the patterns to discover trends or anomalies. Once he came to understand this about himself, it didn't take long before he fell in love with the logic of weaving numer strings.

Lev was in his final year of the Computational Engineering program. He still couldn't believe he'd found someone willing to sponsor his educational expenses. He would happily have spent all he owned to obtain such a blessing.

It was here, at the Court of Learning, where he had discovered pattern recognition methods. They used clustering, in ways very similar to how his mind functioned. The things he'd learned affected him profoundly. A world of self-consciousness fell away when he realized he wasn't broken. In fact, he was gifted.

Lev and Nico headed across the quad towards their final class of the day. Neither of them wanted to be late. Denmount held the title of the most prestigious Court of Learning in the country. It had a waiting list for admission. The most coveted jobs went to Denmount alumni and the people who attended classes there knew it. For the most part, students took their studies seriously. No one wanted to blow their shot at success. Even so, people needed to give their minds an occasional rest. The quickest respite was to exit the buildings and fill the green space. The quad offered a breath of fresh air and a change of scenery. Being a pleasant day, more people ventured outdoors than usual.

Lev had woken on the wrong side of bed and listening to the droning lecture of the Cerebral Therapy instructor hadn't improved his disposition. He moved through the day waiting for it to turn gloomy. A flip of shiny blonde hair from a group of young women provided a moment's relief from his melancholy. He smiled at the scenery. It tipped the scales a little closer to sunshine.

Then he spotted Kade. A storm cloud on two legs headed his way. *Just great* Lev thought. *Maybe he didn't see me.* Lev glanced both ways looking for a way to become less noticeable.

"Hey, where are you going?" Nico asked, swivelling his head.

"Quiet, he might hear you!"

"Who?"

Too late, the jerk was already making a beeline towards them with a scowl on his face. "Never mind," Lev grumbled.

"Hey Radix! Who do you think you are, showing off in class like that?"

"It's not a competition Kade, back off."

Kade had a classic bully mentality and liked to push his way into people's personal space. Lev wasn't particularly intimidated. At six feet one inch with a medium build, he could hold his own, even if he wasn't the biggest guy around.

Kade was smaller, but he seemed to believe otherwise. What bothered Lev was that guys like Kade tended to single him out. He had dealt with the personality type his entire life. They seemed to take offence that he was focused and diligent. It's as if they considered him a personal challenge. He thought it strange since he tried to keep to himself.

"You're the Sage's pet!" Kade continued, ignoring Lev's attempts to walk past. "Why don't you give someone else a chance to contribute once in a while?"

"That's not fair!" Lev snapped, "I can't stop Sage Konish from calling on me. He wouldn't if someone else answered!"

"That's the problem!" Kade retorted, stabbing Lev in the chest with his finger. "Konish only pays attention to his golden boy. The rest of us sit in your shadow looking like idiots, unworthy of his time! You could at least play dumb once in a while!"

"Touch me with that finger again, Kade, and I'll break it for you," Lev warned. "It's not my job to prop you up. Why don't you try studying harder?"

"You're unbelievable Radix. We're not all 'gifted' apprentices on a sponsorship. Some of us have to work hard to pay for our education, and you're jeopardizing our futures."

"What do you expect me to say?"

Kade glared for a full minute before shaking his head. "If you're as smart as you pretend to be, you should be able to figure that out. You're making enemies. Best watch your back," He turned and stormed off the way he had come.

"Can you believe that guy, blaming me for his shortcomings?"

"He did have a point," Nico said.

"You're taking his side?" Lev asked incredulously.

"Come on buddy, you know people find it hard to live in your shadow. Kade's frustration shouldn't come as a surprise."

"That guy needs some serious counselling," Lev muttered, "He must be overcompensating for some shortcoming in his character."

"You see?" Nico chimed in, "That Cerebral Therapy class is paying off already!"

"Arrrgg! Why do I put up with you? Okay, okay, I'll try to play dumb once in a while, but I don't see how the instructor will buy it."

"Your modesty is inspiring." A sadistic smile spread across Nico's face. "I can't wait to hear your perspective on the virtues of humility during our philosophy class next term."

Lev dropped his face into his hands. "Why, oh why didn't I pick my options while some good choices remained? And did you need to remind me of that upcoming misery just as another misery walks away? What kind of friend are you?"

"Best friend?" Nico asked, slapping Lev on the back. "How about I buy you a refresher to make amends?"

"That's definitely not the *best* a friend could do, but I'm thirsty, so I accept."

Nico was laughing openly now. "Well, my considerate companion, I know the perfect spot." Nico spun on his heel and headed off. "But it will have to wait until after class."

Lev quickened his pace to catch up.

Nico truly is my closest friend, Lev thought. *Mom and dad always said that the best friends are those who aren't afraid to tell you what you need to hear whether you want to hear it or not.*

Nico had always been there, helping Lev to understand the nuances of interaction that seemed to go over his head. He always knew what to say to defuse a situation, while at the same time making Lev think about things in a way he hadn't considered.

Nico thinks he lives in my shadow but has no idea how much I admire his patience and compassion. He sees good in people while I go out of my way to avoid them. If I didn't have him as a friend, would I have any friends at all? It wasn't the first time he had wondered.

Lev enjoyed Nico's company in silence for a stretch, taking in their surroundings as they walked at a comfortable pace.

A mature campus, Denmount had plenty of big trees and old architecture. Historians argued over the date it was founded. Many records were lost during the Trantor uprising when zealots burned the archives to the ground. The age of the school was lost, along with the many historical documents that went up in flames. The Maker alone knew the truth but an impression of longevity was palpable everywhere you walked. It left one with a comfortable sense of accumulated wisdom that exuded rightness and safety, but also hidden secrets.

He froze. What had made him think that? Suddenly all notions of comfort evaporated leaving a sense of what? Fear? No, anticipation perhaps.

Nico found himself several steps ahead before noticing his friend's absence. Looking back, he saw Lev standing stock still with a curious expression on his face.

"Hey bud, are you okay?" Nico asked, returning to his side. He waved his hand in front of Lev's face. "Leviticus, you in there?"

"Something is out of balance," Lev whispered.

"What do you mean?" Nico asked, suddenly concerned. "Are you feeling ill?"

"Not ill, no. I feel as if we've been here before — done this before."

Nico relaxed visibly. "I should hope so! We attend classes here, remember? You walk this path daily. Of course it feels familiar!"

Lev shook his head. "No. It's more as if something is about to happen, something expected, like I've experienced it before, but can't quite remember."

Nico squinted. "Are you sure you're not feeling ill?"

Lev struggled to explain. Something was out of place, or had changed. It didn't fit into the pattern of this place that he had in his mind, even while it felt familiar somehow. It disturbed his ordered universe in a way that made him very uncomfortable. He could live with the disorder of things out of his control, but he didn't like it when his mental mapping of the static things was in disarray.

Everything had a pattern, but the pattern had changed in some unaccountable way. He couldn't explain it to someone unable to perceive what he saw. The flexibility of patterns allowed them to flow and change over time, but they remained predictable. He was bewildered. A bit like when you discover a bruise and can't account for it. Lev couldn't put his finger on it, but like a bruise, he would keep touching it until he either remembered the cause or it faded.

"It's probably nothing," Lev muttered. "Let's get to our classes."

"Yeah," Nico agreed. "It's just Deja vu. Everyone experiences it occasionally. I bet the Cerebral Therapy Sage could offer an explanation."

"So we're back to that?" Lev laughed. "I believe I will allow you to buy me a meat roll to go with that mug of refresher. Consider it an opportunity to make appropriate reparation for your compounded abuse of our friendship."

"You got it!" Nico smirked. "I just happen to have a discount scrip."

Lev said nothing, just quirked an eyebrow. Nico, heir to the Callan shipping empire could afford the presses that printed those scrips but that didn't seem to stop him from counting coins.

"What?" Nico asked, "How do you think my family earned its fortune?"

"Riiiight," Lev snorted, "They had a discount scrip for a fleet of ground transports."

Nico responded with a punch to Lev's arm. "That just cost you the meat roll."

As they hurried off to class, they passed the archives. A bench sat out front where Lev often stopped to study on sunny days. Caught up in their banter, neither noticed the crow they startled into flight. It had been investigating a shiny red plaque artfully installed on the backrest of the bench, a plaque that hadn't been there an hour ago.

Chapter 3

The room smelled of exertion. The grunts of sparring partners exchanging blows echoed through the space. Someone hit the mat beside her and she glanced involuntarily. Her opponent took advantage of her distraction but Kayla saw the punch coming. She threw her forearm up to deflect the blow while dropping to sweep her leg behind the knee of her opponent. He buckled, and in one smooth motion she was behind him with her arms around his neck in a choke hold.

"I yield!" He croaked, straining to speak past the pressure on his throat.

Kayla released him and he fell to the mat. Del won most matches in the novice class, but Kayla was advancing quickly and had bested him three times now.

"That was well-executed Kayla!"

She beamed at the praise from her instructor. Jabin Pelle, a level twelve practitioner of warkata, was well known for his skill. As her mentor, he also was the wisest, most patient person Kayla knew. His approval meant a great deal to her.

"Better luck next time, Del." Del scowled at her and she laughed in response. Jabin ordered the class to practise the fourth kata, as he pulled her aside.

"That was dishonourable! You already had the victory. Taunting is completely unnecessary. I thought I taught you better."

Kayla wilted. "I'm sorry Jabin, you're right, of course. I don't know what I was thinking."

"Well, I do. You're far too aggressive in your quest to be the best at everything. When it doesn't come fast or naturally enough, you try to diminish those you feel are in your way. It's beneath you Kayla!"

"I..."

"I don't want to hear it, we've discussed this before. Consequences follow impulsiveness. What do I always tell you?"

"Be patient, weigh the cost of every action, wait for the right moment, and when it comes, commit."

"Praise the Maker! You actually listened! Remember, that's not just advice for battle, it's good advice for life."

"I'm sorry — really — it's just that it's taking soooo long. You know how my mother is, she'll never give me a chance in the field!"

"I do know your mother Kayla and you're too hard on her. Cello is the Chief Sentry and as such, she must listen to the counsel of her staff in these matters. She doesn't decide alone. Each instructor and mentor contributes to the conversation and we must all agree before a novice can move to the next level. We look for well-rounded character and skill in our agents. If the bar seems high, it's not that your mother placed it there but rather those who came before you."

Kayla's shoulders drooped in resignation as she considered the many times she'd lost her temper, or talked back to an instructor.

Jabin's lips twitched into a knowing smile. He whispered in her ear. "Just know that I'm proud of your accomplishments. Personally, I feel you're ready."

Kayla gave him a shove. He staggered back, laughing.

"You know something!"

"I merely said that I felt you were ready. I'm only one voice."

"A dregs churner is what you are! You wouldn't tell me that unless you knew something. Your voice wasn't the only one."

"I'm afraid you'll have to be patient, my dear."

Kayla screwed up her face in mock consternation. She jabbed her finger in his direction. "Only you would use this as a teaching moment."

Jabin just smiled. "I believe our lessons are concluded for the day."

Trying to learn more from Jabin was pointless. When he dug in, he was the proverbial immovable object.

It didn't matter. Something was about to change! She grabbed her pack and ran to the baths. She needed to be presentable if the summons came.

***

The call hadn't arrived until the following morning. Kayla slept in fits and starts and finally gave up three hours before the kitchen began preparing breakfast. That had given her time to bathe and dress, and plenty of time to fret.

When the dining hall finally opened, it was vacant save for a few guards coming off the night watch. The aroma of fresh bread filled the hall. Preparations had begun for the morning meal. Trenchers of meat, cheese, baking and fruit were on offer. It all smelled marvellous, but she was too nervous to eat and only managed a small biscuit with her mug of kofa.

She found the bottom of the mug far too quickly. That was disappointing. With nothing to occupy her mind, her anxiety began to creep up again.

Maybe it would have been better if Jabin hadn't suggested anything. He probably did that intentionally, another lesson in patience. She did need to work on that, but now wasn't the time.

Her Q-view began to buzz. It almost made her jump from her seat and it took a moment before she remembered to accept the incoming transmission.

"Novice Vantos."

She recognized the sharp tenor immediately, it was her mother's assistant, Joff. This was really happening.

"Please report to the Chief Sentry's office immediately."

"I'm on my way." Truth be told, she was halfway there at a dead run before she realized that it might not be dignified to arrive covered in a sheen of sweat. *Calm yourself Kayla.*

She forced herself to repeat the maxim Jabin had been drilling into her head. *Weigh the cost of every action, wait for the right moment.* By the time she arrived at the door to her mother's office, she had collected herself.

Announcing her arrival was unnecessary. Novices were always prompt. It didn't matter that she was the daughter of the Chief Sentry, the expectations remained the same.

Kayla waited at attention in the antechamber entrance. Joff finished inscribing something before standing and inviting her to take a seat.

"Chief Sentry Vantos is just finishing with First Token Ward Bosto. She will be with you shortly."

Joff sat back down at his desk and continued the work he had been doing before she arrived.

Great, more waiting, Kayla stifled a yawn. She looked around the room for something to occupy her mind. Her mother was a spartan woman with little interest in decorating. Her outer office walls were almost bare. The only bit of colour was a woven blanket given to her by her late husband on their wedding day.

Kayla missed her father. They had been very close. A Sicari had taken his life while on a dangerous assignment. Until that day, she had thought her father invulnerable. The memory filled her with rage. She would never say it aloud since it went against the Servator code, but it was part of the reason she was so driven. Her thirst for revenge ran deep. Her mother would be disturbed if she knew how often she daydreamed about it.

The door to her mother's office opened, bringing Kayla back to the present. This was no time for brooding.

"I'll have the monitoring station cleared and ready, Chief Sentry."

"Thank you, Deak."

Cello Vantos turned towards her daughter with a proud smile. "Novice Vantos. Please come in and have a seat."

Kayla entered and sat down while her mother closed the door behind them. The office was familiar ground. Kayla was one of the few children who had grown up on the base. She spent many hours as a child playing around that desk. Everyone in the compound knew her well. She had been the little darling who skipped around the base, always underfoot, filling the halls with smiles and giggles. The base staff were like one large family to her, but it made life difficult now that she was trying to make a name for herself.

People had trouble looking past the little girl they once knew to recognize the talent and skills she possessed as an adult. Or at least that's how it seemed to her.

Cello Vantos watched her daughter, saying nothing. Kayla had never been able to still her features. It fascinated Cello how her daughter's lip quirks and eyebrow twitches flowed over her face in any given moment. It was endearing, and she'd made the mistake of mentioning that — once. The animation was pronounced this morning. What she wouldn't give to know what was going through the girl's mind.

"Really, Mom?" Kayla burst in exasperation, one eyebrow flying heavenward. "Are you going to keep me in the dark too? Did Jabin put you up to this? Why am I here?"

Cello smiled, imagining what Jabin might have said, or rather didn't say. "Jabin didn't put me up to anything. Although, his was the final vote that brought you here today, Novice Vantos."

Kayla's face froze.

Has that ever happened before? Cello wondered.

"You mean I've finally completed my novice training?" Kayla couldn't keep the excitement from her voice. "What's my designation? Where will I be posted? What will I be doing?"

"Normally, people allow me to give instructions before they ask questions."

"Sorry."

"We have an assignment for you in the role of Token Ward."

Token Ward! That was a higher post than she would have expected. "Will I get to run a solo assignment? Is that what you and Deak were discussing?"

Her mother raised an eyebrow until Kayla stopped talking. "Deak? I think you meant to ask about the presence of *First Token Ward Bosto.*"

Kayla squeezed her hands together until her knuckles turned white in an attempt to still her body.

"As I was about to say, this will be a probationary role until you can prove yourself. You will keep in touch with your instructors and seek their council at all times.

"Normally, we wouldn't consider granting a solo mission to a novice. However, a time-sensitive matter has come up and our agents are all currently deployed.

"This is a bit unorthodox, but since it's a fairly straightforward mission, your instructors felt you could handle it. If you perform well, you may find yourself continuing in the capacity of Token Ward. I don't need to tell you how rare an opportunity this is. You must treat it very seriously."

"Yes! Yes, of course! I've been training hard, you won't be disappointed."

"I know you have, but Kayla, you understand how it is. Any impression of favouritism towards my daughter must be avoided. I've had to be sterner with you, and slow to reward. I know it's been hard on you, but it *is* necessary. It must be apparent to all that you receive no special treatment. Exaggerated measures help maintain that perception. One day you'll have the respect of your peers based on your own merit, and then things will be different. Until that day, you will be under intense scrutiny by everyone. You can't afford to make a mistake."

"I understand. Where will this mission take place? Jaihuwan? Kemetica? Sumakad?"

Cello pointed at the ceiling. "Denmount."

Kayla shook her head, not sure if she heard correctly. "You don't mean the city above this base?"

"Do you know of any other Denmount?"

"You must be joking! Mother! I don't need a babysitter! My first mission in the field and I only get to go as far as my own backyard?"

A stern expression crossed her mother's face. A familiar visage that said hold your tongue and listen. "Novice Vantos, and let me be clear, you can very easily remain a novice. When I'm off duty, I

am your mother, but at this moment you are addressing the Chief Sentry of the Caralithican Host! Shall I seek another novice for this task?"

Kayla jumped to attention in a panic. She couldn't lose this opportunity. Why couldn't she ever control her tongue? "Yes Ma'am! Sorry Ma'am!"

"Too often you forget yourself. You'd do well to remember your rank. I understand that you know many on this base as though they were family, but you *will* show the proper respect for their well-earned authority. Do you understand?"

"Understood, Chief Sentry Vantos!"

"Very well, be seated and let me continue. As you know, we keep an eye on all Centres of Learning, especially those with areas of study that attract certain qualities, studies that require high visual acuity and attention to detail. The chance of finding the type of people we prefer to recruit is greater in those settings."

"So, you want me to set a token to test a person of interest. You want to see if they can detect a small anomaly in their surroundings?"

"Yes, but this will *not* be a standard assessment. The subject has been monitored for some time. His name is Leviticus Radix, a soon-to-be graduate of the Computational Engineering program. He's extremely proficient in pattern recognition and we have high hopes for his potential.

"Normally, we prefer to begin the process as you have described and gradually build to a first contact. Typically, a screening process takes place before we let a subject know much about our organization. Unfortunately, we don't have time in this case.

"The Breachers have learned about the facial recognition algorithm Radix's team has been working on. We know the Breachers have been trying to develop something similar for their monitoring network. It would be disastrous if they reached their goals.

"Currently, our quantum communications give us a big advantage, but if the Breachers gain this facial recognition technology it would greatly curtail our freedom of movement. We would no longer be able to place tokens unobserved, or protect those tokens from activation by our enemies. We'd lose our greatest advantage."

Kayla was shocked. She hadn't realized the Breachers were so close to such a disruptive technology. "We need to get to Radix before they do." She realized.

"Precisely. You'll need to bring him in raw, and hope for the best."

"When do I begin?"

"Immediately. We've reserved a token monitoring station for your use." Cello slid a bundle of documents across the desk. "Here are the files we have on Mr. Radix. Study them today and inform First TokenWard Bosto of your plans first thing in the morning."

"Anything else I should know?"

"Kayla, this is more important than you can imagine. Breachers have been spotted scouting the campus. We don't have a lot of time before others join them. This could become dangerous. The only

reason I'm even considering letting a novice do this is because of the resources close at hand. Make sure you're familiar with our escape routes and don't take necessary risks."

"Understood, Chief Sentry Vantos!"

"Alright then," her mother softened visibly, "I'm officially off duty for however long it takes for you to give me a hug."

Kayla crossed the distance to embrace her mother. "Thank you, Mom, I won't let you down."

"Just be careful, please."

"I will," Kayla promised, as she stepped out of her mother's arms.

"TokenWard Vantos, you are dismissed."

She knew it was supposed to be a sober moment, but Kayla just couldn't keep the big grin off her face.

The briefing had taken longer than she'd thought and it was now part way through the noon meal. Her stomach growled, reminding her that she hadn't eaten a proper breakfast. Kayla wanted to start digging into the Radix files right away, so she only allowed herself a quick stop at the dining hall.

She grabbed something to go, and headed straight back to her room, ignoring an invitation to join some friends at a table. She would explain it to them later — they'd understand. Kayla had prepared for this her entire life and she wasn't about to waste another minute.

Chapter 4

Kade was still fuming over his confrontation with Radix earlier. How could that guy be so oblivious and self-centred? He had to admit, grudgingly, that Radix was talented, but Kade was good too. Oh, he wasn't anywhere near the top of the class, more like in the bottom five, but only the best of the best made it this far. The fact that he was even in the program put him far above the average student. So why couldn't he accept his accomplishment and be satisfied?

Kade glared at the path, knowing the answer. His father. That insufferable man whom he could never please. Kade would prove him wrong, and he'd do it despite Radix's annoying one-upmanship.

A buzz came from his tote-comm. Kade grabbed it from his back pocket and flipped the switch to answer the call.

"Hello Kade, it's Geoff."

"Hey uncle Geoff, how are things?"

"Not ideal. Listen Kade, the funds in your account are frozen."

"What do you mean frozen? I was just on my way to retrieve those funds so I can make payment for the final semester of classes!"

"Well, unless you're coming down to make a deposit on the loan interest, you might as well head back the way you came."

"What are you talking about? I made this month's deposit. I've never missed a payment. You know that!"

"I explained this possibility to you when you signed the loan contract. It's a variable interest loan, and the rates fluctuate with the markets, which are performing very poorly at the moment. The rates have risen and you need to make up the difference."

"This is unbelievable," Kade fumed, "you told me it was unlikely to happen any time soon!"

"Well, I was wrong." Geoff didn't sound all that apologetic.

"How much more do I owe?" Kade asked.

"Another seventy-nine silvers is due in the next twenty-four hours. Failure to meet the deadline will see the funds withdrawn from your frozen assets. The bank will release the remaining funds at that time."

"I can't believe this. I don't have another seventy-nine silvers! You know I budget to the copper Geoff! I need to pay for my final semester of school by the end of the week, and I only had enough in my savings to make that payment! You have to help me."

"I'm sorry, Kade — I wish I could, but I took losses in the markets too and I'm a little strapped at the moment."

"That's just great! Thanks for nothing!" Kade closed the connection abruptly, wishing for something more dramatic and satisfying than a flick of his thumb.

What was he going to do? He couldn't delay his school payment. He'd been late paying the school twice before, and they'd warned him if it happened a third time he would be expelled.

Scraping enough money together to make that extra loan payment on time was impossible. Kade groaned. He was so close! One more semester and he would graduate. He couldn't lose it all now.

Kade wracked his brain trying to come up with a solution. He'd worn out his credit with friends and he couldn't get an extra shift at work on such short notice.

Kade saw no alternatives. He would have to grovel to his father when he went home for Ma's birthday party. The thought made him sick to his stomach. Why did the world hate him so much?

Chapter 5

It was a lazy Saturday afternoon. Nico had invited Lev to the estate so they could hang out for the day. Lev arrived with flatbread, cheese and mead from the market. They enjoyed it for lunch while sitting in the shade of the giant cedar trees surrounding Nico's house. Many years ago, Nico's dad had paved an area beneath the trees with flagstones. A circular fire pit, ten hand spans in diameter, occupied the centre. Lev had fond memories of roasting fish on a stick while lounging in comfortable wooden chairs. They enjoyed that setting now. The smell of cedar and fresh air enhanced the taste of their simple meal.

"So Lev, do you want to tell me what happened to you the other day in the quad?"

Lev shook his head slightly, with a knowing smile. He'd thought maybe Nico had an ulterior motive for inviting him today. "Nothing," Lev replied.

"It was definitely something. You haven't zoned out like that since you were a kid."

Nico was like a brother to Lev. When Nico's parents died, he came to live with Leviticus's family until he was old enough to live on his own. Lev had been there for Nico as he struggled to come to grips with the loss of his family. Nico reciprocated by defending Lev when others teased him for his peculiarities. Nico was quite familiar with Lev's episodes, and the associated parental drama in their home.

As a child, Lev's parents worried about the things he was *seeing*. They had made him visit a Cerebral Therapist against his wishes. He couldn't believe they thought he needed fixing and he responded with rebellion. Unfortunately, that only served to convince them of a problem.

At first the specialist thought Lev might be suffering from a reality disconnect disorder. Lev learned quickly not to verbalize what he was seeing. After a few years went by and no harmful behaviour manifested, the doctor decided on a variation of Interpretive Optical Interference as a diagnosis; A condition where the mind interprets specific pieces of information incorrectly and in a consistent manner. The affected individual must learn to recognize the problem areas and apply the correct perception.

The assessment proved inaccurate and unhelpful. The patterns Lev saw weren't *misinterpreted optical interferences*. They existed. He could prove every instance. For a long time, Nico was the only one who believed him. Eventually the doctor had to admit that he could find nothing wrong with Lev. Having no other explanation, they began to label him a savant. That wasn't precisely accurate either, but at least it held less of a stigma than the earlier attempts at diagnosis.

It still galled him to think of all the coins his parents had needlessly wasted. He shuddered to think how badly his life could have been derailed if a misdiagnosis had resulted in a lifetime of mind-dulling medications. It would have robbed him of his abilities and the joy it now brought him.

Of course, such prowess came with disadvantages. For example, playing strategy games with his peers wasn't advisable if he wanted to keep them as friends. Nor was he allowed anywhere near the local gaming establishment, something He and Nico had learned the hard way. Lev could still hear Nico insisting, "We'll be rich!"

"You're already rich." Lev had reminded him. That didn't seem to be a logical argument as far as Nico's teenage brain was concerned. They had made a tidy sum of money at the gaming tables before some very large men took notice. Lev and Nico were tossed out the door without their winnings, leaving them poorer than when they'd entered. The owner warned them never to return, adding some very colourful descriptions of bodily harm to drive the point home. For the next two years, they walked far out of their way to avoid passing too near the place.

The lack of table games didn't bother him much. He did still manage to find challenges against like-minded opponents in Jumkano competitions.

Lev's abilities had gotten them in trouble on a few other occasions but for the most part it had only improved their youthful adventures.

Lev's thoughts brought him back to the present. Denmount was an amazing city to grow up in. Just big enough to offer everything you'd need or want but still small enough to feel like a community. Mountains rose to the east and towering cliffs overlooked the sea to the west. You didn't need to travel far to experience a different landscape.

The winters were mild and the summers hot, moderated by cool breezes from the sea. It was the perfect environment for two young men escaping their troubles. They explored every nook and cranny within a day's walk — that covered pretty much the entire city, small as it was.

Those were days filled with exuberant adventure. Lev used the distraction to escape from himself, and Nico used it to avoid his grief. They shared a bond. Each knew when something was troubling the other. It's why he'd been invited here. He loved Nico for it, but Lev didn't have a way to explain things yet, so he turned the tables instead, knowing Nico was troubled as well. "I'm not ready to talk about it yet. I have to work out a few details. I think you're just avoiding talking about what's been bothering you." Nico didn't try to deny it.

"It's just that graduation is coming up and I have to make some big decisions about the family business. I can't avoid it any longer and it dredges up so many painful memories."

"You know I'm here for you."

"I know. I appreciate it. I guess I just wanted a day like we used to have. Hanging around without a care in the world."

"Nico, you and I have weathered many storms. We always come out the other side. Everything will be okay." Lev wished he felt as confident as he sounded. He couldn't help thinking a storm was building. One that wouldn't pass so easily. The familiar patterns of his youth had changed somehow and he didn't understand what it meant.

Chapter 6

Kayla had worked all day on her operational plan, and by the time she finally let her head hit the pillow, she felt satisfied that she had considered every angle.

She woke from a good night's rest, excited to begin and was waiting in front of First TokenWard Bosto's office when he arrived to start his workday.

A knowing smile crossed Deak's face, but he spoke in a no-nonsense commanding tone. "Probationary TokenWard Vantos. I hope your early arrival means you're prepared to brief me and not to ask for an extension like some fresh novice who forgot to do her homework."

"I am prepared, First TokenWard."

"Then, let me start the kofa brewing and we'll get down to business." Deak opened his office door and bade her enter with a sweep of his hand towards a stool in front of his desk. He started the kofa, then beckoned for the report in her hand as he sat down across from her in a wobbly chair that creaked in protest.

Kayla sat quietly as he read, watching him carefully as he nodded or grunted in turn. When nothing in his demeanour promised to reveal his thoughts, she let her gaze drift around the office.

Unlike her mother's preference for a clean empty space, Deak Bosto seemed to thrive in disarray that matched his slightly dishevelled attire. Most would call it clutter, but not to his face. He seemed to know where everything was when he needed it. Wherever she looked, loose pieces of parchment or items of questionable value were strewn about. Three empty mugs sat on the corner of his desk, each looked less clean than the one he currently held in his hand.

Is that a mouldy piece of flatbread peeking out from under a report? She was about to lean forward to take a closer look, when she realized that his eyes were no longer on the paper, but on her instead.

"Something on your mind Vantos?"

"No, Sir! Do you have any concerns about my recommendations, sir?"

"The report is fine. You seem to have covered the essentials."

"Thank you, sir. What's next?"

"You're not familiar with your own recommendations?"

"No, sir! I mean yes, sir, but — well, can I just get started now, or?" Arg, Kayla hated the way she sounded right then.

Deak burst out laughing. "Sorry, Miss Vantos, just giving the new kid a hard time. I approve of your plan. I've reserved monitoring station twelve for your use until the conclusion of your operation."

"Thank you, sir!"

"Before you go, I'm obliged to remind you that you're not to leave a token unobserved under any circumstances."

"First rule of surveillance."

"That's right. I know it gets drilled into your heads during training, but it's surprising how easily your eyes drift after staring at a Q-view screen for hours at a time. Keep your hand on the switch and learn to turn it off any time you notice your attention slipping. I've found that if I do that, I can't easily get up or walk away without noticing where my hand is. Practise keeping your hand there whenever you're at a monitoring station, even if you're not actively monitoring. Do it until it becomes second nature."

"Good advice, sir. Thank you."

"Good luck, and don't hesitate to come to me with questions. We don't expect a novice to have everything figured out on their first assignment. You are dismissed to your task."

"It begins." Kayla said, quoting the customary response. She stood, bowed her head slightly in the expected recognition of authority, then turned smartly on her heel and left the office.

Chapter 7

Kayla had grown up on the base, but she didn't know this section. It was off-limits except to qualified personnel. She found monitoring station twelve after a few wrong turns and some hastily explained directions from a field ranger rushing by on a task of his own. It proved to be little more than an alcove off the hall with a curtain to draw for privacy.

Novices trained on a similar station, but Kayla felt a thrill at the thought of being at the controls without an instructor watching over her shoulder. It was a big responsibility and a bigger opportunity.

The Q-tech involved was mind-boggling. It had been in use by the Servators for as long as Kayla could remember. Sometimes she wondered how their technology was so advanced compared to the rest of the world, but then again, the Servators were an ancient organization. They lived in the world yet remained apart, allowing their knowledge to grow unimpeded. Other civilizations rose and fell, taking their advancements to the grave. Servators shared some technology with the public for the betterment of all, but Q-tech remained classified — reserved for Servator use only.

Q-Tech allowed for the placement of tokens. A Token Ward could use such tokens for communication, concealment, recording and monitoring. The observational capabilities of potential recruits were also tested using tokens. Kayla would be testing Leviticus Radix in this manner.

She could hear the voice of her tech instructor as she remembered details.

"A token is a mass of quantum entangled particles. Using a simplistic analogy, one might think of it as a 'projection' of solid particles. An entangled pair required a template for the first half to provide a blueprint for the second half of the pair which, at the moment of being observed, gathered elements from its new environment to take a solid form — a token."

The classes had been fascinating, but not nearly so much as the wrist-mounted Quantum Viewer, or Q-view for short. Every qualified Servator received one.

Kayla remembered when she was handed her first Q-view. She couldn't put it down for a week. It appealed to the child in her. The idea that she could cause something to materialize from thin air felt like making a wish, and seeing it come true. However, it quickly became nothing more than a tool after being drilled in its use for hours on end.

Larger Q-view monitoring stations like the one Kayla was about to use were dedicated to analysts and field operatives. Each viewing device accessed coordinates from a sophisticated quantum positioning network or QPN.

Coordinates plotted materialization points for the quantum particles that would form a token. Particle placement was possible for any location that had been previously mapped and entered into the system. By clustering adjacent particles using particle location maps, it was possible to render a physical likeness of any static image or object. Since the token was particle-based rather than light-based, for all practical purposes it looked and felt like the original object. The particles would exist in that location and form until the template was revised or reversed.

Total processing power of the computational hardware and the Quantum Positioning Network posed the only limiting factors for the transfer of data and the size of the token.

Using a Q-view device, a person could set a token to appear at a predetermined location and monitor it.

Direct observation of an *active* token would trigger it to react in a predefined way. One of the reasons for vigilant monitoring was to prevent the discovery of an active token through accidental triggering by the wrong person, or occasionally an observant animal.

Kayla snorted thinking of the stories she had heard of missions gone hilariously wrong when some curious forest creature started investigating a token at the worst possible moment. What was it one instructor had said? "Don't model your token as a tree where mongrels might lift a leg."

Best to use a simple pattern for the initial token placement. Something that could belong without being overtly obvious.

It was up to the TokenWard or a field ranger to devise some method of drawing attention so the intended viewer would look towards the trigger particles and activate the cluster.

Designing a successful encounter was an art form. It was one of the reasons Servators sought observant, inventive individuals for recruitment.

Kayla glanced at her notes. Field rangers regularly patrolled Denmount campus due to its location above the Servator base and they had compiled an extensive account on the habits of Leviticus.

Kayla had studied the Radix file carefully. She knew that he would have a break between classes mid-morning today, and that he liked to use that time to sit on a particular bench to study.

She had slipped out the night before and used her Q-view to map coordinates for a spot on the back of that bench. She'd also mapped coordinates for both sight and sound tokens across from the bench and in a few other locations, giving her a wide field of view to monitor. Now, she just needed to set up templates for the tokens and her trigger.

She had already decided to manifest a simple dedication plaque. It was a common enough sight and even if it hadn't been there previously, people would just think it was a new addition. It was perfectly plausible. She decided to colour it red instead of the typical bronze, just to make it stand out a bit more. She did need to catch Mr. Radix's attention after all.

After a few minutes browsing through existing patterns from the catalogue on the viewscreen, she settled on a rectangular shaped plate. It was a design intended for placement beneath an artwork of some sort. It would do.

She called up the coordinates that she'd hastily scanned the previous night. The system was smart enough to extrapolate on a plane from her scan and calculate nearby coordinates. It allowed her to centre the token on the bench when she was ready to materialize it.

That done, she proceeded to format the text that she wanted to appear on the token. First, she composed a generic dedication to a fictional character, then she paused to consider the message she should direct to Mr. Radix. The space on the plaque was small so the message needed to be brief.

In the plan she had submitted to the First Token Ward, she had chosen the archives building as the place to meet Leviticus. It had several secret entrances to the base, so she had options if something went wrong and she needed to disappear.

Having selected that venue, it was logical that her first choice for a token placement would be the bench conveniently located near the front entrance to the building.

Kayla knew from the reports that Leviticus frequented the archives, so he would be familiar with the layout and the cataloguing system. She decided to wait for him in an aisle equidistant from two potential escape routes. She could spend as much time as she needed browsing the shelves without raising suspicion.

Studying her copied floor plan, she found a suitable spot. That decided, she composed a simple message for the token to display when triggered. "Leviticus Radix. We need to meet. Aisle thirty-nine, section five." She set the token to revert to its original state, after one minute.

Next came the tricky part. She couldn't just materialize the token. She had to make sure no one was around to see it happen. That's where her sight and sound tokens came in. She'd scanned coordinates for several locations in shaded corners or bushes where she could materialize her monitoring tokens without anyone noticing. Once those were in place, she could watch the bench and surrounding area. Then, she would choose an opportune moment to place the visible token.

She looked at her wrist chrono. It was almost time for first classes to begin. She waited ten minutes for the quad to empty as students headed to their classes, then sent the signal to materialize her monitoring tokens.

Kayla held her breath as the feeds came up on her screen. This was a critical moment. If anyone had noticed, she would need to reverse the tokens quickly before anyone could approach for a closer look. She let out her breath in relief and satisfaction. The quad was empty and she could continue without blind guesswork.

It all took longer than anticipated and she wasn't prepared in time to place the token before Leviticus claimed the bench for a study break.

It was frustrating at first, watching him on the monitor knowing she couldn't do anything to get his attention. She was briefly tempted to materialize it while he was sitting there, but too many people were wandering through the area and that would have been foolish.

Eventually she realized it was an opportunity. She could see where he sat and how he adjusted himself when he was uncomfortable. It gave her confidence that he would indeed notice a token in the spot she had selected.

After her target left, she spent the rest of the afternoon scrutinizing her field of view, getting a feel for the ebb and flow of the students. She learned how long it took to clear the quad and how quickly it filled up between classes.

During the second-to-last class of the day, she performed a final inspection of the area and placed the bench token. All was ready. Unfortunately, she would have to wait until the next day for Radix to revisit the bench. Even so, it was all coming together rather nicely and she was pleased with her success.

Voices drifted down the hall, coming closer.

"Kayla! There you are! Have you been hiding here all day? A bunch of us are heading out for refreshers and pan pies, care to join?"

Why not? Kayla thought. *I'm tired of staring at this screen and Leviticus will be heading home. Nothing more to do until tomorrow and I feel like celebrating!*

"Sure! Just give me a moment to gather my things." She quickly shoved everything into her pack, slung it over her shoulder, and joined her new co-workers for a well-deserved break.

She hadn't noticed the blinking light on the console indicating an active token. She wasn't there when the monitoring tokens captured a crow cocking its head to get a better view of the shiny metal plaque that had captured its attention. Nor was she present to see a figure in the background watching the bird.

Chapter 8

Nico felt a flutter in his stomach as he hesitated in front of the open door.

"Come in, come in," a voice called from inside the office.

Stepping through the door was like stepping into another world. Large tropical plants flanked an aquarium on the interior wall and floor to ceiling glass made up the exterior walls of the corner office. It provided a spectacular view of the Sea.

Tenika Sheridan sat comfortably behind the desk. Immaculately attired, her salt and pepper hair was trimmed in a sensible shoulder-length cut. Nico recognized her from several years ago when he had visited his father's office. This very office, in fact.

She tapped a manicured nail on the desktop while her eyes made an appraising head to toe pass. "You've grown quite a bit since I saw you last." She observed. "You take after your father."

Nico felt uncomfortable under her scrutiny. He tried to remember that she was technically his employee, or could be at some point, but it was hard to feel that way about someone twenty-five years his senior. She had kept the company running after his parents' death and likely commanded the respect of everyone who worked here. He imagined she'd earned it.

Nico tried to picture himself directing people and making the types of decisions Tenika made daily. Something inside quailed at the thought. It must have shown on his face.

"You look as if you've just bitten into a lemon," she grinned. "Relax Nico, you have nothing to feel nervous about. I just invited you here to get to know you a bit and chat about your plans for the future."

"My plans?" Nico stuffed his sweaty palms into his pockets, hoping she didn't notice.

Tenika rose from her chair and motioned towards the couch. "Make yourself comfortable. Can I offer you something to drink?"

"Um, just water, please."

"Would you like a slice of lemon with that?" Tenika asked.

Was that a joke? Nico didn't think the head of a major international corporation would tell jokes. Actually, that was inaccurate, his father used to kid around all the time.

She was right, this was silly. Why should he feel nervous?

Tenika leaned over and spoke into the desk-comm. "Marret? Could you bring some water for Mr. Callan and tea for myself, please?"

She walked over to the couch and sat beside Nico — uncomfortably close he thought.

"So, Mr. Callan, I understand you're entering your final term at Denmount."

"Yes ma'am."

"Oh dear no, you make me sound so old. Tenika, will do fine. I have a few good years left in me yet."

Nico's cheeks reddened. "Oh! I'm so sorry, I didn't mean..."

Tenika laughed. "I wasn't offended. No, I should apologize for having fun at your expense. I seldom have an opportunity to sit and chat like this without distraction. Perhaps my social skills have become rusty." She looked wistful for a moment, as if she was recalling something pleasant. "Nes was like that too. So easy to tease. I miss him."

She brought her eyes back into focus. "Your father was also very meticulous. He always had everything arranged, long before the rest of us could imagine the need."

"Yeah," Nico replied, smiling at a memory, "Dad used to have our vacations planned to the minute, and five years in advance. It drove Mom crazy."

"That sounds about right," Tenika laughed. "So, you shouldn't be surprised to learn that he had quite specific plans for you and your place in this company."

"Um, yeah," Nico started, not sure how to proceed. "My lawvocate explained the condition that I complete business training before receiving full control of my inheritance. I also know that the company is in my name, but not much beyond that."

He was suddenly worried she might get the wrong impression, and quickly amended his comment. "I mean, I never expected to step in and immediately take over the company or anything like that!"

"You'll be happy to know that your father didn't expect that either. He had a comprehensive plan in place to groom you for the role. Of course he was hoping to do that himself, but..." Tenika made a nervous coughing sound. "Sorry."

"No, it's fine, ma'am... I mean, Tenika. Enough years have passed, but to be honest I'm not even sure if I want to run a business."

"I'm sorry Nico, perhaps your lawvocate didn't provide you with all of the details. In the event you choose not to take ownership, your father has made arrangements to parcel out the company and sell all its assets. I suppose, if it were your desire, you could just walk away. Your financial security would be assured for life. However, it would also mean that a lot of good people would lose their jobs."

Nico was shocked. He never imagined that he would literally have to fill his father's shoes. "Why would my dad do something like that?" He shook his head at a loss for anything else to say.

"I don't know his reasons, Nico, but I know the goal. That's why I arranged for this meeting. We need to do some planning — arrange schedules — set up a mentor...."

Nico stood up, too quickly. He leaned forward with a hand on one knee while waving the other hand in the air between them.

"Wait — just wait — slow down!"

Tenika had a concerned look on her face. "Are you all right, Nico? Maybe you should sit back down for a bit."

"No, I'm fine. This is just a lot to take in all at once. I need to clear my head."

"Take a few days and let it sink in, but you need to make some decisions soon. The clock starts ticking when you graduate and we need to be prepared."

Tenika stood up as well. "I do have another meeting to attend, so we'll need to continue our discussion at a later date. One more thing before you go, Nico..." She headed for her desk and opened a drawer.

Nico didn't think he could handle much more, but he managed to reply, "Yes?"

"Your father instructed that you receive this when the time came for this conversation." She handed him a message tube sealed with wax.

Nico accepted it with shaking hands. A letter from his father? After so many years? It was too much.

Some part of his brain enabled him to offer a mechanical goodbye, then he walked briskly for the exit. He needed to get outside where the walls weren't closing in on him.

Chapter 9

Kade stood on the doorstep and looked down at the package in his hand. It was for his mother. He hoped she liked it. It wasn't much, but it was what he could afford when he had purchased it. Ironically, if he hadn't bought the gift, he would have had enough money to cover the extra interest payment on his loan.

"What am I doing here?" Kade wondered aloud. "This is the last place I want to be right now."

I don't need this, Kade thought, but that wasn't true. He did need it. He couldn't risk losing everything he'd fought for. He had to swallow his pride and ask for help.

It would be so much easier to go back to his little apartment and wash away the stress of the day with a flagon of wine.

He almost lost his nerve, and was about to turn away but hesitated. This wasn't just about him. It was his mother's birthday and she had been begging for him to visit for some time.

He'd eventually agreed to come to her party since all of his siblings would be there. He hoped their added presence would put his father in a more amenable mood. Screwing up his nerve, he lifted his arm to knock, but the door opened before his knuckles met wood. Any opportunity for escape vanished.

"Kade!" His mother exclaimed, gathering him in for a hug. "I'm so glad you made it!" She kissed him on the cheek and held him tight for a long moment.

"Ma... Ma... I can't breathe!"

"Oh dear, I'm sorry. I guess I got caught up in the moment. I've missed you so."

"I know Ma, I've missed you too. Uh, where's Dad?"

"He's in the backyard cooking up some sausages. Now, Kade," she pleaded, "Please try not to upset him. Let's just share a nice family dinner, okay?"

"I'm not the one you have to worry about."

"Will you do it for me, Kade? Please?"

Kade slumped his shoulders. "I'll try." He sighed as he followed her into the kitchen.

Almost everyone else was there. Thom and his wife Kait were standing at the stove arguing over what spices to stir into the gravy. Jen and Dex were setting up a folding table for the kids.

Boisterous noises filtered in from the living room where Brett had Juke in a headlock on the couch. Their wives looked on, shaking their heads in amusement. Some things never changed.

"Tina, Paulo, and the kids will be here shortly," his mother assured him. "Paulo had to work late today."

"Hey Kade," Thom motioned with his hand, "bring that big brain over here and explain to my wife why pepper root does *not* belong in gravy."

"It needs some heat," she insisted.

"Gravy appreciates a little salt and nothing more," Thom argued. "The meat juices have all the necessary flavour. Anything more is sacrilege."

Kait turned towards Kade, thrust her chin out and narrowed her eyes in her best big sister glare.

"Um — I think I'll stay out of this one." Kade lifted both hands in mock surrender and slowly backed away.

"Coward!" Thom muttered, knowing he'd already lost the argument. Kade wasn't sure to which one of them he was referring.

Maybe this won't be so bad, Kade thought. Time had passed since his last visit. Perhaps his father had learned to accept things as they were. He stood quietly in the dining room entrance and took in the sounds of family.

The back door opened and Brun Brixton crossed the threshold. "Clear the way, sausages coming through," he announced in his deep baritone. "Everyone to the table. Get them while they're hot."

A mad scramble ensued as everyone jostled for chairs while Brun set down the meat laden platter.

Once things had settled a bit, Kade realized the only empty chair remaining was the one right next to his own. His father stared silently at the empty chair for a moment before sitting.

Kade closed his eyes and with a mental sigh reminded himself of the promise he'd made his mother.

"Thank you all for coming," Brun began, "your mother has been looking forward to this all week."

Right, Kade thought, it was just like his father to take credit. As if he had anything to do with suggesting this gathering. More likely, Ma had begged for a week to get his permission.

"We can share this meal thanks to the contributions each of you has made to the family's financial well-being," Brun finished. "Enjoy."

Kade stiffened and the table went silent. His mother turned her face towards him with pleading eyes. Kade bit his tongue and pushed his retort into a little box in the back of his mind.

"So, Kade," his father continued, "how's life out there on your own? It must be nice having no one to worry about but yourself."

There it was. He shouldn't have been surprised, but he had hoped. "You couldn't make it five minutes Dad? Not even for Ma?" Kade shook his head in disgust.

"Don't you shake your head at me young man! Everyone at this table contributes to the finances of this family! Well, almost everyone." Brun looked pointedly at Kade. "It's how we survive. We're all working towards a better future for our children. I've explained this."

"I know Dad! You've told this story so many times, how could any of us forget? Gran and Gramps fled to this country to make a fresh start and we all need to pull our weight — blah, blah, blah!"

Brun surged to his feet. "How dare you disparage their sacrifice. The sacrifices of everyone around this table!"

"I'm not!" Kade yelled. "I'm trying to honour that vision by getting an education! I'm claiming that 'better life' you keep talking about. Am I not one of the children of that future you preach? Why can't you be supportive?"

"You know full well that we could only afford a higher education for one child from this generation. It's up to the rest of us to carry the financial burden!"

Brun thundered.

Kade took a moment to calm his breathing. "I haven't asked for anything from the family. I've worked several jobs and saved every coin to pay for my education and support myself."

"To support yourself — yes," his father replied, ice in his tone, "but nothing to support the rest of the family."

"How can you be so short-sighted Dad? With an education comes better pay. I'll be in a better position to contribute to the family once I graduate."

"Doing what exactly?" Brun asked. "Looking at pictures and telling people what you see? That's not a real job!"

"Patterns Dad, not pictures! Algorithms, predictive writ weaves. It's the future!"

"You're gambling on unproven technology, Kade."

"Whenever you don't understand something, you think it's a gamble!" Kade retorted. "We came to this country for a new life, and you need to accept that people do things differently here. Look at uncle Geoff. He struck out on his own and you see how well he's doing."

"Don't bring your uncle into this. He never supported the family either! He's no example to follow!"

"What?" Kade asked, disbelief on his face. "Uncle Geoff has offered financial support many times. You just refuse to accept it!"

Kade didn't know why he even needed to defend his uncle Geoff. "He's a successful financial consultant. If anyone could help this family, it's him."

"I'd never accept a single coin from your uncle!" Brun stabbed the table with his finger for emphasis. "Money lenders are the very reason we had to leave our homeland in the first place. Those criminals stole the savings of countless good folk, causing needless suffering. To think your uncle threw in with the likes of them. It's a disgrace!

"Do you think I'm unaware that your uncle helped you to procure loans to subsidize your education? Mark my words boy, a time will come when they will demand payment, and they won't care one whit about your circumstances. When that day comes, don't expect assistance from those of us you were unwilling to help."

Kade stared, dumbfounded. Did his father already know about the conversation he'd had with Uncle Geoff about the extra loan payment? Did it matter? He had his answer. No help was coming. At least he wouldn't need to grovel.

Kade stepped away from the table and tucked his chair back in place. Winning this argument was hopeless, and admitting that his father had been correct about money lenders would only lead to a long lecture of 'I told you so.' The price was too high for his pride to accept.

Kade turned sorry eyes to his mother and walked to her side. "I'm sorry, Ma," he whispered, "I have to leave, but I wanted to give you this."

She reached for the small gift box he offered and smiled sadly. "Let me walk you to the door."

They walked in silence down the hall and stepped outside.

"Don't be too hard on your father," She started.

"Wait, Ma. Just tell me — is the family really in such dire straits?"

"No, we're doing fine," his mother assured him.

"Then why can't he let it go Ma? It's been years and still he acts as if I've destroyed the family."

"Your father is a proud man. He won't admit it, but he had dreams too when he was young. You're more like him than you realize."

Kade bristled. "I'm nothing like him!"

"Oh, yes you are." His mother smirked.

"He didn't have the opportunities you do," she explained. "You need to understand that honour and sacrifice were drilled into him his entire life. It's who he is and he clutches to those tenets because they bring meaning to the drudgery of labour without end.

"You did what he always wished in his heart to do — what he couldn't. Instead, he gave up his dreams, believing it the honourable thing to do. Your father cherishes that honour because without that token of respect his sacrifice was meaningless. He couldn't live with that.

"Your dad obeyed his father but you don't obey him. He thinks you don't respect him. It seems unfair to him that he paid such a high price, while from his perspective, you don't appear to think you need to pay anything."

Kade had never heard his father described this way. It was difficult to reconcile with the man he knew. "I don't think Dad's life was pointless."

"Nor does he think your efforts hold no value," his mother interrupted.

She reached for Kade's hands and held them in her own. She looked into his eyes and made sure she had his attention.

"Kade, I'm very proud of you. I always knew you were destined for great things. I believe your father feels the same, but doesn't know how to separate his feelings from his pride."

Kade glanced back at the house. The rest of the family was visible through the window. They were continuing on without him as if he were an afterthought. It stung, and his heart hardened.

"If Dad really feels that way, he'll have to tell me himself." Kade's lower lip trembled. Tears threatening to flow. He quickly turned away so his mother wouldn't see.

Laughter floated through the screen door of the house.

"I'll think about what you've said Ma, but from the sound of things, the family doesn't miss having me around." He turned and walked briskly away. When he got home, he'd open that flagon of wine.

Tilde Brixton sat on the front step and gazed after her son until he was out of sight. She looked down at the small package in her hand. It was neatly wrapped with a small bow on top. She carefully unwrapped it and peered into the box.

A thin gold chain with a pendant rested inside. She lifted it out of the box to take a closer look and gasped when she saw the tiny carved bear. Bear was her pet name for him as an infant because of his tenacity. He was very young when she used that term of affection — unable to speak yet. She could

hardly believe that he would have understood her words at the time, let alone remembered. Yet here it was in the form of a plea that he not be blotted out of their lives.

She wept silently but said aloud, "You're not forgotten, little bear."

She placed the chain around her neck, under her shirt and close to her heart. Then she walked back inside to join the family, minus one.

Chapter 10

Kayla overslept, having spent a late night with her co-workers. The incessant buzzing of her Q-view was an unwelcome interruption.

She groped on the floor beside her bed, searching blindly for the device. After a moment she found it tangled in her shirt and hit the connect button.

"What?"

"Novice Vantos, you're to report to my office immediately!"

Lead TokenWard Bosto sounded angry. Kayla bounded out of bed and made her way to the wash basin to splash some water on her face. *What could be wrong?*

Yanking her hair into a ponytail, she looked for some clean clothes to pull on and paused with a tunic halfway over her head. *He called me Novice, not TokenWard!* Panic rose in her chest as she dressed quickly and ran out the door.

It took Kayla five minutes to get to Deak's office. She lost another minute standing in front of the closed door, not sure she wanted to know what awaited on the other side. She sighed and pushed the door open.

Deak looked up from his desk. He did not appear happy.

She checked to see if it was because he hadn't had his morning kofa. No such luck, the pot was already half empty.

"Sit down, Novice Vantos."

There it was again... Novice.

"You're late!"

"I can explain, sir."

"I don't have time for excuses. I'm too busy dealing with the potential consequences of your actions."

"My actions? I don't understand, sir. The mission has gone flawlessly so far."

"If that were true, we wouldn't be having this conversation. I find the fact that you don't know what has occurred disturbing. Equally disappointing, is that you were not at your station first thing this morning to catch your mistake."

"What mistake? What's happened?"

"Field Ranger Vale was walking past your designated station and noticed that the active token alert was blinking."

Kayla blanched, lost for words.

"I had one of the analysts comb through the viewcording. Would you care to see what she found?"

Kayla hesitantly got up from the stool and came around the desk so she could look at Deak's Q-view screen. He'd paused it at the moment of concern. A crow sat on the bench looking up at the token she had placed.

No. Maker, please, no. It couldn't be that on her very first mission, some stupid creature could have messed things up for her. She'd be a laughingstock. An example to novices for decades!

She looked around to see if this was perhaps some initiation prank. No one jumped out, laughing, to pat her on the back.

Deak was still glowering as he pushed the button to resume playback of the viewcording. The crow was hopping up and down, cocking its head from side to side. Somehow — some way — it had managed to activate the token. The token bubbled furiously as it reconfigured to display her message. After a minute it returned to its original state.

Kayla felt a little relief knowing that her message had not remained visible. Her auto-revert implementation had functioned correctly. There didn't seem to be anyone close enough to read it.

Deak continued to stare at her, one eyebrow lifted.

Yes, it was a beginner's mistake. Leaving a token activated was serious, to be sure. Yet Deak didn't seem to be interested in fast-forwarding to any other moment of the viewcording. He was waiting for her to notice something.

She completed a closer inspection of the other sight token angles. Wait —

something was there in the background, about twenty feet away. She suddenly felt uneasy. A man was standing there, looking at the token, or perhaps the crow. *Maker please let it be the crow!*

Kayla slowly turned her head to look at Deak who was nodding.

"You see?"

"Yes, sir, but surely he couldn't have read the message from that distance. With that bird hopping around, he may not even have noticed the plaque activating."

"Pray that's the case."

"Does the viewcording show the man approaching or activating the token? Does anyone else appear later?"

"Are you attempting to downplay the seriousness of this matter? I'm pretty sure I reminded you, just yesterday, that you're never to leave an active token unattended."

"Sir! I accept full responsibility! It was a foolish mistake, one that I will not repeat!"

"Oh, we're not finished yet. The analyst conducted some research on the identity of that person in the viewcording. We recognize the man. He's one of the Breacher scouts whom the field rangers have spotted around the campus!"

Kayla's lower lip began to tremble. How could this happen? It was so unfair! What were the odds a bird would activate her token in front of a Breacher who just happened by? She wouldn't cry. She would not! Her nails dug into her palms as she struggled to compose herself.

"Do you suppose a trained Breacher scout wouldn't find the antics of that crow suspicious? That his training wouldn't urge him to search for a cause?"

She remained standing ramrod straight and silent, waiting for the discipline sure to follow.

"Finally, you understand the gravity of the situation. When it comes to the use of tokens, no mistake is a minor one. You will spend the rest of this day monitoring that token and the surrounding area for any suspicious activity. You will *not* reactivate the token without my express permission. I advised you to keep your hand on the switch while the token was active. You didn't follow that advice.

"I'm giving you an order this time and I hope you're paying attention. You will *not* place your hand anywhere near that switch now that the token is safely off! If you see anything suspicious, you will alert me at once. Are my instructions clear?"

"Yes, Lead TokenWard!"

"If nothing more serious happens before the end of the day, I will consider your discipline and keep this between the two of us. However, if this escalates, I will report it to the Chief Sentry. Do I make myself clear?"

"Understood, Sir! Thank you, Lead TokenWard."

"You're dismissed to your duties. Remain vigilant!"

Kayla bowed her head and quickly left, eager to get away before embarrassing herself more.

***

Sitting at the monitoring console felt like punishment enough. It provided a relentless reminder of her failure. She wanted nothing more than to flee to her room and weep in frustration.

So many thoughts were buzzing around in her head that it was difficult to focus on the screen. It was tiring, but she couldn't afford to fail at this task. What if she had missed something else? What if something even worse happened as a result? How would she redeem herself?

Memories of the previous evening haunted her. Everyone congratulating her on her promotion — her prideful demeanour as she accepted their praises.

"We always knew you'd succeed, Kayla — you'll do great, Kayla." A groan escaped her lips as she sank lower in her chair. How would she live this down? It was humiliating! And her mother! If this got back to her mother, it would all be over. The Chief Sentry wouldn't overlook her daughter's error. No justification would suffice. Her mother had warned her often enough that she had to live up to a much higher standard.

Deak had shown her a great mercy by responding as he had. If she made it through this, she would make sure to thank him properly when she had the chance.

Chapter 11

Rage boiled through Toller's veins. These Sicari proved useful, but they presumed too much. They were like untrained dogs always pulling at their leash, testing their reach.

They seemed to have no rank among themselves, often working independently. They were assassins who took pleasure in sowing chaos and he supposed their temperament suited the work. Still, he despised them and their lack of respect.

This one had burst into his presence in total disregard of his rank and authority. A Third Anarch should command respect! The interruption came at a critical moment in his interrogation of a prisoner. Now he'd have to begin again.

He restrained his impulse to lash out and strike the brute for his insolence. *One must tread carefully when dealing with wild creatures.*

The Sicari handled the darker side of Breacher business. Toller needed them as allies when it came time to take his place as Second Anarch. They might lack political finesse but Toller excelled in wielding blunt tools with a skill that compensated for defects.

That old fool, Kenric Trantor, held the position of Second Anarch for far too long. His claim to fame was a pathetic little uprising in the distant past. Admittedly, raising an army of malcontents to destroy historic archives had created a much-needed disruption at the time. However, Trantor had never taken advantage of the opportunity to insert a revisionist history that could have accomplished so much more. *He lacks foresight and the imagination necessary to lead the Breachers.*

Toller had no such deficiency. *Kenric's incompetence will be his undoing, but I must exercise caution.* The Breacher ranks overflowed with intrigue and duplicity. One didn't achieve a position of authority without wariness as he well knew.

"What's the meaning of this intrusion?" Villecrest yelled. The Sicari seemed unruffled by the outburst. Those lower in rank tended to cower when Toller's ire was up. Everyone knew of his impatience. Yet this man wore a smug smile. *The impudence!*

Useful or not, Toller was prepared to call his guards and order this animal put down. However, before he could voice the command, the Breacher spoke. He said only five words.

"We've spotted a token."

Third Anarch Villecrest's eyes filled with avarice. All rage evaporated as he mentally shifted gears. *At last. My plans can begin.*

When his designs finally saw fruition, even the Sicari would respect and fear him.

Chapter 12

Nico stared at the message tube. It was lying there on the table doing nothing. Why did it feel so portentous? "Maybe because it is." Nico's voice echoed in the empty kitchen.

What could his father have to say in a letter that the lawvocates couldn't have explained directly? He couldn't imagine his father writing something personal or sentimental, knowing an employee would deliver it.

This is ridiculous — just read it already. His life would change one way or the other. He needed to know everything before he made a decision.

Nico reached for the tube as the wall chrono in the hall chimed, startling him. He snatched his hand back and laughed nervously. *Now or never,* he thought as he lifted it off the table and broke the wax seal.

A single sheet of parchment was rolled up inside the message tube. His father's familiar script filled the page.

My dear Nico, if you're reading this, then I have returned to the Maker. I had so wished to be there for you when this day arrived but the Maker waits for no man.

You will need to know a great deal about the family business and I have prepared in advance, as well as I could, to provide you with teachers. I have left instructions with the company lawvocates. Learn what you can, but believe in yourself. I know your heart — you will succeed in all you set your mind to do.

I'm proud of you, Son. Remember, life may place an obstacle in your path, but

*you can always find your way if you follow the true North Star on your journey —
Love, Papa.*

Nico read it three more times to make sure he hadn't missed anything. His father wasn't one to waste valuable parchment and the content of the letter seemed immaterial.

The last paragraph stood out. His father took steps to ensure only Nico would understand. That meant he didn't trust those he had left to carry out his wishes.

Remember, the letter had said, and so he did.

To celebrate Nico's seventh birthday, his father had taken him fishing. The evening breeze felt cool and the boat creaked as it turned into the wind.

"Careful, Nico," his father exhorted, "you need to learn to steer by touch so you can keep your eye on the stars. Finding your way across the water at night can be treacherous, but learning how could save your life one day."

The experience proved nerve-wracking but also glorious! The wind in his face and the smell of the brine was invigorating. He clung to the memory of it as his father tucked him into bed later that night.

"You did well today, Nico. I'm proud of you. I have no doubt that you'll soon navigate by the stars as easily as the sun." His father's eyes had grown serious then. "Son, I want you to remember something."

"Yes Papa?"

His father pointed to the cornice moulding at the top of the wall. It formed a repeating pattern of embossed stars. "Look to the North Star," he proclaimed.

Nico turned his eyes to the place his father directed. When the house was built, his father had noticed that due to the orientation of Nico's bedroom, the star in the very corner of the moulding pointed due north. He had used that coincidence to teach Nico what direction he was facing no matter where he was in the house. It was a lesson later employed in teaching him to pick out landmarks and their relation to the stars in the sky.

"Sometimes in life, you believe you're following a well-charted path, only to discover it's not the *true* path."

"What do you mean, Papa?"

"If you follow the north star in your room, thinking it the true North Star — you will run into a wall."

Nico had giggled at the thought, and his father joined in until they were laughing so hard their sides hurt.

Over the years it became a running joke. Every time Nico hurt himself or did something stupid, his father would tell his mother that Nico had been following his personal north star. The fond memory of them enjoying a laugh together remained to this day. The contrasting moment — when his father had taken on a serious mien — marred the recollection. He wondered anew what it had meant.

Nico felt certain of one thing. His father had a secret. A secret he wanted Nico to discover.

Nico didn't sleep in his old bedroom anymore. He had the whole house to himself and chose to leave his childhood room as it was. He'd visit it whenever he wanted to walk down memory lane. He ran to that room now.

Flinging open the door, Nico headed straight to the northern corner of the room and looked up. He suddenly felt silly. *What are you doing, Nico? You've looked at that star thousands of times over the years. What makes you think it will be different this time?* He shook his head. No, it *was* different, his father had set something in motion this time.

He didn't know what he'd expected. Inspiration maybe? Some clue to his father's vague letter? He looked at the star once more. Really looked. Something shifted.

Nico jerked his head in surprise and stared at the place where the star had been. It seemed to bubble and grow. The corner reshaped itself into an extruded flat panel with his father's familiar script on the surface. It read, *Encrypted 9/10/ Ezra.* Nico spun, and glanced around the room. Was someone playing a joke — waiting to jump out and have a laugh at his expense? He sucked in a steadying breath. That couldn't be it. No one could have known he was coming to his old bedroom at

this particular moment. His parents weren't alive to share secrets and only they knew the family joke about the North Star.

Nico faced the panel again. The message had disappeared and no amount of staring would bring it back. What technology was this? How did it relate to his father? If Nico thought he had a mystery before he read the letter, he certainly had one now.

"I'll figure it out Papa. I promise." He whispered.

Dropping onto his childhood bed, he stared out the window at the stars in the night sky. It had been a trying day and he quickly fell asleep.

Chapter 13

Kade tried, with limited success, to open his eyes for a third time. His mouth felt like a pillow stuffed with wool. He'd had far too much to drink the previous night.

Reflecting on the quarrel with his father, the idea of continuing his consumption had some appeal. It wasn't really an option — he had classes this morning.

"Right — that education won't be continuing much longer," he croaked.

Kade managed to open one eye long enough to glance at the chrono on the table beside his bed. He still had an hour to get ready. His head throbbed as he rolled to a sitting position. The pain seemed more tolerable than his predicament.

I know I was angry last night, but I don't remember tossing things about. He surveyed the room. It looked like a wild boar had been rooting through his belongings. What difference did it make? He'd be on the street soon enough.

The lenders were asking for money he didn't have and the school would soon be asking for his final tuition payment. He had to pay or he wouldn't graduate. *All of my efforts will have been for nothing.* To come so close only to have it ripped away.... He felt like screaming in frustration.

Kade shook his head and immediately regretted it. Stop thinking like that! *Hang on to hope until none remains.*

That's what his mother always told him. Ironic, since no hope remained for help from his parents. Maybe uncle Geoff would come through with an extension on his deadline.

Or maybe I could sell something. Kade looked around the room. *If I haven't broken everything.*

One day at a time. He needed to explore his options. Meanwhile, he couldn't afford to let his grades slip in case something worked out. It served no purpose to discover a financial windfall only to be denied graduation as the result of an incomplete class project.

Kade finished pulling on his clothes, grabbed the last pickled egg from a jar in the kitchen and headed out the door.

Chapter 14

Nico jerked his head to the side, annoyed. What was that light shining in his eyes? He opened them a slit and blinked rapidly as his pupils adjusted. He awoke confused, then remembered where he was. He'd fallen asleep in his old bedroom and the morning light was streaming in the window. "I guess I was more tired than I realized," he muttered. "I'm still fully dressed."

A quick glance at the star moulding in the corner of the room provided no indication of anything peculiar. Nothing suggested that it had ever been anything other than a star-encrusted cornice.

Was I hallucinating? He wondered. He'd never experienced a vision before. Regardless, he'd seen a message and unless this presaged a serious mental health concern, he would assume his eyes were functioning correctly. Nico snorted. *A crazy person might come to the same conclusion.*

It was easy to remember the brief message — Encrypted 9/10/Ezra — likely an encryption key to unlock something. Nico couldn't think of a place to begin looking for answers.

First things first, he decided. I need some breakfast and a mug of kofa. He stopped off at the lavatory to wash up before proceeding to the kitchen.

After a hearty meal of spiced eggs rolled in flat bread and washed down with a cup of kofa, Nico felt refreshed and ready to tackle the problem. He refilled his mug and walked down the hall to the office where his father had built a substantial library over the years.

If he were to have any hope of figuring this out, he had to try to think like his father.

Entering the office disturbed a little swirl of dust that made him sneeze. He hadn't visited the room in some time. *Got to remember to dust in here.*

He smiled thinking how his friend Leviticus would react. Maybe I'll just invite Lev over and leave a broom conspicuously leaning beside the door. He doubted the room would remain dust laden for long if Lev were around. His friend couldn't ignore a mess that was within his power to put in order.

Nico walked over to the window to open the shutters. Then he strode over to the reading chair and sat down. After scrutinizing the room, he closed his eyes to let it soak in.

It was an old trick his father had taught him to help identify landmarks. Take in the horizon and close your eyes. The most prominent thing you saw in your mind was the landmark most recognizable to others when providing directions. He hoped something would jump out at him.

Maps were arranged on the desk and star charts on the walls. A globe stood in the corner next to a small table where his grandfather's first nav sighting instrument was on display. All manner of books on navigation, cartography, topography, landmarks and anything else that might advance the family's shipping business reserved a place on the shelves. Nothing distinctive caught his attention.

Nico recalled his father spending hours in here — studying potential new routes and calculating fuel costs or time savings. Nes Callan was always looking for some way to gain an edge. Travel was a constant of life for the Callan family.

His father's clue included numbers. *What could they represent?* Nico mused, *a date? Distances? Road markers?* "And why did you include Grandfather's name?" Nico asked aloud.

The remaining morning and part of the afternoon flew by as he paged through books and searched for possible hiding places. Frustration settled in as the solution eluded him.

I need to walk and clear my head, Nico decided. It was his habit to stroll to the cliffs at the edge of the estate and look out over the sea. The rolling waves helped him to think. He grabbed a flask of water and headed out the door.

The afternoon sun baked the earth producing heat waves visible in the distance. The chirps and whirs of insects intruded on the silence.

Nico walked briskly despite the heat. Before long, he began to jog. It felt good to move after sitting so long. The tall grass beat a familiar rhythm against his shins. This place was part of him. He smiled as he broke into a sprint covering the last stretch to his destination.

His chest was heaving when he arrived, shirt drenched in sweat. After catching his breath, he dropped to the ground and slung his legs over the edge of the cliff. Goosebumps formed as the updraft cooled his skin and dried his shirt.

Gazing at the water for a time, a seabird caught his attention. It dove into the sea and emerged with a fish in its mouth, then flew to the rocks at the base of the cliffs to feast.

The rocks below brought memories of fishing with his grandfather. At the time he was too young to venture out with the men in the boats. Instead, he and Grandpapa would cast nets from the rocks.

Looking past the bird, he spied the large flat stone where they would spread nets to dry. Grandpapa would teach him songs of the sea as they settled into a comfortable rhythm — sorting the catch and mending nets before heading home. He had so many memories tied to travel on the sea, and land for that matter, but they always began and ended here. Home, business, and family were intertwined.

Nico's grandfather had built up a fleet of fishing vessels — and eventually ground transports — to carry his produce to market. His father had taken that business and built it into a vast transportation network that spanned the globe.

I can't end this Nico realized. I can't walk away from this legacy they've created for me. He knew in that moment he would take over the family business.

Life isn't about getting what you want. It's about being productive and accomplishing something good. What would it say about him if he took everything his family had accomplished and tossed it aside as if it held no value?

"It *does* hold value!" He declared to the sea. "*I* value it!" He meant it with his entire being.

A deep sorrow filled him as he thought of all he had lost. His grandmother had died in childbirth and he never knew her. His grandfather had died of a heart attack while he was fishing alone. They hadn't recovered him until his boat drifted to shore a week later. Nico was eight at the time and it was his first experience with the death of a loved one. He had never wanted to feel such grief again, but he did, when his parents died a few years later. He felt utterly alone and he missed them all.

It struck him as he was sitting there that the catacombs were nearby. Numerous caves riddled the face of the cliff. Over the years, people had joined several of them to form a network of tunnels as more bodies were interred there. The caves provided a natural crypt used for years by the locals as a place to house the bones of their loved ones. Nico's family owned the property, but they continued to make it available to the locals who would regularly visit their loved ones.

Nico hadn't paid respect to his own loved ones in some time. With all the memories that had been dredged up, now seemed like a good time. It was only a ten-minute walk from where he was. He rose and headed toward the caves.

Chapter 15

"Of all the days for an advanced theory lesson!" Kade grumbled as he left the classroom. His head was still throbbing and he wasn't absorbing much or really anything the sage was saying. He'd never been so happy for a lecture to end. *Only four more classes to go.*

He was slowly shuffling his way along the edge of the quad. The sun caused him to blink so rapidly he didn't think he could find his way to the next class.

"Hey Brixton, you lost? I thought you were an expert on maps or something?"

The query came from somewhere about twenty cubits to his right, but he didn't bother looking.

"It's pattern recognition! Not maps," he retorted.

"If your aimless stumbling is part of a pattern, I don't think any of us recognizes it. I guess that's why you're the expert."

Several people guffawed. Apparently, he had an audience. Maybe if he ducked into the shadows between buildings, he could escape the sun long enough to stop blinking and get his bearings.

The bustle of the quad quieted noticeably as he advanced several steps into the alleyway. That and the cool shade offered a welcome respite. He stood motionless and enjoyed a moment of reduced pain.

"Good morning Mr. Brixton."

Kade flinched at the mention of his name and the pain came rushing back.

"Who?"

"Oh, pardon me, I didn't mean to startle you."

Kade squinted, trying to identify this unwelcome intrusion. He imagined one of those buffoons from the quad had followed him.

"Look, I need to get to class." He squeezed his eyes shut willing the person away.

"I'd like to make a proposition."

Kade grabbed a second look. The speaker didn't sound like a student. His voice resonated in the alleyway, smooth and cultivated. Now that his eyes had adjusted to the darker surroundings, he could tell that it definitely wasn't a student. The man was in his forties at least.

"Do I know you?"

"We've never met. My name is Decar Tosh."

Tosh. That's a Sumakadian name. This fellow is far from home. "Well, Mr. Tosh — as I've said, I need to get to class."

"If you'll grant me a few minutes, I'll make it worth your while."

"Look my friend, whatever you're selling I'm not buying. You need to pick your targets better. I don't have a copper to my name."

"Oh, you misunderstand, Mr. Brixton. I'm not selling — I'm buying, so to speak."

"You're not my type."

"Please, no need to be crude. I work for a technology company, and I understand you're a student of computational engineering."

"You're offering me an engineering job? I haven't graduated yet."

"Not exactly. Currently we're more interested in a project you've participated in. We understand you're working on a facial recognition algorithm under the supervision of a prodigy by the name of Leviticus Radix."

Kade felt his face flushing with rage as he spat out the hated name. "Radix?"

Unbelievable! Leviticus hadn't even graduated yet and already he was polluting the corporate waters. Was this what the future looked like? Forever living in the shadow of the golden boy? Always second best?

He thought things would change once they graduated and struck out on their own in the world. Apparently not if this were any indicator of the future.

"Leviticus Radix is *not* my supervisor! We work as a team. I know every bit as much about that project as he does."

"Interesting. You're saying that you have full access? That you don't require Mr. Radix's prior approval to work on the project?"

"Of course not! He isn't even necessary! I could rebuild that algorithm myself if I had to!"

"My profound apologies. I was not aware. In that case, perhaps I can bring my proposal to you directly."

"I'm listening."

"My organization has also been working on facial recognition. As you can imagine, we would prefer to be first in bringing this technology to market. When we learn of people working on similar projects, we're eager to have them join our team. It's so much easier to bring people on board who already have experience in the field."

Kade shrugged. "I believe I've made my credentials clear."

"Yes, yes. Unfortunately, I only have your name listed as someone who might put me in touch with Mr. Radix. You would need to prove your expertise before we could consider an offer."

"What sort of proof would you require?"

"What indeed. You said you have full access to the project?"

"Yes."

"In that case, this is what I propose. Bring a copy of the project for us to review."

Kade shook his head. "That's not possible."

"I thought you said you had access."

"I do, but I'm not about to hand proprietary information over to some guy who approached me in an alley. The project belongs to Denmount. It's not mine to sell."

"Oh, of course! Nor would I ask such a thing. We vigorously protect our own projects and would expect no less from others. However, that's not what I'm suggesting. I'm proposing that you bring a copy of your algorithm to an arranged location where an expert from our team could obtain a look

and ask you a few questions to ascertain your expertise. You would retain possession of the copy. We don't need Denmount's algorithm. As I've said, we have our own. We only wish to ascertain your knowledge of the subject. This is a relatively new and specialized field, as you well know. It's the only practical way for you to offer proof of experience. Based on your interaction, our expert will quickly discern whether you truly understand the technology."

Kade thought quickly. *With Radix as competition, this may be my only opportunity to beat him to a top-ranked position. It's a gamble whether this guy is legitimate or not. I would know more if I could talk to this so-called expert of theirs. Still, how would I get a copy off campus?*

"Mr. Brixton, I realize that this seems a little unorthodox. I wish that I had caught up with you on a bench in the quad rather than this dark alley. I imagine it all seems a little suspicious to you.

"As I suggested earlier," Decar continued, "I'm willing to compensate you for your time. If you agree to my proposal, my company has authorized me to offer five hundred silvers to potential hires for the inconvenience of our vetting process. Here is a card with contact information and a few details about our company. Please conduct a little research. You'll find that we're top-ranked in the field and well respected.

"If you're interested, show up at this location within the next two days. Bring your copy of the algorithm and hand this card to the gentleman at the front desk. He will arrange for you to talk with my expert who is staying there while we're in town. If you don't show up, I understand completely. We will continue our search for other talent. Perhaps we can convince Mr. Radix, when we locate him.

"It was a pleasure meeting you, Mr. Brixton. I have already taken far too much of your time. I'm sure you're very busy so close to graduation. I do hope we can work together. Goodbye for now."

Kade stared after the man as he walked back out into the sunshine of the quad. Seeing him in the sunlight. He looked every bit the genuine businessman. Nothing sinister at all. He found himself reassessing any reservations he'd initially held.

His line of reasoning was interrupted when the offer hit home. *Five hundred silvers?* That would pay for his tuition and several loan payments while he looked for work after graduation. Better yet, if this were the real deal, he might have a job offer right after graduation. He couldn't believe it — could he?

If it turned out to be a genuine opportunity and he waited until they talked to Leviticus, they would choose Radix — no doubt in his mind. Kade was an excellent writ weaver, but no one could compete with Radix in a side-by-side comparison. Oh, how it would gall him if Leviticus stole this opportunity away from him!

Kade had a lot to think about. He didn't have much time but some hope remained for him to cling to.

Chapter 16

Nico walked the cliff edge to the catacombs. He could smell the green of growing things on his left and the salty brine on his right.

Something about the border of land and sea pulled him in two directions at once. Part of him wanted stability and a set path while another part yearned for adventure. The land anchored him in the present and the sea called out with promises of the future. The dichotomy suited him. It felt right, somehow.

The sun was beginning to set by the time he arrived. That would help, Nico recalled. The cave's interior would brighten with the sun lower in the sky. Lamps were available at the cave entrance, so he wasn't concerned about finding his way around, but the red glow of the setting sun made the place less gloomy.

It wasn't easy for a person to find the catacombs. Patches of scrub brush dotted the cliff edge and overgrowth often hid the entrance. You had to know where to look.

Nico stopped to get his bearings. A rock outcropping stood about fifty yards back from the cliff edge. He knew to look for the entrance in the bushes on the edge of the cliff — opposite and to the right of the rock.

He'd travelled a bit too far. Nico turned around and wandered back, recovering his steps. Searching between the shrubs, he spotted the telltale depression. Nico tried to protect his exposed arms from the thorny branches as he gingerly picked his way past. Someone usually trimmed back the bramble when a body was to be interred. Enough time had passed without loss of life that the brush had filled in.

A stairway had been carved into the face of the cliff. The steps were wide enough for two to walk abreast. A stone parapet provided security. Pausing at the entrance, Nico looked out over the sea once more to check the sun on the horizon. It was setting faster than he'd expected, but the cave interior remained well lit. Nevertheless, he thought it wise to grab one of the lanterns from the wall.

The crypt was much as he remembered. Alcoves were carved into the sides of the cave. Roll-up doors protected the ossuaries from vandals or grave robbers who might stumble across the hidden steps. Nico walked quickly to the rear of the sanctum, conscious of the dwindling light. The caves were connected at the back, and he needed to cross over to cave nine. His grandfather had chosen that particular cave because it was angled in such a way that the North Star was visible from within the cave. Grandpapa wanted his bones laid to rest in sight of the guiding star. It appealed to his seafaring nature.

Nico found his way to his family's alcove and pressed in the combination to unlock the rolling door. The lock used a simple letter-to-number cipher based on his grandfather's name — Ezra. Rolling

up the door left a void in his heart and a lump in his throat. The bones of his family were in these boxes, but they offered poor companionship.

Placing one hand on each of his parents' ossuaries, he said a prayer to the Maker as silent tears rolled down his face.

"What were you trying to tell me in your letter Papa?" As if in answer to his question, he had a sudden memory of another time his father had told him to *look to the North Star*. It had occurred right here in this cave when they had laid his grandfather to rest.

The family had stayed after the ceremony to wait for nightfall so they could pray Grandfather on his way as he made his final sojourn. The North Star wouldn't serve as his waymark on this journey beyond those twinkling lights. His guide would be the Maker Himself.

Nico remembered they had been sitting in the cave entrance with a perfect view of the sky. For some odd reason, his father had led him to the back of the cave and turned him to face the night sky. He had asked Nico if he could pick out the North Star from where they stood. He couldn't see it until his father had repositioned him a few times.

"I see it now Papa, it's right there." Nico had dutifully pointed it out.

"That's right Nico. Remember the North Star."

Nico had been absently tracing his finger over the number carved on his father's bone box as the memory played out. He looked to his hand and the number jumped out at him. Box number twelve. His mother's box was next to it — box number eleven.

Blood drained from his face and he felt a chill go through his body as his eyes moved to the next box — number ten. The box of his grandfather. The answer was right there in front of him. Ezra — cave nine — box 10.

The message from his father wasn't an encryption key at all. That wording served to distract people. He had actually been hinting at the ossuaries, which were, in a manner of speaking, en - crypted!

Look to the North Star, Nico remembered. His father had made him stand in that exact spot at the back of the cave for a reason. Nico made his way to where he thought the spot might be and turned to face the entrance of the cave. The sun had almost set and the first stars were becoming visible.

Feeling around on the floor, he found a sharp stone and stood back up. He held the stone in his hand as he waited for darkness.

When the stars stood out clearly, he experimented with his position. "There!" he exclaimed. The echo startled him.

Using the stone in his hand, he carefully scratched a line on either side of his head in the stone wall at his back. He wanted to mark the area that approximated where the North Star was discernible. He scuffed the ground with his feet, leaving a mark in the dirt to show where he had been standing. Using the lantern, Nico gave a cursory inspection but the light was failing. He'd have to wait until daybreak.

It had grown dark. There was no way he would find his way back to the house. He was too filled with anticipation to leave anyway. That suited Nico. The night was warm. He'd sleep in the cave.

Settling at the opening to the sea. Nico stared up at the night sky. Maybe Papa was looking down at him right now. He fell asleep with a peace he hadn't felt in a long time. He was finally going to get some answers.

Chapter 17

Nico's eyes sprang open at first light. A breeze off the water brought a salt tang to his nose. Sitting up, he yawned, stretched and worked out a knot that had developed in his neck from sleeping on the hard ground.

A seabird called out, looking for a fish no doubt. The thought caused his stomach to growl and he searched through his pack, retrieving a flagon of water and an apple. *This is it.* Nico thought as he finished the apple and threw the core into the sea. *Today I find answers.* After a final mouthful of water, he walked to the back of the cave and started his investigation.

The back of the cave appeared much as one would expect of a rock wall. No obvious markings stood out other than the scratches he had made the previous night. He drew closer to scrutinize that patch in particular. Nothing unique caught his attention.

He tried staring at the spot duplicating his experience with the star moulding in his old bedroom — still nothing. Maybe he'd missed some hidden instruction on the ossuary?

Jogging back to the family alcove, he entered the code to unlock it and rolled up the door once more. He couldn't discern anything different about his grandfather's box from what he recalled seeing the first time.

Having no better ideas, he glanced around feeling foolish and tried staring at the numbers or anything else that looked promising in case the bedroom incident was repeatable here. *I probably look like a lunatic,* he thought. *Staring at things like a madman as if doing so will magically transform them by the power of my mind.* He chuckled at the mental image.

His eyes began to burn and nothing was happening anyway. *Enough of that.* He closed the door and walked back to the rear wall running a hand over his face and rubbing his eyes. He looked up at the spot he had marked, not expecting to see anything different.

The wall began to bubble and transform just as the cornice moulding had in his bedroom. This time it didn't form a message, however. The cave wall dissolved and an entrance appeared, revealing a tunnel leading deeper into the cliff.

The rock face had vanished! How was that possible? Solid rock didn't disappear like that. He'd felt the cold stone and had carved into the surface with a rock.

After about thirty seconds, stone began to re-form. The tunnel entrance sealed ten seconds later. *What on earth?* Try as he might, he could find no seams or any other evidence that an opening had ever appeared. Pounding at the entrance was like pounding on a rock wall. No surprise, he already knew it was more than an illusion.

I wonder... Nico grabbed a larger stone from the corner of the cave and hurled it at the covered entrance. It bounced back as expected, but he did hear a hollow sound when it struck. *Aha!* The tunnel behind the wall remained.

He stared at the spot again — nothing. What had he done differently? Of course! He had opened and then closed the roll-up door on his family's crypt. He ran back and repeated the process. Just as he'd guessed — when he stared at the spot on the rock face it dissolved once more. It seemed that by opening and closing the crypt he could trigger a response.

After about thirty seconds the tunnel entrance closed once more. It provided an elegant way to maintain secrecy. The delay afforded just enough time for someone to walk from the closed crypt and pass through the tunnel entrance before it sealed, leaving no evidence that anyone had been there.

Nico shivered as he tried to imagine what would happen if someone weren't fast enough. Would they get stuck inside the rock face as it re-formed? *Yeah, let's not test that.*

Nico desperately wanted to explore but he wasn't properly provisioned. He might find numerous branching tunnels to map. Or, the tunnel could take a day to traverse, only to end in a locked exit at the far end. That last possibility hardly seemed likely now that he understood the trigger mechanism, but he wasn't comfortable with the risk of so many unknowns.

He'd need food and water to last for a several days at least. He'd also want to bring some excavating equipment in case he needed to dig his way out should his passage become blocked. It wouldn't hurt to have some way to mark his passage in case the tunnels became a maze. He mentally added that to the list he was forming.

His stomach gurgled. It was getting dark again and he hadn't eaten since morning. Had he truly been here that long? *Time to head home and prepare a plan.*

***

It was friday afternoon, the last day of school before the start of a week-long break for the business program at Denmount. Sages would be grading papers and with no looming project deadlines, he could enjoy some free time.

It presented a perfect opportunity to explore the mystery of his father's hidden tunnel. Since that first visit, his obsession with the mystery had grown. The implications had distracted him from his schoolwork all morning. It would be good to get some answers so he could focus after the break.

His mind drifted again — walls that materialize out of thin air.... He couldn't fathom how his father would have access to equipment of that nature, technology unknown to most of the world. What other secrets did his father keep? *Maybe I'll find more answers this weekend.*

Chapter 18

Kade darted his eyes nervously around the room. Everyone from the team seemed occupied with their viewscreens and the instructor had left the room. His hand clutched the storage device in his pocket. Could he do this?

The viewscreens lined one long table against the wall across from the classroom door. Kade had chosen the screen at the end so no one could sit on his left side.

He set his pack on the chair to his right, discouraging anyone from claiming that spot. A few angry sneers thrown towards those who approached, convinced everyone that he was 'in a mood' and that it might be best to give him some space.

Anyone walking into the room had a direct view of all screens at once, but that was unavoidable.

The instructor had said he needed to attend a meeting so Kade calculated he had at least a half hour for unsupervised activity. Other than the instructor, only project team members ever came into this room — Kade didn't expect any surprises.

Five hundred silvers. That number ran through his mind every few minutes. It felt as if he was selling out somehow, but what choice did he have? His final tuition payment was due in two days. It was the only way to earn the money he needed in time.

If he missed the deadline for payment, he would be expelled. All those years of hard work and education wasted. He would be stuck in some low-paying job for the rest of his life. The notion of that failure was too much to contemplate. His father would never let him live it down. No, the humiliation would be unbearable. If it came to that, he would leave his family behind, never to return.

He needed to procure a copy of the project files. It would be all right. He would show the files to Decar Tosh's expert, answer a few questions, and quickly destroy the files when the interview was over. *Or maybe I should keep the files as an insurance policy — something to sell if everything goes wrong.* What was he thinking? It wasn't like he was participating in espionage.

Kade had done his research — Decar's company was legitimate. This was just for a job interview. So why did he feel so guilty? *Enough!* Whatever this was, it remained his only option. He could get caught copying the files and be expelled, or he could miss his payment and be expelled. Either way, he had nothing to lose and everything to gain. Kade steeled his resolve. He had put almost four years into this project, it belonged to him as much as anyone.

He looked down the line of students staring at their screens. Leviticus sat seven spaces down the row pecking away at his keypad. *Supervisor? As if!* No way was he going to let Radix rob him of this opportunity or get credit for Kade's own hard work on this project! He caught himself sneering and quickly composed his features. The decision solidified in his mind.

Kade casually reached over to his pack on the seat and pulled it up onto the table beside his viewscreen. He placed it so it would block his classmate's view. He made a show of rummaging

through the pack and pulled out some bread, cheese and an apple and set them out on the table for all to see.

He bit into the apple and chewed loudly. Every head snapped up and stared at him. Ducking his head into his shoulders, he made a sheepish expression and slowly lowered his apple to the table picking up the bread instead. He waved it a bit as though asking permission to proceed then gingerly nibbled quietly. Everyone turned back to their tasks and ignored him as he'd hoped. Now they would judiciously continue to ignore him knowing he still had a noisy apple to munch.

The instructor had left, and the rest of the project team focused on their individual tasks. It was now or never.

The storage device was out of his pocket and plugged into the network in a few heartbeats. He stole a quick peek to assure himself that no one had noticed. So far, so good.

Everyone on the team had joint access to the files. Security measures weren't a concern once you were in the system, since they were all working together on the project.

He had considered coming to the classroom while no one else was present, but that might raise suspicion. He risked more by taking this route, but it meant that everyone was logged into the system at the same time. Nobody recorded which station they worked at on any particular day. If questions arose down the road, it would be difficult to place guilt on any one person. He had decided this option was preferable.

If he were caught in the act, denial wouldn't be an option and he would bear the consequences immediately. However, if he managed to leave with the files at the end of class — well, he would still worry, but much less. The possibility remained that someone might notice a record of copied files, but by then too much time would have passed and he could claim innocence along with everyone else. The trail would be cold.

Kade selected files he personally worked on since he was most familiar with those specific components. It would be easier to answer questions about his own writ weaving during an interview.

A few subtle keystrokes started the transfer. If someone happened to notice the progress indicator, he had decided he would say he was test compiling his work. It wouldn't pass careful scrutiny, but was plausible enough.

The transfer completed more quickly than expected. Kade stared dumbly at the screen. It seemed too anticlimactic. He half expected security to come charging into the room. Another minute passed and nothing happened.

A second thought intruded. What if the interviewer was expecting something more? Kade tried to remember his contributions. Did he work on enough critical components to make it clear that his writs were part of a facial recognition algorithm? Of course he had! In four years, he must have.

Still, did he want to take that chance having come this far? He selected all of the remaining project files and started transferring those as well. He quickly regretted it when he saw the much slower pace of the progress indicator.

How much time has passed? Kade looked at the wall chrono. The instructor had left fifteen minutes ago. He needed to wrap this up.

Why did I start that second transfer? So stupid! A kink was forming in his neck from ducking his head behind the cover of his pack. *That probably looks a little suspicious* he thought, straightening his spine.

His movement attracted the attention of Selica Lor, across the room. She took it as a cue to perform a languorous stretch of her own. She looked over and gifted him with a wink. *Oh no. Please, not now!* Selica had been flirting with him the last few days. She was a recent transfer to Denmount.

When she had first arrived, he had the impression she was interested in Leviticus. Kade wasn't sure why she had suddenly turned her attention to him. Normally he wouldn't have minded, but this was the worst possible moment. He averted his eyes, hoping she'd take the hint, but she stood up and moved in his direction.

Kade stood up in a panic as heads turned in their direction. He said the first thing that came to mind. "Um, yeah, I could use some kofa too."

That seemed to satisfy the others, but Selica was staring at him, one eyebrow raised in query. He shared a conspiratorial look and nodded at the kofa machine under the pretense that he wanted to speak with her privately. He grabbed her elbow and steered her away from his viewscreen. She looked mildly surprised but didn't pull away from his touch. Kade positioned Selica so her back was to the workstations. "Can I pour you a cup?" He asked, while looking over her shoulder at his screen.

"Sure."

He poured a mug of kofa and offered it to Selica. She accepted it with a question in her eyes that didn't match her words. "I wonder who brews the kofa for the lab? It tastes like mud."

Glancing at his viewscreen, he noticed the progress indicator nearing completion. He needed to hold her attention for a few more minutes. Kade slowly poured a second mug for himself and made a show of looking for some cream. "I know. It's pretty bitter, but it does keep me awake."

"There's a little stall about a block from the campus that serves a great mug of kofa."

Was she suggesting a date? He'd considered asking her out in the past, maybe she'd say yes.

Selica looked as though she was considering heading back to her seat so he laid his hand on her forearm and leaned forward to whisper in her ear, so he wouldn't disturb the others. Once again, she didn't pull away so he took that as a good sign. This seemed to be a day for risk taking.

"Selica," he began quietly.

"Yes?" She asked in a similarly hushed tone, leaning forward a bit.

"Well, we're nearing graduation and none of us knows what the future will bring or whether we'll see each other again. Anyway, I've always admired you, I mean your work..." He felt his cheeks flush as he fumbled his words.

Selica had a pleased expression on her face as she drew close enough to brush against him. "I know what you meant."

Kade mentally rolled his eyes. *I've always admired you? Good grief! Just ask her out before you say something worse.* "Yes, well, uh, would you like to join me for a meal sometime?"

Kade didn't think she could get any closer, but she pressed against him and whispered in his ear. "I'd like that very much."

It sounded more like a promise than an answer. A little shocked, Kade didn't know where to direct his eyes. They fell on his viewscreen and he saw that the file transfer had completed.

His relief was so complete that he found himself smiling and suddenly realized he was hugging Selica. She winked again, pulled away from his embrace, and walked with a little sway in her hips back to her chair.

The rest of the team was vigorously pretending that they hadn't seen the exchange. He couldn't have dreamed up a more effective way to draw attention away from his viewscreen.

Kade rushed back to his station. He surreptitiously disconnected and pocketed his storage device just as a chime announced the end of class. Shoving everything back into his pack, Kade flashed Selica a quick smile and rushed out of the room. The day had turned out pretty well so far. He had succeeded in getting the files and as a bonus, he had a date with Selica.

Kade decided to skip his study period. If he hurried, he could make it to the location on the card Decar had given him and get this interview over with. He'd feel much better once he had that five hundred silvers in his pocket, then he could start planning for his future.

Chapter 19

The wait for the weekend was near unbearable. Every class had dragged on, each minute longer than the last. Nico's upcoming expedition filled his every waking moment. By the time the final class of the week arrived, he felt ready to explode.

Now he sat contemplating everything except philosophy in the class he had convinced Lev to join. Lev had been glaring at him with accusing eyes through the whole lecture, leaning over at one point to whisper something. Nico assumed the muttering involved threats to his well-being, but all he heard was, "can't believe... If you... Just wait until..."

Nico didn't have a response. He was stewing a little himself. Of all the potential philosophical discussions available, the sage had chosen patience as the topic. The Maker was surely testing him.

After what felt like a lifetime, the class finally ended. Nico bolted for the door and Lev was hard on his heels. "Why are we running? Nico? I was just blowing off steam. I wasn't really going to hurt you — much." Lev increased his pace to catch up.

The comment stopped Nico short as he started laughing.

"And why are you laughing now?" Lev asked.

"As if I would run from you in fear. You punch like a six-year-old."

"Oh, really?" Lev arched an eyebrow. "You mean like that time I knocked you on your backside during boxing class?"

"You sucker punched me!"

"I didn't sucker punch you. You took that ill-advised moment to wave at Janissa."

Nico groaned. "Don't remind me. That was the most humiliating moment of my life. I was hoping for hero worship, not laughter."

"Awww — you're still *my* hero."

"Shut up!"

"She was way out of your league anyway." Lev squinted. "Seriously Nico what's up? You've been acting antsy all week."

Nico thought quickly. He wasn't ready to share this with Lev. Not before he knew more about what his father had been hiding. "I don't know. I guess that meeting I had with Tenika at Callan International has me wound up. This is the final term of school and I need to make some decisions that will affect the rest of my life."

"Yeah, I'm sorry man. That's a lot of responsibility they heaped on your shoulders. I hadn't considered how it might be affecting you."

"It's okay." *Got to downplay this.*

Lev put a hand on Nico's shoulder, a look of concern in his eyes. "Listen, if you want to hang out this weekend and get your mind off things...."

"No!" *Way to go Nico, that didn't sound at all suspicious.* "I mean thanks, but I just need to be alone with my thoughts for a while. I figured the school break would give me time to wrap my head around — everything." He hoped his face showed the right mix of innocence and solemnity.

"Okay — well, you know how to reach me if you change your mind. I need to head to the lab to help out with a project. Catch up with you later?"

And just like that, Nico found himself alone. A big stupid grin spread across his face. He hadn't had an adventure in years. In the past he'd always explored new places with his parents, but on the day they died his wanderlust had died with them.

Now, though — now he was going on one last trip, planned by his father. He'd forgotten how much he enjoyed the anticipation. Nico ran for his electric tri-wheel. He couldn't wait to start the weekend.

Chapter 20

Nico gathered the last of his things and set them at the front door. The pile was modest — just the perishable foods that he'd held back until the last moment. The rest of his gear was already in the tunnel. He'd carted a load to the catacombs each day over the past week in preparation for the weekend.

Placing everything within the hidden tunnel had involved a little trial and error at first. Each time the tunnel opened he had thirty seconds to get his equipment through before it closed again. The thought of getting trapped inside before he had transferred all his provisions was worrisome, but not as terrifying as imagining what might happen if it closed while he was in the way.

His transfer efforts mostly involved frantic tossing, but some fragile items required a quick sprint in and out. He tried to practise caution, but one time he dropped a fuel cell right at the threshold just as the wall began to re-form. He watched in resignation, stepping back in case the cell ruptured. His fears were unfounded. The process originated from the edges of the tunnel, growing inward. At the same time, the wall thickened from the central plane of the projection, outward. The process made an almost silent crackling sound similar to fine gravel when it's poured out on a hard surface. Clusters built upon each other like a fast-growing crystal that just pushed objects out of its path.

Experimenting, he'd tried holding a pick axe directly in the way, only to have it push back. After gaining some confidence he'd tried pushing against the still forming matrix with his hand, hoping to get a sense of whether it was malleable at any point. As far as he could tell, it proved solid from the beginning of the process to completion. Or at least he imagined it to be so. It happened so quickly he couldn't be certain.

That was yesterday. Today he felt as prepared as he could be. It was time. He slung the pack with the last of his supplies over his shoulder, locked the front door of his house, and began his adventure.

***

When he arrived at the crypt, it was early evening. He wasn't worried about losing light as the sun set. Any exploration would occur in dark tunnels regardless. He had plenty of charge for the lanterns. His plan was to enter the tunnel and let the entrance close behind him. Then, he would set up a base camp of sorts and organize everything he had frantically tossed in over the course of the week.

Entering cave nine, Nico walked to the opening in the cliff face overlooking the sea. He spent some time sitting on the edge watching the sunset. When the sky dimmed enough that he could make out the North Star, he turned and headed back to his family's alcove.

Opening the rolling door, Nico placed his hands on the ossuaries of his parents. "Okay, Papa. I'm following your lead here. I hope I'm up to the task. I guess you wanted me to find something you knew I'd need to see, so here goes." He shut and locked the alcove and glanced over at the patch of wall to trigger the tunnel entrance. When it opened, he ran to his destiny.

Nico spun around and stared out the opening, an adrenaline rush coursing through his veins. *This suddenly seems foolish, Am I really going through with this?* The entrance sealed. *I guess so.* "Great planning Nico. It's pitch-black and you didn't turn on a lamp before walking in." He wasn't sure why he'd said that aloud except perhaps as a way to push back at the eerie black silence. It felt like he'd been searching in the dark for an hour before he finally located a lantern.

First order of business was to see if he could open the entrance from the inside. *It would be impossible to find a spot to stare at without a light to see,* Nico mused. If he found himself dealing with this technology on a regular basis, he'd need to make sure he always had a light source handy. Switching on the porta-lamp, he began searching the wall for clues.

He hoped that the intent of the trigger design was only to keep wanderers *out* of the tunnel and not to keep people in the tunnel from entering the crypt.

By that hypothesis, the key should be obvious from this side. That assumption was soon dismissed. A quick perusal revealed nothing, so he drew close to the surface and began systematically searching smaller areas from the bottom up.

He was starting to think that maybe he needed to do something further back in the tunnel first. Perhaps a primary trigger action was involved. He'd needed to open his parents' alcove before the secondary trigger spot was enabled. This might be the same.

Convincing himself of that likelihood, he rushed his scan of the final section of wall. Then, something in his peripheral vision caught his attention. There! up in the ceiling nestled in a hollow. A person might never see it unless they happened to stand right against the wall and look up. A symbol had been carved into the rock. It looked like a stylized letter 's' within a circle. He stared at it for a moment and the entrance opened.

"Yes!" Nico pumped his fist. He wouldn't be trapped in here after all. The logical part of his brain assured him that, of course, it had to be so. His father wouldn't have led him here without a way to get out. Regardless, when the entrance sealed once more, relief washed over him.

Setting the lantern on the ground, Nico took in the haphazard gear scattered about and finished preparing his base camp. The last thing he set up was his bedding. That done, he settled in for his evening meal. For dinner, he munched on some meat rolls and a piece of fruit while considering his plan of attack for charting the tunnel.

I should probably get some sleep and start early in the morning, Nico thought, but he wasn't tired yet. Besides, he needed to find some place to relieve himself. That urgency in mind, he determined to explore just a bit before bedding down.

Nico shoved a few fluorescent wax marking sticks into his pockets and grabbed a second lantern, before heading down the tunnel. After walking for twenty minutes, the tunnel widened into a cavern. The ceiling rose thirty cubits above him. He estimated the width of the cave at roughly eighty cubits and ovate in shape.

Executing a slow turn, he let the light from his lantern play against the far walls. Some odd shadows wavered off to the right and he started moving cautiously in that direction. The shadows quickly resolved into a shape. Nico couldn't believe his eyes. "A tunnelling machine," he whispered in awe. He'd read about machines like this as a child, but as far as he knew they only existed on the other side of the world. *How could it be here?*

About twenty steps from the machine a larger tunnel loomed. It appeared to be the point of egress for the massive vehicle. He'd search that tomorrow.

Nico spent the next half hour exploring the engine, the cab, and the diamond cutting disks of the exotic machine. It was parked against the undulating cave wall. Loose rock and earth lay in piles where the cutting heads must have grazed as it was manoeuvring.

Alcoves appeared sporadically in the cavern walls. He found one conveniently situated behind the tunnelling machine alongside some loose piles of earth. It would do for a temporary latrine.

Having successfully accomplished his first objective, he realized he was getting tired. Time to return to his makeshift camp. Curiosity got the better of him. *Maybe I'll just walk over to the mouth of the other tunnel and have a quick look before heading back.*

The new tunnel was much larger than the one he had travelled from the crypt. A pattern of score marks in the tunnel walls confirmed the tunnelling machine as the culprit.

Nico walked about fifteen steps into the tunnel, feeling the grooves in the tunnel wall as he dragged his fingers across the surface. Suddenly, a familiar sound disturbed the silence and he spun in time to see that the entrance from the cavern to this new tunnel had sealed. He let out an involuntary cry and ran towards the newly formed wall. Before he took five steps, the same crackling notes reached his ears again, this time from where he had just been. He was trapped, the tunnel sealed on either side of him.

Chapter 21

Kayla stared at the viewscreen. Her eyes burned with exhaustion and hours of boredom made it difficult to keep them open. Even so, she was relieved that no one in the quad seemed interested in her token. Perhaps a Breacher presence in the vicinity had only been a coincidence after all.

Her stomach rumbled. She hadn't found time to eat after the rude awakening. The day began with a reprimand from her superior officer and the misery continued with the endless monotony of babysitting the screen before her. Not knowing how long her penance would last was the worst part. Another gurgle punctuated the thought. *It serves me right.* With any luck she could get through this day, start proving her worth, and forget the whole thing ever happened.

Kayla had reconfigured her sight tokens to add motion sensors. She turned them off whenever the quad filled with people, but during classes she left them active. It meant she had to deal with the distraction of endless false flags due to insects, squirrels and birds. She gladly endured it, wanting to ensure that she missed nothing.

An alert was signalling from sight token five, positioned within a bush. It sat seven cubits behind the study bench which held the contact token intended for Leviticus Radix. Sight token five recorded a view parallel to the length of the bench towards the next structure beyond the archive building.

Movement was visible in the space between buildings. Kayla zoomed in for a closer look. A head popped out briefly, then returned to the shadows. A moment later, another alarm went off in the opposite direction. She recognized the Breacher. He was the one Deak had identified in the recorded footage from the night before. They were watching the bench.

Leviticus had been on the bench earlier during his study period. Did the Breachers know that? Were they interested in the token, or in Radix? Or, did they realize that Radix was the intended recipient of the token?

In her briefing she had been told of the concern that Breachers might attempt to approach Leviticus, but no one anticipated it happening so soon after the scouting party had been spotted.

The quad was emptying as students began to leave for the day. A moment later, Leviticus came into view. He made his way to the bench. *What was he doing returning to the bench at this time of the day?* He sat down and idly stared up at the clouds. Both Breachers had eyes on him. It seemed as if they expected Leviticus to show up.

"Get out of there," Kayla whispered.

The timing of the motion alerts couldn't have been a coincidence. Something was definitely going down. The Breachers were waiting for the quad to empty.

What should she do? Deak had left for an early dinner break. He had promised to watch the monitoring station for a bit when he returned, so she could find something to eat as well.

If she didn't wait for Deak, he'd be furious, but if she let the Breachers grab Leviticus, it would put another black mark on her record. Not that it would matter since it would also presage the end of the shortest career in history. Why did she keep finding herself in situations with impossible choices?

Kayla ran some quick calculations in her head. If she left immediately, she could get into position inside the archive building and follow through on her original mission before the quad emptied.

The threat was clear and present. She didn't need to monitor all the sight tokens anymore. She only needed to keep eyes on the ones recording the Breachers — and the bench where Radix sat. She could monitor those remotely using her wrist Q-view.

I wouldn't be leaving my post. Kayla convinced herself. *Not really, just relocating it.* More importantly she would be in position to help if necessary. It seemed like the type of initiative expected from a TokenWard. Once she was in position, she could place a call and interrupt Deak's meal to update him.

The more she thought about it, the more sense it made given the time constraints. Speaking of which, she was out of time. It was now or never. She made her decision. *Now!*

Kayla ran hard towards the tunnels leading to the archive building. People jumped out of her path, and more than a few threw questioning looks her way. The odds were that Deak would hear of it before she was prepared to contact him. She hoped she would get a chance to explain things to him first. The thought made her run a little faster.

The archive building was an ancient structure. Servators had built it more than six hundred years ago. Over the centuries, a city had sprung up around it. The Servator base of operations was hidden below the surface, growing or changing to keep pace with the sprawl of life above it.

A relatively recent addition to the city by comparison, the Denmount Court of Learning was far more intentional in its expansion. Servators encouraged its development in subtle and sometimes not so subtle ways from behind the scenes. Anonymous donations provided the most obvious incentive but not the most important. Famous lecturers were enticed to visit. Prominent sages were lured to teach. Facilities remained up to date with the latest texts and equipment. The efforts helped establish an enviable reputation and with it, longevity.

Servators placed a high value on enduring architecture as surrounding buildings provided numerous places of egress from the Servator base. Additionally, a large population made it easier to slip in and out unseen. It had served well, allowing the Servators to operate in secrecy for generations. Kayla ran for one of those exits now.

Her chest was heaving as she arrived and it took a few minutes to calm her breathing. A sedate study environment wasn't the place for a spontaneous appearance. Particularly while gasping like someone who had just run a marathon. Kayla smiled at the mental image of her covert operations instructor frowning furiously.

She glanced at her Q-view to monitor the situation outside. The Breachers hadn't moved. *Good.*

Servators typically placed exits in low traffic areas. Even so, every exit had both a sight and motion sensing token hidden in the public area beyond the tunnel. Checking the tokens to verify that a public space remained clear was protocol before deactivating a false wall.

Kayla switched to a view of the exit token and watched carefully. The exit appeared clear for passage. A door activation token was always in a hidden spot above the exit. The false wall would instantly re-form after an operative crossed the threshold. A necessary precaution in such a public place.

She pressed as close as she could to the exit and prepared to dart through as she eyed the appropriate spot to activate the token. A few seconds later she was safely on the other side, the wall already re-forming behind her.

Before proceeding, she contacted Deak. "Lead TokenWard," she whispered, "this is TokenWard — um — Novice Vantos. Breachers are on an intercept course for Leviticus Radix. I repeat, Breachers are on an intercept course for Radix. I'm in position according to my submitted field operation plan, ready to intervene."

"Vantos. Hold position! I'm on my way! Field rangers can be at the quad in ten minutes! You're to monitor only!"

Kayla switched the Q-view back to her hidden sight tokens. The quad had emptied and the Breachers were stepping out of concealment. One was waving the other to his side. The rangers would never make it in time.

"Lead TokenWard, we're out of time. Operation is a go!"

Leviticus had shifted position on the bench. He was staring right at the plaque. She'd never have a better opportunity.

"Vantos! Hold Position! Do *not* engage!"

Here goes everything or nothing she thought as she activated the token. She watched as a startled Leviticus jumped up from the bench. He stood motionless for a moment as though making his mind up about something.

"Come on, come on," Kayla urged.

Leviticus began to look around and spotted the Breachers. No longer having the element of surprise, they began to walk briskly towards him. He stiffened.

"That's right Radix, you should be very concerned. Run to the archive building — now!"

As if he could hear the command, Leviticus made a beeline for the archive entrance.

Chapter 22

Leviticus couldn't stop thinking about his strange experience on campus. It left him feeling off balance, a puzzle he needed to solve before he could move forward. The compulsion to know had driven him back to this spot near the archive building.

He was facing the front entrance about ten paces away. The sensation had first manifested here. Closing his eyes, he slowly breathed in and out, clearing his mind of distractions. When he opened his eyes, he looked straight ahead and slowly turned one hundred and eighty degrees.

He could feel his mind soaking in the surroundings. There it was, that same sense of something both familiar and out of place at the same time. The exact location wasn't immediately obvious. He stepped forward and bumped into someone hurrying down the path.

"Hey! Watch where you're going!"

"Sorry!" *Way to go Lev, you're trying so hard to observe your surroundings, you're not even seeing what's directly in front of you.*

Lev decided to return to his original location. Now that classes had ended for the day, the quad was almost empty, but a small group remained behind, sharing an animated discussion. *Of all the places for them to stop. Of course they would choose that very spot.* Lev rolled his eyes.

He moved slightly to the left of the group, still facing the archive entrance from approximately the same distance as before. Lev began the process again.

Alarms went off in his head immediately. A bench sat beside the path between him and the entrance to the archive building. It hadn't been directly in his line of sight the first time around.

Something seemed different about the bench. That idea seemed strange in and of itself. It was his favourite spot to sit and study. He knew it well. That would explain his sense of familiarity, but what was it that felt out of place? He sat on the bench and threw his arm over the back.

Looking up to the sky, his fingers danced a metallic tappity-tap on the back of the bench while he pondered. After a moment his fingers stopped. *Metallic? This is a wooden bench.* Lev slowly turned his head to view the red metal plate beneath his fingers. It appeared that the bench was now dedicated to a generous donor.

It made sense. Something had indeed changed. The bench was both familiar and now different. Even so, it didn't bring him any comfort having an answer to the mystery.

Lev, you idiot! If every little change to your surroundings is going to affect you this way, how will you get through a day? The thought worried him. Had his childhood therapist been correct all along? Was his 'gift' going to turn on him now and become a crippling curse?

He shifted his position on the bench so he could better read the plaque. Shading his eyes from the reflection and focusing on the text, he began to read. "This bench is dedicated to..." He couldn't make out the words anymore. The plaque began to bubble and what he had been reading changed into

something entirely different as he finished. "...Leviticus Radix. We need to meet. Aisle thirty-nine, section five."

Lev sprang to his feet and frantically looked around to see if anyone else had witnessed what had just occurred. No one had noticed the plaque, nor his peculiar antics.

He held his head between his hands, not sure how to react. How could someone know he would be here at this moment? Was he being watched?

"Oh, that's just great, Lev," he muttered. "Seriously? Your first question is whether someone is watching you, rather than how a metal plaque just transformed before your eyes? Paranoia isn't a good indicator for your current state of mind." He quickly closed his mouth. *Talking to yourself in public isn't helping.*

Okay, think this through. Assuming you're not losing your mind, who would want to meet you under mysterious circumstances? His thoughts went to something the head of his development team had mentioned earlier in the week. Corporate spies had been questioning people on campus, attempting to learn something about the facial recognition algorithm his team was working on. Maybe that's what this was about. If that were true, maybe he should try to find out more about this person so he could alert campus security.

Lev looked around and spotted two large men watching him. They didn't look like corporate spies and were walking purposefully in his direction. His mind raced. If the person who wanted to meet him was in the archive building, who were these two characters?

He didn't have time to sort it out. He definitely did *not* intend to confront two intimidating strangers. He chose the lesser threat of the moment and ran toward a rendezvous with only the Maker knew whom.

Lev hurried to aisle thirty-nine and stopped at section five. He glanced over his shoulder to see if his pursuers had followed him into the building.

"Leviticus Radix?"

Lev spun back around. A young, fit-looking woman was standing in the middle of the aisle.

"If you value your life, you'll come with me."

Lev almost laughed. "If I value my life? Seriously? I think you've watched one too many theatre troupes."

"Look, we don't have time for this. Those two men you spotted outside are coming for you and they don't have your best interests in mind."

"Now, that I believe." Lev glanced nervously over his shoulder in time to see one of them at the end of the aisle.

"There he is," one of his pursuers bellowed.

Lev looked back to his would-be rescuer with a question in his eyes. She was already sprinting in the other direction.

"Run!" She yelled.

Leviticus ran. He had to push hard to keep up. She turned right at the first break in the rows of shelving and then left again in an attempt to throw off their pursuers. When they reached the end of the aisle, she ran for a stairwell beyond the rows of shelving. Lev picked up his pace trying to catch up. She didn't slow, racing to a lower level three steps at a time. Lev was right on her heels, almost falling on top of her as he tried to catch his footing.

They descended five flights of steps before reaching the bottom. Lev followed her into a sub-basement. Every usable space appeared full of pallets piled with parchment — stacked to the ceiling. A heavy scent of ink and leather filled the air. He usually enjoyed that aroma, but mixed with the adrenaline it made him feel slightly queasy.

He shouldn't have stopped to look around, because he lost sight of his guide. Lev opened his mouth to call out, but a hand reached from between stacks of parchment and yanked him into the shadows. They were behind a row of towering pallets near the wall.

Gruff voices echoed in the stairwell and heavy footfalls pounded down the steps. A moment later he could make out their words.

"You stay here and guard the stairwell. It's the only exit. I'll look around."

Lev started to panic. They couldn't hide here. Any minute they'd be discovered. A porta-lamp lit beside him. What was she doing? They'd see!

The blood drained from his face as it occurred to him that she may have been part of the plan all along. He let her lure him down here where no one could hear him call for help.

In his dread, he didn't notice the wall behind them begin to bubble and disappear. Before he could comprehend what was happening, a pair of hands thrust him into the newly accessible void. In the dim light from the lamp, Lev was shocked to see a wall sealing them off from the archive basement.

The woman he'd been following dropped to the ground, exhausted. "That was close," she said, between great gulps of air.

She lifted her arm and spoke into a device on her wrist. "Objective is secure. Repeat — objective is secure."

Lev didn't have words. First, because he was breathing heavily himself, but then because his brain was still trying to catch up with everything that had happened. "Who are you?" He finally asked.

"My name is Kayla Vantos, TokenWard of the Caralithican Host. I know you probably have many questions, but I'm not the best person to answer them."

"That's it? After all we just went through — that's all you're going to say?"

Kayla stood up and started walking down the tunnel they had entered.

"Follow me. All of your questions will be answered."

"What makes you think I'd follow you anywhere?"

"Oh you'll follow, that much I know."

Lev couldn't believe the arrogance. He turned to walk in the opposite direction and ran into a dark wall. Twisting back, he saw Kayla watching him with a smirk on her face and a dramatic lift of one eyebrow. She pointed her porta-lamp down the tunnel and started walking again.

Lev sheepishly followed. At least he knew he wasn't losing his mind. Everything that had occurred in the last fifteen minutes was real.

Chapter 23

Toller's grip tightened on his tote-comm. "I haven't excused your incompetence for losing the Radix boy. You knew his importance for expanding our viewcorder network. Once we've added facial recognition, the Servators will no longer be able to hide themselves. It will usher in a new age for the Breachers. I will *not* see my plans derailed!"

"Of course, Third Anarch. Failure is inexcusable. I have already disciplined the responsible personnel. It won't happen again."

"You barely escaped discipline yourself. You were in charge of this operation and you failed the mission objective. Fortunately, your people uncovered something of value to me. You always were a lucky soul, Decar. The fates have spared you once again."

"I accept full responsibility for my failure and have accelerated our response. We've been installing viewcorders all across the campus."

"Excellent! The mysterious escape of Radix from a room with only one guarded exit was an unprecedented slip up by our old enemy. Clearly Servator secrets lay beneath the archive building."

"I would remind my lord that our search for hidden exits revealed nothing."

"Didn't you say your men got a good look at the girl — that she's the same individual as the one we captured on the viewcorder during the surveillance of Radix for your original operation?"

"Indeed, sir."

"She not only placed a token during your operation but is familiar with hidden passages on the campus. Don't you find that suspicious? This woman clearly operates in the area. It's the only explanation for her repeat appearance. She was ready to act quickly when needed!"

"I have anticipated your interest. Network engineers have been sent to place viewcorders at other courts of learning around the world."

"Don't presume to know my mind! Servators won't operate at every court. The thing of import here is the archive building. That structure is ancient, as our enemy is ancient. We don't need to waste resources blanketing the planet. I want you to identify a pattern. Once we capture a few of the Servators, they will reveal other locations readily enough. Focus your efforts on courts with ancient structures."

"As you wish, sir."

"That Servator intervention wasn't a coincidence. They must have known of our plans for Mr. Radix. Find those responsible for leaking information and bring them to me."

"It will be done."

"Oh, and Decar, I expect you to complete your original mission. If we can't have Radix, find someone else with intimate knowledge of the facial recognition project at Denmount."

"Miss Lor is already working on a contingency."

"Don't disappoint me a second time."

Toller disconnected his tote-comm and allowed himself a genuine smile. Perhaps he had been too easy on Decar. It was important to reinforce one's reputation or people would perceive a weakness. Truth was, Decar was his most trustworthy servant. A competent man who usually brought results.

Toller was actually very pleased. The Servators had made a costly mistake. Such errors occurred once in a hundred years. Not a man to miss opportunities, serendipitous though they may be, he intended to seize full advantage.

They now possessed a starting point for their search. If he could implement facial recognition on his viewcorder network, he would bring the Servators to their knees. It would be a route unlike anything the Breachers had achieved before, and he would be the one responsible. Today was a very good day.

Chapter 24

As they neared their destination, Kayla slowed to tug her uniform into place and tighten the ponytail at the base of her neck. She wanted to look every bit the part of a seasoned agent as she entered the base proper with her charge. She glanced at the token trigger to open the false wall and checked to make sure Leviticus was still behind her.

"Stay close and step quickly through the entrance. The wall will re-form in fifteen seconds."

"What happens if someone doesn't get through in time?"

Kayla produced a popping sound with her mouth and Lev's eyes widened. She shouldn't be messing with his head like that, but he had been hesitant to go with her and she worried about him lagging behind when she was so near to completing her mission.

She stepped into the alcove on the other side. Lev was so close behind her, they may as well have been dancing. She almost laughed out loud. *Not professional Kayla — Not professional at all.*

Exiting the alcove into the large open space of the common area filled Kayla with relief. They were safe now. Nothing more could go wrong. The base kept tight security at this particular ingress where several tunnels converged. Numerous stun cannon emplacements and other security measures stood ready to protect the base.

A second tier situated twenty cubits above, ran the perimeter of this space.

Rangers patrolled regularly, taking advantage of the benefit bestowed by higher ground in the event of an enemy infiltration. All entrances to the cavern itself could instantly seal, forming a large containment cell.

The cavern formed one of the larger pockets on the base and staff often used it for gatherings and other temporary installations. Alcoves had been excavated in the walls around the perimeter over the years. These provided stalls used for a small market, popular with staff. During work hours, people shared snacks or beverages at tables pulled out from the alcoves.

The place was a hive of activity — more than usual. Everyone was rushing about attempting to avoid collisions with each other as they rushed to the main tunnel leading to the sub-earth rail transport.

Kayla spotted a familiar face and grabbed her arm as she was rushing past. "Tam, what's happening?"

"Oh! Kayla! I didn't notice you standing there — I'm in a bit of a rush. The Chief Sentry has ordered the evacuation of all nonessential staff."

"Evacuation? Why?"

"I don't know — just following orders. I need to go, I'm helping coordinate the transport of equipment."

She ran off before Kayla could ask any more questions. Lev threw her a sideways glance. She shrugged, just as bewildered as he was. "Come on, I'll get you settled in and find out what's happening."

They threaded the crowd to a less busy path along the walls and found their way to an exit that would take them to First TokenWard Bosto's Office. The halls were quieter here and they moved at a good pace.

Deak was sitting at his desk with the door to his office open. His head whipped up when he spotted Kayla entering. He shot her a dark look and then turned his head to address Leviticus. "Mr. Radix, I'm greatly relieved to see you unharmed — welcome. I'm First TokenWard Deak Bosto. I can answer some of your questions and will get you situated shortly. If you would excuse us for a moment?"

"Uh, sure?"

Deak stood up and grabbed Kayla by the elbow a little more firmly than she would have liked, as he led her out into the hall.

"You're hurting my arm."

Deak released her, looking more frustrated than she had ever seen him.

"Kayla, your mother is waiting for you. Go! Now!"

He used a personal address, not her formal title.

Remembering her mother's admonition about respecting the office of her betters, she chose to respond in a formal manner. "First TokenWard Bosto, what has happened?"

Deak became even more stone-faced and said nothing. His arm pointed down the hall. She would obtain no answers from him.

Kayla tossed him a miffed look, which she probably shouldn't have directed at a superior officer. She was tired of the poor treatment she'd received since her return. She had successfully completed her mission, yet so far, all she'd received was attitude for her efforts. Granted, the base appeared to be in the middle of an emergency, but she would have expected at least a quick congratulatory pat on the back from Deak.

His stony expression softened somewhat and turned to sadness. Kayla found his new expression far more alarming. She needed to find out what had happened and that meant getting to her mother as quickly as possible.

***

Kayla had barely stepped into the office of the Chief Sentry before her mother embraced her in a fierce hug. "Thank the Maker! Are you alright?"

"Of course I'm alright, Mother. Stop treating me like a child! I trained for this!"

Cello stepped out of the embrace, her face hardening. She said nothing as she closed the office door and walked to her desk.

"What's happening, Chief Sentry? Why are you evacuating the base?"

"Very well, *Novice* Vantos," the heavy emphasis on a junior title wasn't lost on Kayla, "we'll dispense with familiarity and focus on business."

Kayla didn't like her mother's accusing tone. She knew it well and braced herself.

"I hereby revoke your conditional title of TokenWard and place you on indeterminate suspension."

"What?" This was unbelievable. "For what possible reason? I've successfully completed my mission objective and saved a man's life!"

"At the cost of another!" The fury on Cello's face forced Kayla back a step. She had never seen her mother this way. Cello Vantos was a very patient woman by nature.

"What are you talking about?"

"Toshi is dead."

That couldn't be right. Kayla had just spent time with him and the gang last night.

"Char is devastated."

Kayla placed her hand over her mouth. "I need to go to her!"

"I think you should steer clear of her for a while."

"Steer clear ... Mother, what are you talking about? Why is everyone looking at me strangely?"

"Your actions brought about Toshi's death!"

Kayla held up her hands, a bewildered expression on her face quickly followed by anger. Instead of recognition for saving a man's life, her mother accused her of a friend's death?

Cello let out an uncharacteristic grunt of frustration before spelling things out. "Kayla, you disobeyed a direct order from your superior! You showed no regard for rank! Your reckless action endangered everyone on this base!"

"Waiting wasn't an option! I had to act immediately or Leviticus would have been abducted!"

"No! He would *not* have! Backup was on the way."

"Deak said they were ten minutes out. That would have been too late."

"Backup for *you* was ten minutes away, but Deak already had the perimeter secured. The Breachers couldn't have left the campus with Radix."

"I didn't know..." Kayla started.

Cello immediately cut her off. "First TokenWard Bosto gives orders, not explanations. He gained his position by proving himself over the course of years. People trust him with their lives because they have faith in his tactical abilities. *Your* job is to trust your superior and obey orders — immediately and without question. If you had, Leviticus would still be safe, and Toshi would be alive. Instead, you decided you knew better. You — with all the experience of your first mission!"

"Okay, I messed up, but how does that lead to Toshi's death?"

"It's my fault." Cello shook her head in dismay. "I knew you weren't ready for the field. I never should have allowed it and I will tell that to Toshi's family when we have time to grieve. I'll accept the consequences of that failure."

That failure? It infuriated Kayla when her mother treated her like an incompetent child! She kept that to herself for the moment. She was still missing some pieces to the puzzle.

"Toshi?" She prompted.

"When you disappeared into the archive basement — a room with only one guarded exit — the Breachers immediately suspected a hidden Servator safe room. I don't know what you were thinking. That was a serious violation of protocol. The Breachers took a head count of everyone in the building and were monitoring entrances. When someone who shouldn't have been there exited...."

"Toshi." Kayla gasped.

"He was supposed to disassemble the tokens you placed and return immediately. When he didn't report in on time, a ranger was sent to look for him. They found Toshi's body in a copse just beyond campus."

"Oh, no!" Toshi had died because she exposed a Servator base entrance? Kayla's knees went weak as she considered the ramifications.

Her mother continued, unrelenting. "Having two confirmed Servator sightings, the Breachers called in reinforcements. They have been setting up viewcorders all across the campus. Apparently they now believe Denmount Court of Learning operates as a Servator hub. We can no longer come and go freely without even greater risk. Your actions have compromised the base."

"Hence the evacuation of noncritical personnel."

"Precisely. By week's end the evacuation order will apply to all remaining personnel and it's likely the base will undergo a long-term lock down."

Kayla clung to some small hope that this would resolve itself. "We don't know for certain that the Breachers suspect this campus as a major Servator hub." She knew it was a weak argument the moment she said it and her mother stared at her for a long minute before speaking.

"One more thing, Kayla...."

More? Kayla wasn't sure she could take any more.

"Just prior to the onset of evacuation procedures, we discovered a Breacher viewcorder. Evidence suggests placement occurred several days ago. It was pointing towards the bench where you placed your token. You obviously missed it when you performed your site assessment. The Breachers must have come to a similar conclusion about the best location to monitor Mr. Radix. Unfortunately, your appearance tipped them to the fact that we knew about their interest."

Kayla wrung her hands in disbelief. Her eye was twitching and her lower lip trembled.

"The ranger who made the discovery pulled a copy of a viewcording taken by the device. He transmitted it to our analysts with his Q-view. It shows you placing the token. Your face is clearly visible. I suspect your likeness is finding its way to memory stashes across the globe as we speak. You can never operate in the field again. You're now most likely on a Breacher watch list.

"While you were *rescuing*, Mr. Radix, those Breachers no doubt recognized you from that viewcording. Your quick appearance to rescue Leviticus confirms close proximity of Servator operations. Toshi's appearance added to that suspicion.

"The ranger who transmitted the copy of that viewcording has gone missing. A second death may follow this debacle, but not before he endures a painful interrogation." Cello's face told Kayla that her mother knew more about Breacher interrogation techniques than she'd like.

"We have little choice but to assume the security of this base is in jeopardy. We certainly can't risk more exposure."

It was too much. The full weight of Kayla's failure pressed her to her knees. She was responsible for uprooting all of these people's lives. For hundreds of years, Servators had built up this base and she had single-handedly depleted that investment. Toshi was gone forever and Char might never forgive her. A ranger was missing, possibly suffering torture. No wonder Deak looked at her in that way. His disappointment had been palpable.

Everyone would soon know. Kayla Vantos, daughter of the Chief Sentry, promising novice, couldn't live up to expectations. She had been warned that her impulsiveness, quick temper, and pride would be her undoing if she didn't get them under control. She hadn't listened, not really. How could they forgive her? For the remainder of her days, whenever someone looked at her, she would wonder what they thought of her. Kayla Vantos, scorner of the Maker's Way — destroyer of the Servator cause.

Tears streamed down her face. How could this have happened? How could she have been the cause? *I have shamed my mother*, she thought. Yet when she looked into the Chief Sentry's face, she found only compassion there.

If such compassion was born of following the Maker's Way, then that path was more valuable than she had ever imagined. Was there anyone alive who didn't need compassion and forgiveness at some point? Right now she needed it more than life. Her mother's eyes filled with tears as well. *For her? For Toshi? For...*

"What is his name?"

Cello was caught off guard. "Pardon me?"

"His name, the missing ranger?"

Her mother nodded in understanding. Or was that approval?

"Marcon — Field Ranger Marcon Fenris, of the fourth division." It sounded too much like a memorial to a man already dead. Would she ever feel hopeful again? Kayla didn't have an answer. She did know she would never forget those whom she had failed.

Chapter 25

Kade read the address off the card a third time. It was the right place, but in a bad part of town. A major corporation wouldn't put their representative up in a place like this, would they? Then he remembered Decar saying that this was the location of his expert, not necessarily Decar himself. Whatever, they were foreigners, maybe where they came from this was considered luxury. Who was he to judge?

He stepped over someone who had overindulged and was sleeping it off. Just enough space remained to open the front door. When he entered, a malodorous cloud assailed his nostrils. He almost ran back outside, but someone from behind a desk said, "You must be Kade Brixton."

"That's correct. How did you know?"

"We don't see many people like you in these parts."

"People like me?"

"Yeah, educated uppity types."

Kade almost burst out laughing. No one in his circle of peers had ever been referred to in such a manner. Least of all himself. He and his kin were pretty low on the social ladder. Then again, he hadn't ever come to this part of the city to see how much lower people could get.

"I've been told to wait for you. Now that you're here, hopefully I can get back to my own business. I'm a busy man. Come this way."

Following the fellow meant traversing an obstacle course of refuse. No wonder it smelled so bad. They continued to the end of the hall and his guide knocked on a door. "Enoch, your three o'clock appointment is here," he said with a snicker.

A cacophony emanated from Enoch's office. The tune of someone rearranging furnishings. Angry verbosity provided accompaniment. Silence followed on the heels of a loud crash. A few moments later the door opened to reveal a small balding figure about ten years Kade's senior with a disgruntled look on his face.

"Well?" The impatient little man was tapping his foot vigorously. "Stop your gaping and get in here. Let's see whatcha got!"

Kade slowly handed over his storage device, afraid to get too near to the man. The guy looked as if he might be contagious. Kade hadn't known what to expect. It wasn't this.

The 'expert' hobbled over to his viewscreen and plugged in the device. As the screen filled with Kade's files, the man gestured for him to sit. Kade searched for a chair and stepped towards one that looked relatively clean.

"No! Sit there! It has to be there!" the little man insisted, pointing to a stool.

Kade shrugged and sat on the stool. He didn't want to draw this out any longer than he had to.

"Explain what I'm lookin' at," the fellow demanded.

"It's a facial recognition algorithm."

Kade thought both the question and the person, odd.

"The one from Denmount Court?"

"Of course."

"Tell me about it."

Kade proceeded to explain details about the algorithm — how it worked and anything he thought might prove his knowledge on the subject.

"That's enough."

"Do you have any questions for me?" Kade asked.

"Nope. Heard everything I need to hear." The man handed Kade a heavy pouch.

He accepted it and looked inside. Silvers filled the bag.

"It's all there. You can count it." He pushed a small table towards Kade.

"No, that's okay, I trust you."

"Don't trust nobody! Count it," he insisted.

Kade obliged. When he finished counting, he wore a big smile on his face.

"As promised — now leave!" He handed the storage device back to Kade and pushed him towards the door."

"Wait, that's it? Do I get the job?"

"The boss will contact you. Now get out and don't be comin' back here!" He awarded Kade with one final shove and slammed the door behind him. It didn't take long for the smell to drive him the rest of the way out of the building.

Once outside, a few deep breaths helped clear his nose, but his clothes had picked up the reek. They'd need a good washing. His eyes were drawn to the pouch he gripped. The heft felt reassuring in his hand. He would call Selica and take her out for a celebration! Tomorrow, he could settle his tuition fee and maybe pay off part of his loan.

Decar was as good as his word, and why shouldn't he be? The man worked for a large reputable company after all. Decar's expert, on the other hand, was very peculiar. Kade didn't think he was truly an expert at all. Enoch, was it? The fellow didn't seem to understand what Kade had shown him. It was troubling.

Don't over think things Kade. You have five hundred silvers in your pocket and soon you'll have an attractive woman on your arm. He smiled, and then frowned at the offensive odour clinging to his shirt. First, he needed a bath and some fresh clothes.

He started off with a skip in his step, but it soon turned into a jog when he remembered that this wasn't the best part of town to be strolling with a bag full of coins.

Chapter 26

Second Anarch, Kenric Trantor, shook his head in disgust. That fool Toller was still plotting his downfall. Why couldn't he be satisfied with the status quo? He overreached, coveting something undesirable. If only he knew the truth.

Kenric would happily trade places with Toller if it were possible. Unfortunately, such options weren't open to him. If he wanted to avoid a direct confrontation with the overlords, he had to maintain his position and he would rather die than face the wastrels.

It galled him that the upstart would think him too senile to spot his machinations. Didn't the man realize the wealth of resources available to a Second Anarch? Very little took place under his purview that escaped his notice.

Admittedly, he had been much like Toller Villecrest in his youth, but he no longer held such childish illusions. He remembered well his own rise to power. He had instigated the Trantor uprising, a plot he had designed to gain attention from the wastrel overlords of Sumakad. It was part of his bid to win favour.

Following the initial uprising, long-term plans designed to facilitate his rise sat ready to be executed, but it proved unnecessary. His predecessor suddenly died and Kenric advanced in rank through no effort of his own. His plans continued, but while the prior intent was to gain the attention of his masters, they now served to appease.

When Kenric first gained the seat, he read through the Annals of the Anarchs. Apart from a few who reigned very briefly, the majority offered the same admonition. Under no circumstances should the Second Anarch ever seek an audience with the wastrel overlords.

Second Anarchs traditionally held the role of gatekeepers to the doorways of the overlords. In the past, he'd wondered how he was to receive instructions if it was unwise to pass through those doors. He had chosen to err on the side of caution. Lacking wastrel oversight, he decided to continue with his original schemes until he heard otherwise.

Kenric had spent a great deal of time listening at the door in his charge. He discovered that when his efforts lead to chaos and suffering, and especially when it drove humanity away from the Maker's Way, the response beyond that door was savage glee and maniacal laughter.

Conversely, when his efforts did not produce such results, or worse, led to an increase in those seeking the Maker's Way, the sounds changed to raging and cursing. It was a strange discordant noise that filled him with dread.

He had learned that it wasn't necessary to consult with the overlords, only to satisfy them. They were insane and he hoped never to face them. It was bad enough to be able to hear their deranged howling.

They didn't seem to value a war-winning strategy so much as ever-increasing suffering. Kenric had joined the Breachers in their battle against the Servator Host thinking he had picked the winning side. He had come to realize that his masters cared not at all if both sides suffered.

The Breachers maintained a military structure because it offered a convenient way to establish unquestioned obedience. Every Second Anarch understood that the overlords provided little by way of strategy. Breachers had no grand design to lead them, only the pursuit of pandemonium in an attempt to appease the wastrel overlord's hatred of the Maker.

As it turned out, Trantor's task had become rather simple. No need for a great deal of planning. Where temptation existed, lust and avarice followed. One needed only provide the opportunities and the rest would take care of itself. The only thing that required a little more work was sowing seeds of doubt about the Maker, but humanity was suspicious by nature and easily swayed with ideology that would bring selfish gain.

It was a terrifying line between the pleasure or rage of his masters, but as long as he managed to straddle that line, they left him to do as he pleased. He ruled within an organization of great power. It was the closest thing to a kingdom he was likely to achieve.

Was it the kingdom of his dreams? No, but it was the best he could expect in his lifetime. He wasn't about to give it up — certainly not to that upstart Third Anarch. Villecrest could have his seat after he died but he wasn't about to let that happen anytime soon. Toller would learn to regret his ambition in due time, just as he had himself.

Kenric held no illusions about his joyless slavery. The best he could hope for were fleeting pleasures in the time remaining to him, so he took full advantage of his position to indulge every desire within his opulent chambers. All the while, beyond the door, the overlords cackled with glee.

Chapter 27

Kade caught himself woolgathering in class. Who could blame him? Last night had been amazing. Selica was smart, pretty, and seemed to have a great sense of humour. Or at least she laughed at all of his jokes.

Kade and Selica had indulged themselves. After what was probably the best meal of his life, they walked along the beach and talked into the small hours of the morning. He should be exhausted, but he felt energized. *Why did I take so long to ask her out?* He wasn't paying much attention to the sage. His thoughts kept returning to Selica's goodnight kiss.

Kade's pleasant reverie was interrupted when he was called out of his first class — summoned to the Court Master's office. No doubt they would ask about his tuition. It was curious that they would pull him out of class, but he was happy to oblige. It meant getting this weight out of his pack that much sooner. He felt like a target was painted on his back, walking around with so many coins.

A security guard stood outside the Court Master's office. That didn't surprise Kade. A lot of money passed through those doors. It actually comforted him knowing that someone would witness the transaction.

Kade sat in the outer office for a few minutes before the door opened and he was ushered to a seat in front of the Master's desk. The security guard left and closed the door behind him.

Tuition payments hadn't been such a serious business in the past. Maybe they were expecting him to ask for an extension again. Were they preparing to expel him if he didn't have the money? He thought to put the Master's mind at ease immediately. "Good morning, Court Master. I had intended to visit you sometime today. I'm prepared to pay the final instalment of my tuition."

The Court Master stared at him, mouth slightly agape as though he were looking at a madman. Kade didn't know what to make of it.

Finally, the Court Master broke the silence.

"Mr. Brixton, let me be brief and to the point. Several witnesses saw you conversing with a stranger in the shadows. I know you were present when I met with the special projects team earlier this term. I warned the group that a corporate spy had been spotted hanging around the quad. You were all explicitly ordered to avoid him."

Actually, Kade didn't remember that warning. He had been up all night studying and had been so fatigued, he wasn't really paying attention.

"You signed a covenant when you joined the team, promising not to reveal any information about the project under threat of expulsion and possible criminal charges."

"What? No, wait, this is all a big misunderstanding!"

"We have no proof that you divulged anything at this point. Rest assured that if evidence of that nature comes to light, we *will* bring criminal charges against you. I know your financial situation. As part of our investigation, the lenders have confirmed that your account is currently in arrears. The fact that you're suddenly prepared to settle your tuition is highly suspicious. I assure you, we won't be accepting a copper from you until we can verify where that money came from."

"I can explain everything."

"I don't need an explanation, I need proof. If you can prove that the money came from a legitimate source unrelated to your conversation with this corporate spy, and if you can prove that you did not divulge any information, then we can revisit this conversation. As things stand, according to your covenant agreement, suspicion is enough to warrant expulsion.

"Further, your tuition deadline is today and we can't accept payment until you have proven its legitimacy. You currently have two strikes against you and I can't see how you will meet the requirement of proof before the end of day. Or am I wrong?"

Kade hung his head. "No, Sir."

"Then you leave me no choice but to expel you. I'm exceedingly disappointed. I have a soft spot for those who work hard to raise their station in life. I had high hopes for you. I'm saddened that you would prove me wrong when you were so close to succeeding."

"If I could just have a little more time," Kade pleaded.

"You will be escorted off campus. If you return, I'll have you arrested for trespassing. I sincerely hope no criminal charges are forthcoming. That would bring shame to you, your family, and this institution."

Kade sat in a daze, astonished by the swiftness of it all. The Court Master made it clear that their meeting had concluded by pointing to the exit. Any uncertainty fled when the security guard hoisted him to his feet and paraded him out the door.

Chapter 28

Lev scanned the cluttered office. He couldn't find anywhere to sit in this hoarder's paradise. Not that he felt comfortable enough to relax. His nerves were screaming for him to run, but he didn't know his way out of this place and he needed answers.

It comforted him somewhat to think that if he was to be interrogated, they probably wouldn't have chosen this cramped little office. Surely if he were a prisoner, they wouldn't leave the door wide open without a guard in sight. Lev snorted at the thought. Did they even require guards? He'd seen the security measures when they came in. It's not like he could just stroll out of this maze of tunnels. Even if he tried, how would he stop them from dragging him right back?

The number of people and wealth of resources he had seen on his way to this office was astonishing. How could such an enterprise exist below the small city of Denmount? How could it remain hidden? It spoke of skill and influence. He doubted he could evade such an agency for long were he to try escaping. His head swam with the implications, and the shambles around him added to his discomfort. How could anyone work in such a mess? Lev smiled to himself *Maybe they know me better than I realize and this is some subtle form of torture.*

Leviticus had already neatly piled three stacks of parchment on the desk and was holding a fourth stack when the owner of the office returned.

The man froze for a moment looking first at the documents in Lev's hands, then at the stacks on the desk and finally back to Lev. There was a mixture of confusion and exasperation on his face. The fellow slowly shook his head and held out his hand in greeting. "Hello, my name is Deak Bosto, Lead TokenWard for the Caralithican Host of the Servators."

He offered a genuine smile as he shook Leviticus's hand. "It's good to see you in person, Mr. Radix. This has been a long time coming. I wish it had been under different circumstances but here we are."

"And where exactly is here, Mr. Token Servant of Caralithica, or whatever you just called yourself?"

"TokenWard of the Servators. But please, just call me Deak, or TokenWard Bosto if you prefer. In answer to your question. This is a Servator base of operations. I imagine you have many questions. Don't worry, you will have your answers. We have nothing to hide."

Lev's mouth hung open in disbelief. He closed it with a click and stared at the man, taking a moment to gather his thoughts before speaking. *Don't antagonize the friendly secret agent Lev.* "Mr. ... Deak. I've lived in Denmount my entire life and am only now discovering the existence of a 'Servator' base beneath the city. Neither I nor anyone I know has ever heard of a Servator, let alone a host of them who exist for purposes only the Maker knows.

"In my recollection, a construction project of the magnitude that could account for such a large underground facility hasn't happened in my lifetime. Which means that this place must have been here for quite some time. Apparently, it predates my parents and grandparents who also grew up here and never mentioned a group known as the Servators. Forgive me for saying so, but it seems to me that you have a great deal to hide."

"From the general public, yes, but not from you."

"And to what do I owe this distinction?"

"To the fact that we wish to recruit you. We've had our eye on you for some time, Mr. Radix. You have a unique gift and it's our hope that you're willing to use it for the benefit of mankind."

Lev shook his head in annoyance. "You couldn't just knock on my door like normal folk? Did you consider telling me about your organization and following up with an offer? This whole thing is outrageous!"

"I apologize for the way of our first meeting. This isn't how we normally do things."

"And how do you *normally* do things?"

"Typically, we would approach you in a manner very similar to what you just described. We start by introducing ourselves and explain a little about a career offer that might interest you. Over the course of a few meetings, the two sides feel each other out. We share a little more about the culture and values of our organization and determine if you hold similar views. It's important to know if we can work together, you understand. If it appears that everyone is on the same page, we take a leap of faith and explain who we are and what we do."

"So why didn't you? Why am I only now hearing of this? Am I supposed to believe that when you approach people in your normal way, they don't find it bizarre that a recruiter has impossible technology and a secret underground citadel? Nothing about this is remotely typical!"

Deak waved placating arms. "As I said, we have a process. We prefer to reveal things at a slower pace with explanations along the way. At every stage, candidates have the option to step away or to proceed. It can take many years before someone is exposed to the things you have witnessed. Our organization employs people who have never seen this base and live ordinary lives while working for an important cause. Unfortunately, a very dangerous organization has targeted you for abduction — slow wasn't an option."

"Those thugs who were chasing me?"

"Exactly so, and while you may find all of this uncomfortable, I assure you that had you fallen into their hands, this would feel like a day at the town fair by comparison."

"So you say. Do I trust the intentions of those who were chasing me? No, but your intentions are equally mysterious to me."

Deak conferred an approving nod. "Good! Always seek the truth before coming to conclusions. I have little doubt you will come to trust us once you have the full picture. I certainly hope you will come to trust me. I'm in charge of your protection. That will be easier for me if I know you're willing to wait for answers. It will be immeasurably more difficult if I need to worry about you foolishly placing yourself at risk."

Lev cocked his head to one side. "I evidently don't have a choice at the moment. I might ask for you to let me go, just to see if you would, but I don't know if those thugs would be waiting for me. I need more information."

"And you'll have it. The Chief Sentry will be free to meet with you in about two hours and she can answer all of your questions. Meanwhile, you look like you could eat. How does a visit to the kitchen sound? Afterward, I can show you to a bunk room where you can wash up or rest while you're waiting."

Lev's stomach growled in response. Deak laughed,

"Alright then."

Chapter 29

Lev felt better with a full belly and a good scrub. The bunk room was empty at the moment and he was grateful for the opportunity to process his thoughts in silence.

A cat he hadn't noticed, rose from one of the bunks and padded over to him. It rubbed against his legs and purred. "Hey little buddy, where did you come from? Are you my designated guard?"

Many of the bunks were in disarray as if they had been quickly vacated. That made sense since an evacuation was underway when he'd arrived. I wonder what that was about? *Am I in danger here?* His furry companion mewed but it wasn't the answer he was looking for.

Lev began unconsciously tucking in bed sheets as he wandered between the bunks, deep in thought. He had so many questions. Deak the 'TokenWard' had said that Servators on this hidden base belonged to the Caralithican Host. Denmount was, of course, located in the nation of Caralithica, but the way he said it suggested that Servator Hosts might exist in other nations.

How could a globe-spanning organization remain entirely unheard of? Correction, a lot of people knew about it, but how could they all keep it secret from everyone else?

These people knew who he was and that he had talent in his chosen field of study. They also knew that some other unknown faction held plans to abduct him. It would seem two opposing groups had been watching him for some time.

The very idea sent shivers down his spine.

Lev preferred structure and this new reality stripped away any pretense of order that he held. He felt adrift, not knowing how to fit this new truth into the pattern of what he thought he knew. Actually, now that he considered it, there had always been an undercurrent of something he couldn't quite grasp. A sense that he wasn't seeing the whole picture.

He was reaching for another bed sheet when a voice from the doorway announced the presence of a visitor, unless he truly *was* losing his mind and the cat was speaking to him now.

"We have staff for that you know." It was an authoritative voice and Lev knew without looking that this must be the Chief Sentry. He wasn't sure what to expect when he turned around. It wasn't the friendly face he saw smirking back at him.

Two intimidating men stood at her sides and slightly behind her. Everything about her spoke of power and he doubted she really needed protection from the two who trailed in her wake. Even so, he felt at ease in her presence — safe.

She had IndoAsian features and black hair cropped short. Someone who aged well, looking both wise and youthful at the same time. *If it weren't for the business-like demeanour, she would be quite beautiful*, Lev thought.

"Ah, young Mr. Radix. We meet at last. My name is Cello Vantos, Chief Sentry of the Caralithican Host. I know that Deak has already expressed his regret for the abruptness of your introduction to our little family. I apologize that I couldn't meet you when you first arrived, but as I'm sure you surmised, we're currently dealing with a situation that required my attention."

"The evacuation you mean?" Lev hadn't meant to speak out of turn, but he was tiring of mysteries.

"And again, I must apologize. We're in uncharted waters here. Normally I would be meeting potential recruits under very different circumstances. You must have a great many unanswered questions as a result. Know that as the Commander of the Host, I answer to very few people. You can expect that my responses to your questions will be free of the obfuscations you might receive from those of a lower rank. To be blunt, we lack time and have much to discuss. I hope you don't mind if I'm direct and to the point."

"I would appreciate that."

"Well then, please, walk with me."

Lev joined her side as they left the bunk room. Chief Sentry Vantos walked quietly for a while, gathering her thoughts. "Perhaps it would be best if I gave you a little history lesson for context. You're familiar with the Maker's Way?"

"Yes, I know of it, I wouldn't say I'm a follower of it."

"But you understand that some follow it and others oppose it?"

"Well, I know many hold an agnostic position but I can't say that I've ever heard of a group actively opposing it."

Cello stopped and turned to him with a little smile. "You've also never heard of the Servator Host — correct?" She shrugged and continued walking. "Have you never felt that the world around you was experiencing social decline? A lack of concern for others? Moral decay?"

Lev felt uncomfortable with the direction of the conversation and interrupted. "I have friends who follow the Way — people I respect and admire." It wasn't really an answer to her question.

"You speak of the Callan family."

Lev stopped walking, his shock apparent. "Enough with the games! You obviously know a great deal about me, but I still know very little about you!"

"Calm yourself, Mr. Radix. Nes Callan was a very close friend of mine. Someone I knew long before you were born. I sorely miss that man. I bring his name into the conversation because he's known to both of us. He was a valued and well-loved member of our organization. I want you to understand the sort of people you're currently dealing with and I want you to consider the shade of those who tried to abduct you."

"Woah — wait — backup ... Nes Callan was a Servator? Does Nico know?"

"Yes, Nico's parents were both strong supporters of our work. They lost their lives in a roto-wing 'accident' orchestrated by the same group who tried to abduct you."

"Nico's parents were murdered? Does he know *that*?"

"Nico knows neither of those truths, but he will. Very soon he'll take over the family business and much will come to light."

Lev was furious. When Nico lost his parents it devastated him. It had taken years for his friend to come to terms with the grief. Lev suddenly wished he could confront his would-be kidnappers and make them pay for the misery his friend had suffered.

When Lev had last spoken with Nico he was going through a bit of a crisis with the pressure of taking over the family business. Now he would learn that the world was a very different place. Could he handle this new revelation about his parents on top of it all? Lev's heart went out to his friend.

The Chief Sentry must have seen the look on his face. Compassion was evident in her eyes when she spoke. "Trust me when I tell you that Nico won't have to go through this alone. He has many friends among the Servators. Friends that he's not yet aware of. Some are familiar to him and will help him through this transition."

Lev gave her a grateful nod.

"Back to our little history lesson. The Servator Host is an ancient order. We have existed since the genesis of our world. We hold at bay, a group who call themselves the Breachers. Their name is apt since they insert themselves for one purpose. To tear apart. They exist only to seed chaos and destroy. They're the authors of all that is wrong with this world. Their every decision is a blind rush to oppose the Maker's Way. If you were friends with the Callans, you have known a shining example of what we strive to protect."

Lev nodded in agreement. The Callans were wonderful people. The Chief Sentry stopped again and gestured to an engraved plaque on the wall. Written in large letters were four lines of text.

If anything you do or say
would sway a heart and mind today,
then you have served to pave the way
to truth and life or death's decay.

Lev gave her a sideways glance, eyebrows raised in question.

"This is a motto of ours. Something we strive to live by. It's a reminder that whatever we say or do has consequences that affect others. We ask ourselves whether the decisions we make in a given moment will alter another's path towards a life lived in truth and joy, or one that spirals towards darkness and death. The Maker's Way is truth and the Servators are both servants and protectors of truth."

"So everyone in your organization is a follower of the Way?"

"It would be more accurate to say that no one in our organization is an enemy of the Way. Some agree with our goals and that is as far as it goes for them. They're satisfied to see good established in this world. Their involvement is usually limited in scope. Others, however, continually seek truth and as a result they understand and invest a great deal more. Nes Callan is an example of the latter. I like to think that I'm also a continual seeker of the truth. The things I've seen convince me that the Maker's Way is our only hope.

"In like manner, some support the efforts of the Breachers. A surprising number are oblivious, merely consumers of guilty pleasures that darken their minds. They hurt others without a thought, easily swayed by selfishness. Their only goal is to gain more for themselves. The small wounds they inflict serve to fortify Breacher plots. Death, from many small wounds.

"Breacher's sway many with false promises of power and wealth. When morals and ethics produce guilt at odds with their desires, they begin to associate with those who can appease their conscience — like-minded individuals who have learned to lie to themselves. Once started down this path, people inevitably begin to hate anything and anyone to question the morality of their choices. The Maker's Way, being the most painful reminder to them. Some of these will choose to become enemies of the Maker and find themselves in Breacher ranks. We try to help those who have started down that dark path to learn the truth before the Breachers gain too much influence over them."

Lev tried to imagine such a scenario and an image of Archivist Gilad sprang to mind. He remembered the look on Nico's face when the sage used her position to promote an anti-Maker sentiment. It was unprofessional and completely unrelated to the curriculum. Yet, she had mocked people who believed as Nico did. Her voice filled with scorn as though they were, well, an enemy. The idea that she might actually hate good people like the Callans shocked him. He said nothing as he followed his tour guide, deep in thought.

Before long, they turned into a larger tunnel. It was wide enough for heavy equipment to pass and terminated with a large vault-like door.

The Chief Sentry stared at a spot on the wall. He couldn't understand what she was looking for until a keypad suddenly materialized. *More of this mysterious technology. I'd love to study it.* She entered a code and the big door began to open.

The fragrance of greenery and earth washed over him. They were in another cavern. Not as large as the one he had first entered, but filled with a riot of plant life. It was a jungle of fruit trees, flowering plants, and vines that filled the space and clung to the rock walls. He felt the Chief Sentry watching him.

"This is The Garden. It was one of the first installations on the base. Some of these plants are from the time of genesis. They no longer survive on the surface. Vaults like these exist all over the world to preserve such flora."

"It's beautiful."

"Tell me, Leviticus, what do you see?"

He wasn't sure what she wanted to hear. He wasn't a gardener, and knew little about plants. "It looks like a nice place to get away and think."

"No, Mr. Radix. What do you *see* in that way others cannot?"

Oh! Now he understood what she was asking. How could she be aware that he saw things differently? Lev stepped tentatively into the garden, closed his eyes and inhaled a deep breath. He relaxed, opened his eyes, slowly turned his head, and took in the sense of his surroundings.

His eyes opened in surprise. "It's strange. I'm not sure how to explain, but it's perfect. Like nothing has touched it, yet it's obviously a cultivated garden."

"Perhaps not so strange. It's true that this garden is maintained, but at its sowing, the seeds were randomly scattered and left to grow as they would, with no interference. Generations of caretakers have tended these plants, but they've found their own balance in this contained ecology. This garden may appear haphazard, but a deeper look exposes the order of plant life as it would be when left alone. It follows a logical template."

Lev nodded in sudden understanding. Yes, that was it. The garden seemed erratic, but at the same time, it was ordered and sensible. It held a complex pattern with none of the abrupt pattern changes found where people settled and built homes.

"If someone were to seed an invasive plant in this place, it would be difficult to calculate the ultimate cost until after the damage was done. It's a good analogy for how the Breachers operate. They plant a disruptive seed and then stand back to see what damage it causes. But let's continue, I have more to show you."

The next stop seemed to be a cross between a storage room and a laboratory. Technology was on display, the likes of which Leviticus had never seen nor heard. He stared longingly like a child at the sweets stand in the market. How he would love to get his hands on even one item in this room and study it.

"Chief Vantos had a twinkle in her eye. "Does any of this interest you, Mr. Radix?"

"If you truly have been keeping an eye on me, which is pretty disturbing by the way, then you know that it does. How can this exist? Why horde it? Why keep it to yourselves?"

"We do share technology to benefit the world. Among the more recent examples, Exotic Particle Reactors and Lighter Than Air craft. However, much of the technology available to us could be incredibly destructive in the wrong hands and so we keep it contained."

Lev's eyes narrowed with suspicion as he surveyed a section of the room that was clearly an armoury. "If you're so altruistic, then why the weapons?"

"As I've mentioned, we're protectors and must counter force with force. These provide a way to defend ourselves as well as others. However, all of our weapons are non-lethal."

Leviticus made to reach for one of the weapons. The guards took a step forward and he carefully withdrew his hand. "May I?"

She nodded. The two guards remained where they were, but looked ready to leap into action at the slightest provocation.

Lev picked up a baton-like device. "What does this do?"

"That is a stun baton. It temporarily disrupts the nervous system, rendering an assailant immobile. Lev carefully set it back down with slow deliberate motions. "And this?"

"That one is a sonic cannon. It severely disrupts the balance of those who are within its range. Very effective against large crowds."

"And this?"

"A flash charge that emits a very bright light. It can temporarily blind an adversary."

Lev shook his head in wonder. The technology he had just held in his hand was enough to topple empires. Cello voiced what he was thinking.

"As you can see, we have advantages that would allow us to rule if we wished, but never in our history have we forced our ideals on the world."

"With such a great temptation, surely someone..." Lev began.

"And yet it has never happened," she finished for him. "Which should tell you a great deal about who we are and what we represent."

One of the guards checked a device on his wrist and whispered into the Chief Sentry's ear.

"Mr. Radix, would you indulge me in one more visit to the garden?"

Lev shrugged his shoulders and nodded in agreement — this was their show, he'd see it to the end. When they arrived, the door was already open.

"Leviticus, could you tell me what you see this time?"

He repeated the steps he took on their first visit. His forehead creased in confusion. "Something is wrong, or at least different."

"Look closer, deeper if you can. Can you tell me the location of the difference?"

Lev didn't have to try. The disturbance shouted its presence in this pristine place. He pointed without hesitation. "There, above that bush on the cavern wall."

One of the guards spoke into the device on his wrist and a red light began blinking at the spot where Lev was pointing. The Chief Sentry nodded and Lev realized he'd just participated in some sort of test.

"As First Token Ward Bosto explained to you, we have a process for vetting potential recruits. One is to determine the level of sensitivity to one's surroundings. In your case a plaque on a bench in front of the archive building was to provide that initial assessment. Unfortunately, precipitous events prevented that test from occurring in the proper manner. Sorry for the current subterfuge, but it wouldn't be much of a test if you knew what to expect. Thank you for your patience."

"Did I pass?"

"Beyond expectations. Please, follow me to my office where we can discuss your future."

"We've come this far. Why not? Lead on."

Chapter 30

Kade was escorted to his room in campus housing and given thirty minutes to collect his things before he was evicted. It required less than fifteen minutes to gather his few belongings. He hadn't owned much to begin with, living on a meagre part-time wage. It didn't help that he had turned his place upside down in a drunken rage a few days earlier. It gave him a little satisfaction knowing that he was leaving a mess behind for someone else to clean up.

Then, just like that, he was sitting on the street with two travel packs, wondering how things could have gone so wrong so quickly. At least he still had most of five hundred silvers. He silently chastised himself for his extravagance on that date with Selica.

Kade sighed heavily, standing up and shouldering his belongings. He faced a half hour walk to the nearest public boarding house where he could get a bed for the night.

As he walked, his mind filled with frustration. *It just isn't fair. I worked hard to pay the bills, I did well in class, I burdened no one.* He tried desperately to find someone to blame, but found no way to deny responsibility for his current predicament. He had taken a risk for a big payoff knowing that it felt wrong, that something like this could happen.

Maybe I can still salvage something. The Court Master had said they didn't yet have proof of wrongdoing. They had given him the opportunity to prove his innocence. He hadn't given away the algorithm. In fact, the storage device was still in his pocket.

Kade stiffened in shock as he suddenly realized how much worse things could have gone. If they had searched him, he wouldn't be walking the street looking for a place to spend the night. Instead he would be settling into a permanent new home with steel bars for decor. He shivered at the thought of life in prison.

What if they uncover more evidence against me before I can find a way to exonerate myself? Unless I can somehow convince them of my innocence, I won't be able to remain in the city.

Maybe if he contacted Decar he could return the remainder of the money in exchange for legal help. Decar's organization must have powerful lawvocates. They probably came up with a legally compelling arguments every day. If that option cost more money than he had, perhaps they would let him work it off. Decar did say they were looking for people with Kade's experience.

It was a small hope and he seized it. Kade dropped his packs and knelt to dig through them, frantically looking for the card with Decar Tosh's contact information. He pulled it out triumphantly and immediately entered the information into his tote-comm.

After a few fearful moments wondering if Decar had already left for his own country, the smooth familiar voice answered.

"Mr. Tosh! I'm so glad I caught you before you left! I need to speak with you. I've been expelled! They're saying terrible things about you!"

"Calm yourself, Mr. Brixton. You're not speaking coherently."

"I'm sorry. Please — I need your help."

"Where are you right now?"

"I'm heading for the boarding house on Eland Street."

"Very well, I will meet you there. Leave a note at the front desk with your room number. I'm sure we can sort this all out."

Kade's shoulders slumped in relief. "Thank you, Mr. Tosh. I'll be waiting."

Chapter 31

The office of the Chief Sentry was spartan. Leviticus liked it immediately. It felt proper for the person in charge to be precise and orderly — not like that Deak fellow. Lev suppressed an urge to go back and finish organizing that disaster of a workspace. How the man could get anything done was a mystery.

"So, Mr. Radix, you have some decisions to make."

"Is this the part where you tell me I know too many of your secrets and will be spending the rest of my life in a dark hole?"

"Nothing so dramatic. As it turns out, we must abandon this base. No one will be operating out of this area in the foreseeable future. Even if we remained, others couldn't find this place if you told them about it.

"If you were to leave and tell everyone the things you've seen, no one would believe you. You'd have no way to prove your tale."

It was true that no one would believe him. Lev still wasn't sure he believed it himself.

"You're no threat to us. To the contrary, I think you would be a tremendous asset to our organization. We were trying to recruit you after all."

"So what are we talking about here?"

The Chief Sentry drew a deep breath and slowly let it out, considering her words. "Perhaps it would be best if we pretended that this was a normal recruitment process taking place in a kofa shop somewhere. Once I've explained the process, we can deal with the extenuating circumstances."

"Can I have a mug of kofa to enhance the illusion?"

That caught her off guard and she laughed. "You know, I think we could both use a mug. Why don't we continue this conversation in the kitchen?"

It was a short walk. Privileges of being the Chief Sentry, Lev supposed. She gestured towards a table for him to grab a seat in the dining area. While he waited, she stuck her head into the kitchen and spoke with someone. She had barely made it back to the table to join him when a portly gentleman hustled out with a cart. It was laden with pastries, two mugs and a decanter of hot kofa. It smelled heavenly and his mouth watered at the sight of the sweet rolls.

The Chief Sentry began her sales pitch while he poured kofa for them both and added some cream to his own mug.

"If things had progressed as we intended, you would have proven your potential for recruitment when you spied the token on the bench in front of the archive building. You did indeed notice, but fleeing for your life shouldn't have been the follow-up.

"Instead, the Court Master would have received correspondence of our interest in you. Not the Servators, mind you, but one of our associated businesses. We do have legitimate business enterprises and regularly take on employees. Not all of them are recruits. Few of our recruits are aware of this base. Even fewer the deeper workings of our organization. Many work for us and live quite normal lives never getting more involved than their daily employment.

"Getting back to the point — we have a standing arrangement with Denmount Court of Learning for right of first offer to talented students. Should a student accept an offer of employment with us before they graduate, we have worked out an agreement whereby credentials can be credited on the basis of work experience. This allows us to proffer job opportunities well before graduation occurs. We prefer this method of recruitment because after graduation, many other companies would be in competition for those same students. In exchange, we provide generous donations to support the school's many programs. You may have noticed some of your peers accepting similar arrangements on occasion."

Lev nodded in agreement. He recalled that exact circumstance during his first year when one of the senior students was offered a job six months before graduation. "And what would you offer me?"

"We already knew that you were a talented computational engineer, and we have an interest in facial recognition algorithms like you have been working on. Even if you hadn't passed the token test, we would have approached you with an offer of employment at one of our technology firms. We pay slightly above industry standard with generous benefits and opportunities for advancement. Having seen some of our technology, you already know that we're on the cutting edge, and our companies are industry leaders. You would not have found a better employer in your chosen field.

"After working with us for a time, those who show aptitude and skill are vetted for special projects. Confidentiality covenants are signed and it usually involves travel to remote research facilities for months at a time. These individuals get first-hand experience on some of our more exotic technology. A rare few prove themselves trustworthy and loyal to the Servator cause. At that point, they gain access to the hidden facets of our organization. Such an offer opens a whole new and amazing world of opportunities and compensation. Benefits include a lifetime guarantee of financial support and cutting-edge health care. Free room and board are available at all our bases and unlimited free travel to any of our facilities located around the world. You were prematurely exposed to the existence of this base, but assuming you weren't, would you have been interested in such an opportunity?"

Lev pulled a long sip of his kofa before answering. Even if he hadn't seen some of that secret technology, he would have jumped at such an offer.

"I'd be lying if I said no. Regardless, that ship has sailed, so why don't you explain the extenuating circumstances you alluded to?"

The Chief Sentry shifted uncomfortably and avoided his eyes. "I'm so sorry, Leviticus. Many options are no longer open to you. The Breachers' interest in abducting you means your safety is a thing of the past. You can't return to your old life. That's no fault of the Servators, but I grieve your loss of choice in the matter. If you were to return, not only would you be in danger, but the lives of your friends and family as well."

She let that sink in. Lev felt a mixture of fear for his family and indignant rage at the theft of his freedom. He wanted to hit something.

A wordless minute passed. His jaw began to hurt from clenching his teeth. He opened his mouth to let out the breath he had been holding. Chief Sentry Vantos took that as a cue to continue.

"On a more pleasant topic, the results from our test of your sensitivity in the garden rated you higher than we've seen in many years. People with your gifts are fast-tracked to special projects. If you had accepted our offer under normal circumstances, it would have only taken you a few years to find yourself making a similar decision to the one that you now face — minus the Breacher threat, of course. I don't know if that's of any consolation."

"So, basically my options are to risk my chances alone, on the run, or avail myself of your offer for employment and protection."

"It saddens me to have our proposal viewed in that light, but it's a fair assessment of your predicament. If you accept our offer, we can arrange to provide an inconspicuous security detail while you tell your friends and family about an amazing career opportunity on another continent and say your goodbyes. It will need to happen quickly. We can provide legitimate details and secure contact information so your family can keep in touch. Once things settle down, we'll find some way to accommodate visits. In the line of work you have chosen for yourself, it's quite common for an engineer to work on remote projects for extended periods of time. So, while your family may miss you, they won't have cause to worry."

"Thank you. I acknowledge the Breacher attempt to grab me wasn't your fault. I appreciate that you're considering ways to make this easier, but it's not just about the job. It's not even the danger. The matter of your existence as an organization gives me pause. Your agency represents a completely different world view. If I do this, my future is confined to one path. I won't have the luxury of turning back even if I wanted to. You're asking me to make a decision based on very limited information, from only one source. A source with its own agenda."

"I do understand your concern. It's wise that you do not wish to jump into something without all of the facts. I'd like you to consider a few more things before you decide.

"You have a great gift, Leviticus. The world doesn't understand the way you see things, but we do, and we can teach you how to harness it. You can't begin to comprehend the applications. I promise you this — if you train with us, you will have answers to questions you have been searching for your whole life. I beseech you now, Leviticus. Don't squander your gift. In joining the Servators, you earn an opportunity to make a real difference in the world — to work alongside a force for good.

"True, you don't know enough to make an informed decision, nor do you possess time, so trust what you already know. You've encountered Breachers — you understand the threat they represent even if you don't really understand the scope. You've seen this base and our technology. You know much of the science that benefits this world can only have come from the same source. Has anyone mistreated you during your time with us? Reflect on the spirit of generosity, our non-lethal methods of defence, the fact that friends of yours — good, good, people — believed in our cause.

"Consider the world around you, Leviticus. Have you really seen a less objectionable path than the one I'm offering? If it came down to a choice between the Servators or the Breachers, which would you choose? Even if you walk the line separating the two, you're never truly neutral. The support you give to one side or the other is only a matter of degree. Are you the type of person who's satisfied with half measures? If not, you'll find yourself closer to one extreme or the other. Of those two options, which do you prefer? Apart from the moral and ethical implications, could you just walk away? With what you now know, could you live out the rest of your days never learning the full truth?"

The woman is so earnest, Lev thought. She was leaning close, staring intently into his eyes, begging him to recognize truth in her own. She was correct. He knew it in his heart. He couldn't walk away without regretting it for the rest of his life. A thought occurred to him then. Nico would be a part of this with him. Lev wasn't alone. He wasn't sure when they might see each other again, but knowing they were fighting for the same cause felt right. He smiled. "I'm in."

Chapter 32

"Okay, first things first. We have to leave this place, so we'll need to wrap things up quickly."

Cello spoke into her Q-view passing orders. "Deak, I need four trusted rangers for protection duty. They will accompany Mr. Radix to collect his belongings and say his goodbyes. Once done, they're to rendezvous at the Caralithica way station and proceed to Ebot in Kemetica. I will secure arrangements for your arrival. Grab Jabin on your way and have him pack his bags to join them. Leviticus will need to begin training in self-defence immediately. Oh, and Deak? Set up an encrypted tote-comm for Leviticus so his family can contact him."

Lev stared dumbly as the Chief Sentry went into leader mode. Was this commanding woman the same who had shown such compassion moments ago? Judging by the responses from her people, they respected her more than they feared her.

"Joff, I need you to contact the Court Master at Denmount. Set up the standard pre-grad hiring arrangement for Leviticus Radix, effective immediately. Inform the Court Master that Mr. Radix won't be returning to class and that we expect credentials in place by week's end." Cello paused for a moment listening to Joff's reply. "I don't care if it's after hours. Drag him out of bed if you have to. If he wants to see any future donations, he'll get this done tonight!

"One more thing, Joff — prepare a letter of offer from InnovaMech to

Leviticus Radix with the standard salary for a computational engineer at the InnovaMech offices in Kemetica. No, wait — make that one and a half times regular salary, an offer too good to turn down. Make it your first priority. I will need that within the hour."

Lev couldn't believe what he was hearing. InnovaMech! The global leader in cutting-edge technology — and did he hear her say one and a half times standard salary? His parents would push him out the door for that kind of opportunity. It was a dream job. They would be very happy for him. Lev hoped he could hide his worry and look excited at the prospect, for their sake. In any other circumstance he wouldn't have to fake his joy, but this was all happening so fast and it felt so permanent.

"I also need you to contact the Chief Sentry at Kemetica base and let him know that we have a high priority candidate headed his way. Have them set up a position for him at InnovaMech as a front, but he'll require living quarters at the base. They'll need to begin sensitivity testing immediately. Tell them that they'll want Akhen Hor involved in his training. That will get their attention. Let the Chief Sentry know that I will contact him shortly with further details."

No sooner had Cello disconnected from her Q-view than four men entered and stood at attention. "Good! Mr. Radix, these four rangers will accompany you at all times until you reach Ebot. They will remain out of sight while you share the good news with your parents. Explain to your family that you were hired with the understanding that we need you immediately and that the ground transport outside your home is waiting to take you to a sea transport leaving within the hour. Give them your tote-comm information."

At her mention of it, one of the rangers handed a tote-comm to Lev — the latest model. Lev smiled wryly knowing he couldn't have afforded such a high-end device a day ago. It was tossed to him like some disposable toy of little value. This was to be his life now. He wondered how long it would take to get used to this new reality.

"Well? Why are you all just standing around? Let's get moving, people!"

Turning to Leviticus, all she said was, "It begins."

He supposed he had better get used to his new life quickly.

Chapter 33

Three anxious hours passed before a gentle knock sounded on his door. Kade rushed to open it.

Decar Tosh was standing in the hall in front of a towering hulk of a man. His thick-necked companion was wearing ill-fitting business attire that looked as though it would tear if he moved too quickly.

"Mr. Tosh! Please come in. Thank you for seeing me."

Decar strode confidently into the small room while his business partner ducked to keep from striking his head on the door frame. The tiny space suddenly felt very full. Decar sat in the only chair while his friend chose to remain standing. The room had limited floor space so unless he wanted to hug the large fellow near the door, Kade had no choice but to sit cross-legged on the bed. Decar set a portable viewscreen on the small table beside the bed, and powered it up. Then he looked expectantly at Kade and waited.

"Mr. Tosh. When I started on the facial recognition project at Denmount, I signed a covenant prohibiting the sharing of information related to that project. Apparently, I was seen speaking with you and rumour has it that you're a corporate spy."

Decar raised a brow but kept silent.

"Of course, *I* know you're a legitimate business man," Kade hastily added, "but you can see how things look from the Court Master's perspective. I've been expelled pending an investigation. I was hoping you might be able to help clear this matter up. Perhaps prove your credentials as a legitimate business man and assure the investigators that you were only recruiting future employees. They suspect that money changed hands and I need you to assure them that it wasn't in exchange for information. Perhaps you have lawvocates who can show that it's common practice in your country, as you've said."

When Decar failed to respond, Kade added, "I've spent a little of the money you gave me, but I will happily return the rest in exchange for your help. I'll pay you the remainder when I'm able."

"Let me summarize what you've just told me, Mr. Brixton. You're under suspicion for sharing proprietary information and breaking a covenant, punishable with criminal charges. As things stand, you have no way to prove your innocence. At this moment you're only a suspect, but if the investigators can prove money changed hands, you will end up in prison."

"Yes, that's it exactly! That's why I need your help!"

"Mr. Brixton, I'd like to show you a viewcording that has come into my possession." Decar pressed a button on the viewscreen and arranged it so Kade could see. It was a viewcording of Kade handing a storage device to a shady looking little man who plugged it into a viewscreen. The screen in the viewcording filled with a familiar writ weaving and Kade didn't doubt that if someone enlarged the image they would recognize the algorithm.

Kade knew what he would see next. The strange little man handed him a sack full of silver coins which Kade proceeded to count. "Where did you get that? Is this the only copy? We can't let the authorities get their hands on this!"

"Indeed. If the investigators were to learn of this viewcording, you would have no defence. You would certainly end up in prison with no hope for a future. It would bring shame to your family."

"But you have powerful lawvocates, right? Information didn't actually change hands. I still have the storage device. That man in the video is obviously running some kind of extortion scam. Surely you want to see him exposed for harming your reputation?"

"Mr. Brixton, I'm a little astonished at your level of naiveté. Or perhaps it's desperation clutching to hope so you can avoid the uncomfortable truth. The information on your storage device was copied the moment my associate plugged it into the viewscreen."

Kade couldn't breathe.

"Ah — I see things are falling into place for you now."

"You! You did this!" Kade lunged for Decar in a fit of rage and ran into a mountain of muscle. *How did someone so large move so fast?* He fell back onto the bed in a sitting position with his back against the wall, momentarily shocked into stillness. His shoulders suddenly slumped as he let the back of his head bump against the wall in defeat.

"Don't look so despondent. We'll be leaving tonight for Sumakad and you'll be joining us. We have different laws in our country and you'll be safe from prosecution. You *will* come to work for our organization. The weavings you provided are very promising and you will help implement them on our network. You'll have the employment you coveted, and if you work hard for us, you'll receive generous compensation."

"I can't just leave!"

"You're not a stupid man, Mr. Brixton. I believe you understand your predicament quite well, but let me spell out your options. If you refuse to come, this recording will find its way to the authorities. I have people here in Caralithica who would keep an eye on you to make sure you couldn't disappear. You wouldn't want to run afoul of the authorities, would you? I hear Caralithica has a swift justice system with lengthy terms of imprisonment.

"I still have the algorithm so I don't really need you, but I suppose that means I'd have to find someone else familiar with the project to join us in Sumakad. Now that I think of it, your friend — Selica, is it? She's much nicer to look at than you are. I think I would enjoy working with her."

"You leave her out of this!"

Decar ignored him and continued. "Alternatively, you can join us. You will be compensated well and live a very comfortable life. We have many technological challenges for you that will engage your mind and provide a fulfilling career. We will provide you with official credentials giving you status as a computational engineer in Sumakad. You'll need to write letters to your friends and family, explaining truthfully, that you received an incredible job opportunity with an international company — an offer that you couldn't afford to refuse. You will never see them again, but after a suitable amount of time has passed, we will begin sending a generous monthly stipend to your family in your name.

"You can have everything you ever wanted. You'll be a hero — earn the respect of your family and provide for their financial well-being. Or, you can go to prison, lose everything you ever worked for and bring shame to your family name. The choice is yours."

"That's not really a choice at all."

"No, not really."

"When do we leave?"

"Immediately. Fogar will carry your packs."

Chapter 34

Akhen Hor fumed as he disconnected from his Q-view. They were pulling him away from important work — for sensitivity testing, no less! A task for a novice analyst. *Is this some form of punishment?* he wondered. Akhen was always in trouble for some imagined slight or another. He was granted a little leeway for his eccentricity, because no one could match his skill as an analyst.

He had better things to do than cater to the hopes of every regional leader who thought one of their novices was the next analyst prodigy. Yet here they were, preparing to parade another candidate of great potential before him.

Couldn't they have the candidate tested by someone else first, to see if the individual were truly worthy of his time? It was maddening. Akhen sighed. Dwelling on it was pointless. He may as well get this over with. The sooner done, the sooner he could get back to his work.

Apparently, the candidate had been sent to testing room three. That was as it should be. He had arranged that room specifically for his purposes. "At least they got that much right," he huffed.

When he entered the room, the test subject was already there. He sat on a stool near the door, just off to one side. *Odd. Why would he move the stool there?* The subject was a young man, Caralithican by the looks of him. Very far from home if that proved true.

"Name, rank, and trainer," Akhen demanded. The last two usually told him all he needed to know.

"My name is Leviticus Radix. Um, I have no rank or training. I assumed that's why I was here."

Akhen was livid. "This is unbelievable! You're telling me you haven't even received baseline testing?"

"Maybe? What's involved in baseline testing?"

"Who?" Akhen demanded.

"Who, what?"

"Don't play games with me young man! Who is the incompetent fool wasting my valuable time by sending an untested, clueless outsider? You must have training of some sort?"

"I was studying computational engineering before I came here."

"Computational engineering?" Akhen couldn't believe his ears. The lad wasn't even a novice analyst associated with the Servators. He was merely a student from some Caralithican public school. The fellow shouldn't even be on the base! Heads would roll for this incompetence.

Akhen was about to drag Leviticus to the nearest guard station when he realized he still didn't have a name to attach to this flagrant security violation. "I ask again. Who sent you here?"

"That would be Chief Sentry Cello Vantos, sir."

Akhen stopped mid-stride on his way to the door. "The Chief Sentry of the Caralithican Host sent you to me?"

"That's correct, sir."

That's interesting, Akhen thought, and a little flattering if he was being honest with himself. "What exactly did she say?

"She said that you would be interested. I don't know why, specifically, except that she seemed to think I was gifted."

Akhen snorted and rolled his eyes as he moved back to the testing table. "They're always gifted. Never mind. If the Chief Sentry sent you here then she has her reasons. We shall see. Well, come closer. My bark is worse than my bite and we can't accomplish much if we're yelling to each other from across the room. What in the name of the Maker prompted you to move the stool over there by the door?"

"It seemed — the least intrusive place to be."

"Least intrusive! I nearly tripped over you coming through the door!"

"I meant least intrusive to the space."

Akhen froze. He looked around the room for the first time. "What have you done?"

"I'm sorry — items were out of place. I just tidied up a bit and put things where they belonged."

"Young man, this is your first visit to this room. You couldn't possibly know where anything belongs!"

Even as he said it Akhen acknowledged that everything was in the correct place. Not one or two things, but literally everything. This was Akhen's testing room. He had gone to great effort to arrange tokens throughout the room in a very specific arrangement. It was why he demanded this room be reserved for his personal use.

It was a test of his own devising. Only someone with a high level of sensitivity would notice the intentional pattern or that things were slightly out of place. Only Akhen knew precisely where they belonged.

Over the years, a few promising candidates had sensed things weren't quite right. Even fewer had been able to point out specific tokens as the source of disorder. This young man — Leviticus, was it? He had found every last one of them! Extraordinary! "Put them back."

"Excuse me?"

"You heard me! Put them all back the way you found them." It was an impossible task, of course, but he wanted to watch the young man in action.

Without hesitation, the young man got up and moved around the room, methodically placing each item back in its original location. Not only location, but orientation as well. If that hadn't been incredible enough, he did it in the same order as Akhen himself would have done. It was the logical order for placement in the pattern.

Akhen's guest displayed no evidence of second-guessing, it appeared as second nature to him. The fellow had no idea what he had just accomplished when he went back to his stool and sat down.

Now that Akhen thought about it, the stool was indeed in the one spot where it was least disruptive to the harmony of the pattern. Well, the pattern as it was before Leviticus had put it back into disarray. Currently, he was squirming on that stool looking particularly uncomfortable.

"You look troubled." Akhen pressed.

"I don't wish to seem disrespectful, sir, but this isn't right."

"You disapprove of my demand? You come into my space and move things about and then think my reaction inappropriate?"

"Oh, no sir! It's the room, sir. Those items don't belong where they are now."

"Indeed they do not." Akhen began to smile. In fact, he was smiling so hard his face began to hurt. "You belong to me now."

If the young Mr. Radix was uncomfortable before, he looked positively alarmed now. Akhen didn't blame him, the way he was grinning and rubbing his hands together probably made him look maniacal.

"From now on, I will be your mentor. We'll be spending a great deal of time together." Finally! A challenge worthy of his abilities. Someone who shared his perspective of the world. He would hone this young man into a formidable analyst.

Akhen made a mental note to send an expression of his gratitude to the leader of the Caralithican Host. *I wonder what sort of gift would please a Chief Sentry?*

Chapter 35

Nico couldn't guess how long he'd been sitting in his stone prison. His chrono sat among the rest of his gear at the tunnel entrance. It felt like hours had passed.

He hadn't told anyone where he was going and the only person who might eventually miss him was Leviticus. That likely wouldn't happen until after the school break. Unfortunately, he had told Lev that he needed some alone time. *If Lev tries to contact me and I don't answer, he'll probably assume I went off hiking or something. It could be weeks before anyone begins looking for me.*

Even if a search party were able to track him to the crypt, they would never find the hidden tunnel entrance. How could he have been so careless? He didn't bring any food or water or even his tote-comm to call for help.

If he had waited until morning and provisioned himself properly, he would be better prepared for exploring. But no, he'd let curiosity get the better of him. He'd thrown caution aside to check out one more tunnel before settling down for the night and now he was trapped.

Who knew how long this trap had been waiting to be sprung? Did its creator even live anymore? Would someone eventually come to check or was this a long-forgotten tunnel? Nico considered the accumulation of dust on the tunnelling machine and guessed no one would be coming. He should have at least left a note or something.

Now he would slowly die, alone in this place. Nico hoped that the lantern wouldn't give out before he did. He couldn't imagine a worse fate than to lay entombed in earth and darkness waiting for the end to come.

He spent the next hour or so scouring every hand span of the place, searching for something, anything that seemed like a switch or trigger to open an escape route. One word ran through his head the whole time. "Stupid... stupid..." He screamed once in frustration and then gave up and sat down. "I'm going to lose my life. Not to a worthy cause, but stupidity."

"Oh, I think you can still contribute to a very worthy cause, Mr. Callan and I believe it will be many years before you leave this world."

Nico's head jerked up in shock. The tunnel was open once more and a regal-looking woman stood before him, guards at either side.

"Hello, Nico, my name is Cello Vantos. We've been expecting you."

Nico leaped to his feet, eyes alight. "I knew it!"

The two men stepped forward lifting some sort of batons. Nico jumped back in alarm. Who were these people? Were they friends or enemies of his father?

"How do you know my name?" Nico demanded.

"Your father and I were close friends."

"If that's true, then why have you brought..." Nico hesitated. These men wore uniforms and held themselves like warriors. Soldiers? Yes, he decided. "Why are you here with soldiers?"

The woman waved for her men to lower their weapons. "I apologize. My companions can be a little overprotective. No harm will come to you. I give you my word."

Nico pointed his chin towards the weapons. "What are those things anyway?" He had never seen a baton that looked like these. They seemed futuristic, machined to finer tolerances than he thought possible.

The woman, Cello, nodded at one of the men.

"Stun batons," the man explained, holding it out for Nico to examine.

Nico raised an eyebrow in query to which the soldier added, "a non-lethal weapon that temporarily disables one's foe."

"No such weapons exist," Nico began, then shook his head remembering the strange technology that had so effectively trapped him. "Never mind, of course it does. I've seen several things beyond my experience lately. It seems such technology was unremarkable to my father."

"Your father produced them, as a matter of fact."

"My father was a fisherman and a transport driver who grew a shipping business. He most definitely was *not* a scientist."

"I didn't say he invented them, I said he produced them. He had many manufacturing enterprises employed to support our efforts."

Nico was staring intently at her as she spoke. Something about her voice seemed familiar. "Do I know you?"

She smiled, looking genuinely pleased. "The last time we met, you were about seven years old."

"You're the disappearing lady! I remember you! I came into my father's study to show him something I had carved and you were there. Papa shooed me out and I waited in the hall for you to leave ... but you never did.

"Papa left his office, hurrying off with a worried expression on his face. He walked right past and didn't notice that I was sitting there. I expected you to follow him. When you didn't exit the study, I looked inside — the room was empty! I searched every corner but you had disappeared, just like that." Nico snapped his fingers. The wonder of it filled him again, and then he put two and two together. "Wait... One of those hidden entrances must have been in my father's study."

"I'm surprised you remember that. Yes, that's correct. One of these tunnels leads there. Your father had it made so we could meet in secret to discuss Servator business."

"That tunnelling machine belongs to my father?"

"That and so very much more. I haven't walked these tunnels since your parents passed away. That was such a tragic loss. I miss them both. They were dear friends.

"Your father was preparing you to take over for him one day. He arranged for you to find this place when the time was right. We set up monitors to wait for that day. I apologize for holding you here like this, but we didn't want you getting lost in the tunnels. For your own safety, you understand. The integrity of these old passages is questionable. Collapses have occurred in spots.

"Had you not discovered this place on your own, we would have eventually approached you in some other manner. I'm happy that you came to us and not the other way around. Some of what we must discuss will seem unbelievable coming from a stranger. It's better that your father was first to introduce you to some of our technology, even if it was posthumously. It will make the rest easier to hear."

"What's a Servator?"

Her laugh filled the air with warmth. "So like your father to ask the most difficult to answer question first."

Nico didn't care which she answered first, so long as he got answers. He had so many questions, he wasn't quite sure where to begin. Cello held up her hand before he could ask.

"Why don't we take this tunnel to your father's study and you can make me something hot to drink before we begin? Maybe a little something to eat as well? I missed dinner."

Chapter 36

"Leviticus, focus!"

"I am focussing!"

"No. You are not! I know your baseline abilities, and this isn't even close. It's like your mind is a thousand leagues away."

Maybe not a thousand but at least several hundred. It had been two months since he left home. Ebot bore no resemblance to Denmount. It was always hot and dry. In Denmount, soothing ocean breezes were the norm. Such respite from the heat was unheard of here. Not that Kemetica was without its charms. The marketplace was always an adventure, filled with bright colours and the scents of exotic spices. Tasting the incredible variety of fruits and vegetables was a treat and the baked goods were wonderful.

The people were friendly and generous, but he missed his family and friends. He yearned for the days when Nico would drag him to an eating establishment, swearing that it had the best soda or meat roll on the planet. The menu never lived up to Nico's endorsement. *Is this what melancholy feels like?* he wondered.

"Again," Akhen prodded.

Lev turned his back to the stage and waited for it to reset. Tokens were projected among a variety of random objects haphazardly strewn about. Akhen expected him to locate as many as possible before the projector disengaged. All objects were mapped on his Q-view and he had to select tokens from among the other items displayed on the map.

Lev located two tokens before the projector shut off. So far, his best had been eight in the time allotted. This wasn't even close. Lev threw his arms up and growled in frustration. "What's the point of all this anyway?"

"The point, young man, is to locate as many tokens as you can in the shortest amount of time possible."

Lev rolled his eyes. "I know *that*, but you're training my mind to respond by reflex as though I were about to enter battle. It's similar to the methods used by the warkata instructors to train physical reflexes. I thought analysts studied static data in a safe room — somewhere far from danger. And why do I need to worry about catching everything the first time around? If I'm analyzing recorded or transcribed events, I can just look over the records a second time if I missed anything."

Akhen looked thoughtful and motioned for Lev to sit. "Rest for a moment. I generally teach more advanced students and I keep forgetting you never attended novice training. This is all new to you. It's true that many analysts study static information sources. Even so, the ability to notice a variance quickly can dramatically decrease the time necessary to wade through data. For the rangers waiting on those results, it can mean the difference between life and death in the field.

"Our best analysts are those who can accurately sift data at a high rate. Those analysts are specialized and called on to assist in field work. They need to apply their skills in real time. Far too few of us can function in that capacity. For that reason, we do our best to elevate those skills in all of our trainees.

"I know you have no reference for comparison, Leviticus, so let me explain something to you. In the exercise you were practising, the average field analyst identifies between three and five tokens in thirty seconds. They learn to do that after years of training. On a good day, you can identify eight tokens in fifteen seconds and your training has only just begun. In our field of expertise, I'm considered the most skilled and I have never been able to surpass ten tokens in ten seconds."

Leviticus stared at his instructor. "What are you saying?"

"What I'm telling you, Leviticus, is that you're no mere analyst. You possess the potential to become a great one like those from our past. We've not seen someone with your promise in hundreds of years."

The excitement in Akhen's eyes unnerved Lev, but Akhen continued before he could respond. "Never mind that, for the moment. I can tell you from personal experience what honing these skills can mean. The areas in which you will excel, and to what degree, are still to be determined. The ability to read a changing pattern in an instant is what every analyst strives to achieve. Consider the possibilities. You gain an advantage with instantaneous recognition — the time to see patterns within patterns. Let's consider warkata since you brought it up. Imagine capturing images of your opponent's attacks in your mind. As the battle progresses, you would begin to recognize indicators of an impending assault before its onset. That would give you a distinct advantage. It's precisely the advantage your warkata instructors are giving you when they train you to watch your opponent for physical signs that give away intent."

Akhen had Lev's attention. He would love to take some of his sparring partners down a notch or two.

Akhen continued. "Picture yourself in the heat of battle. You recognize the telltale movement of a kick about to come, but you also see something more in the eyes and facial expressions of your opponent. Detail revealing hesitation or carelessness that leads to predictable actions. Perhaps your opponent's breathing pattern or scent denotes fear or anger? You could anticipate so much more than the average warrior. If you knew when your adversary would block, and how, you could attack with impunity. If you knew in advance what would provoke an attack, you could block every attempt. At least in theory. Your opponent might begin to believe you can read his mind. I have been able to employ enough of this technique that few will spar with me anymore. I look forward to the challenge you may provide me in that regard some day.

"That's only one example, but I can't emphasize enough the potential of instantaneous pattern recognition. The applications are limitless — political negotiations, large group battle strategy, even discerning what drives people."

Lev didn't think he would ever be able to understand people regardless of his 'gift', but he could understand the strategic application. It had always served him well when playing Jumkano.

He had intuitively done exactly what Akhen was suggesting while playing board games. He would make a move on the board and then watch an opponent's face carefully. It was like he could see their thought processes as they looked at one game piece, and then another. Whenever they came to a decision, a subtle shift in their demeanour always gave them away. Some tiny nuance told him whether they were confident or taking a gamble. Their ploys seemed transparent to him.

Could he really learn to do that in other arenas? The thought intrigued him even while it frightened him a little. Thinking back, Lev had to wonder — why did it come so easily to him when he was playing a game while eluding him during these training sessions? He guessed that he felt less pressure while at play. More than that, he felt self-assured. He didn't question his ability in those moments. Could it really be that simple? Could he learn confidence under pressure? Lev wasn't certain.

Was it possible he was trying to learn the wrong thing during these exercises? Perhaps instead of pushing himself to think faster, he needed to let go. Maybe he needed to trust himself and learn to suppress things that interfered with the process. It was worth a shot. "Can we try it again?" Lev asked.

Akhen smiled. "By all means."

Lev proceeded to identify six tokens on his next try. He grinned in anticipation. He couldn't wait until his next sparring match.

Chapter 37

Nico wasn't sure what to serve for a meal. He didn't normally host dinner guests and a bachelor's pantry was far from glamorous. He decided to go with basic foods that didn't need much preparation. Before long, he had piled a tray with sliced fruit, cheese, prepared meats, a jar of date jam and flat bread.

Nico grabbed a flagon of wine along with the pot of kofa he had been brewing and set them beside the food. *It will do,* he nodded as he looked over his offering. He carried it all into the dining room in two trips. Once everyone was settled at the table, Nico blessed the food and invited them to partake.

The two men dug in with relish. Nico was surprised to note that the woman ate as heartily as her companions. *I guess she wasn't joking when she said she'd missed dinner.* Nico joined them, but ate half-heartedly, more interested in the discussion to follow.

When his guests finally seemed satisfied, he offered them each a refill of kofa or wine, and then quickly cleared the table.

Returning from the kitchen, Nico noticed that the woman, Cello, had found her way to a comfortable chair in the sitting room. One of her companions took a position near the door and the other excused himself to check the perimeter of the house.

Nico guessed at her importance but didn't know how he should be addressing her. He felt out of his depth. Such concerns were beyond his experience. What kind of organization had his father joined? He grabbed a seat opposite and leaned back, considering where to begin. *I suppose it would be good to know the proper form of address.* "You've introduced yourself as Cello Vantos, but perhaps you could tell me what your role is in all of this."

"Of course, how rude of me! It's just that your father preferred to keep things casual. Being back in this house — well, I suppose I fell into old habits. The place hasn't changed. Everything looks much as I remember it."

"I have only fond memories of my home and felt little need to change anything." He held her gaze, waiting for his answer.

She coughed, sensing his impatience. "I apologize for my distraction — I also have many pleasant memories of this place, but you're right, we have much to discuss. I serve as Chief Sentry for the Servator Host in Caralithica. I don't expect that to mean anything to you, but basically I'm in charge of all matters pertaining to our operations here."

"And what matters might those be?"

"We're the Maker's servants, protectors of the Way."

It wasn't really much of an answer, but Nico chose to ignore that for the moment. "Chief Sentry of the Servator Host.... A host is suggestive of a large army," he stated. "I'm unaware of any current wars."

Cello's eyes were roaming the room as she answered, a small smile forming whenever they paused on one memory or another. "Not so great a number. Perhaps in the tens of thousands worldwide. More, if you count the many who serve in logistical roles. Your father was one such. We do have a military structure, but we don't battle flesh and blood so much as destructive ideology."

Nico grabbed onto the tidbit about his father — logistics, she had said. That brought things into perspective. His father was indeed gifted in the movement of people and products. "Are you implying that my father's shipping ventures played a role in supporting your organization?"

"It continues to play a role. Nico, your father was involved in so very many more ventures than you could possibly imagine. The shipping company that was your family's original claim to fame only scratches the surface. If any of our people need to travel — whether by land, sea, or air — it's via one of your family's assets. Food, construction material, equipment, technology — he had his hands in everything. To this day, his efforts remain the single biggest contributor to our daily operations. We should never have allowed ourselves to become so dependent on him, but he succeeded at everything he set his mind to. You know how difficult it was to refuse your father's generosity."

Nico did know. On his seventh birthday, he had been hinting at his interest in a throwing sling. Upon opening his gift, he found a fishing net. His father had proudly displayed the quality of the net and was beginning to explain the intricacies of its modern design when he must have noticed the disappointment on his son's face. Nico would have done anything to remove the hurt from his father's eyes in that moment. His mother had explained, "Nico, the receiver of a gift cannot dictate to the giver, or it becomes the fulfillment of a demand and is no longer a gift."

Thankfully, it was an easy thing to prevent. A simple smile would fill his father with such obvious joy that the true gift became his happiness. Giving was part of Nes Callan's nature and the man would not be who he was without it.

Cello's voice cut through his reverie. "Nes was an exceptionally gifted man. Our accumulated wealth has financed many of his enterprises and we continue to receive a return on our investment as a result. Your family benefited financially as well. It has proven challenging to provide plausible sources for his access to easy capital, without drawing attention to our existence as his benefactor.

"If you take over your father's business enterprises, no doubt you will be surprised to learn the breadth of his investments. Nearly all of the companies under the umbrella of Callan International reserve a segment of their operation for clandestine activities. This is part of the reason we needed to speak with you. You might have seized control of Callan International in ignorance, never knowing all you should know about your newly acquired financial empire. That wouldn't have worked out favourably for either of us. We would like very much to carry on a relationship like we had with your father. Such an arrangement would allow us to continue to quickly meet unexpected needs. It would also give you a source of quick capital to develop ventures of your own interest. Our past partnership with your father was always mutually beneficial.

"More importantly, we hope you will feel as your father did and see the value of contributing to a worthy cause. Your father was more committed to the Maker's Way than anyone I have personally known. He perfected his genius in his zeal. I know he hoped that you would find the same joy that he felt through his work with us."

"Did my Mother know?"

Cello chuckled. "While your father may have been an ideas man, it was your mother who got things done. He would provide the vision and she would — let's just say, gently nudge people in the right direction."

Nico grinned at the accurate depiction of his parents. Cello clearly knew his family well.

"Even old Ezra knew, but he was too long in the tooth to contribute as he might have liked. A man of wisdom, his support came more in the form of blessings and encouragement. Serving the Way was a family affair and helping the Servators was the manner in which your family chose to contribute."

"So, my family was not directly involved in Servator operations, but took on a supporting role?"

Cello's eyes clouded over. She shook her head as her features took on the appearance of someone who had swallowed something distasteful.

"Your parents started out that way, but we underestimated the liability of their proximity to our operations. Over time, the Breachers identified them as part of our organization. I encouraged your parents to leave Caralithica, but I couldn't sway them. I insisted that at the very least they should take field training so they could learn how to defend themselves and move covertly. At the time, I was thinking they would become proficient in the use of our communications equipment and our safe houses — maybe gain some rudimentary skill in warkata. They agreed to the training and surprised us by becoming some of our most skilled rangers."

Cello paused, suddenly seeming at a loss for words. She straightened her back, resolved. "Nico, I must tell you something difficult to hear. Ranger work is dangerous and your parents perished as a result."

"My parents died in a roto-wing accident."

"It was no accident, Nico. Someone tampered with the craft."

Nico couldn't breathe. It had taken years to get over his parents' death. The nightmares that had plagued his youth threatened to come roaring back. He took a calming breath and stood. "Who?" He demanded. "Who killed my parents?"

"I'm so sorry Nico...."

"I don't need your pity!" He interrupted. "I just need to know who!"

"We don't know precisely. We believe it was arranged by someone from within one of your father's companies. The perpetrator covered their tracks well — likely supported by our enemy."

Nico sat back down. "I think you had better tell me a little more about this enemy."

Chapter 38

Life in Sumakad turned out better than Kade expected. He had received credentials as a computational engineer and was leading a small team to implement the facial recognition software stolen from Denmount Court of Learning.

He felt a little guilty about that, but it hadn't been his *intent* to steal anything. He soothed his conscience by telling himself that Decar Tosh was the actual thief. Kade was the ignorant accomplice who hadn't realized what was happening.

It didn't quite solve the moral dilemma of working for Decar now, although the man had forced him into that as well. It really wasn't his fault, or at least that's what he told himself. He preferred not to dwell on the matter.

At least the man had followed through on paying off his loan and sending monthly financial gifts to his family. He supposed the lie was necessary to keep his family from asking questions about their son's absence.

Kade gleaned a little pleasure imagining his father having to accept that his son's efforts were paying off. It must gall the man to admit his error, though his father wasn't actually wrong. Kade had no intention of letting the senior Brixton know that. It was payback for all the misery his father had put him through over the years. At the beginning of each month, Brun Brixton would receive a little reminder that Kade was the largest financial contributor of the family. His father would be on the lookout for ways to discredit the money, but he wouldn't be able to refuse it until he had some evidence to support his suspicions. Kade was confident the fiction would go unchallenged. It wasn't like the man would ever confront him for the truth. Kade could never go home. Decar Tosh had invested heavily in him and held incriminating evidence to keep him in line. *These people own me*, Kade thought. Still, his keepers paid a very generous salary and provided an apartment to live in. His gilded cage was a consolation, however small.

Parties erupted every night with beautiful women and accommodation for any vice imaginable. Kade found some of it disturbing, but who was he to judge? He stuck with what he knew. The alcohol drowned out thoughts that would have otherwise kept him awake at night. If given the choice between guilt and prison, he'd choose guilt every time. *I'll just have to learn to live with it*, he thought for the hundredth time.

All in all it wasn't so bad of a life, at least until he woke and dragged himself to work. This morning was particularly bad. He was behind on his project and he couldn't think clearly. *Not much chance I'll see progress this morning*. He hoped Decar wouldn't show up today. The man had been hounding him lately, pushing for results.

"Brixton!"

Kade groaned, *no such luck.*

"Are you drunk man? It's early morning!"

"No, I'm just suffering last night's aftermath."

"You smell like a brewhouse!" Decar was fuming.

"I just need a mug of kofa and I'll be fine."

"No, you fool! It's not fine. Not fine at all! Villecrest wants to see you. Now! He'll want a report on your progress. Please tell me you have some good news on that front."

"I've told you, writ weaving requires time."

"That's not an answer!"

"I'm streamlining syntax to prepare for aggregation of the current test variant."

Decar said nothing for a full two minutes while staring at Kade, as if to determine whether he was speaking to a man or an infant. His face suggested something with intelligence more akin to a turnip.

"I don't have time for this. Get yourself cleaned up. You have ten minutes to make yourself presentable. Trust me when I tell you that you do *not* want to keep Mr. Villecrest waiting. I swear, if you make me look bad..." Decar shook his head in disgust. "Don't just sit there — go!"

Chapter 39

Nico's reaction to the revelation of his parents' murder left Cello shaken. It brought back memories of her own shock at learning the sad news all those years ago. A tear formed in her eye but she blinked it away. She had to finish this. Nico deserved to know about the Servators. Cello had promised Nes that she would take Nico under her wing when the time came. If she wanted Nico to trust her, she needed to be honest with him.

"Before we go any further, Nico, I need to know something. Are you a follower of the Maker's Way?"

"My parents raised me on those teachings. If you're asking whether I personally adhere to those beliefs, the answer is yes. I have seen the darkness and confusion in the world and have no doubt that the Maker's Way is a better path. Even if I hadn't come to learn that truth for myself, I would have followed my parents' example. I have seen nothing as appealing in the lives of my peers."

"And do you believe in the prophecy of the flood?" Cello became concerned when he didn't answer right away. She worried that he might be one of those who only followed the Way when it was convenient.

When he responded, it was defensively. "I do! Go ahead and laugh if you wish, everyone else does."

Cello sighed inwardly with relief. It would make this so much easier. "I have no intention of mocking you, Nico. According to the prophecy, if the world becomes too filled with darkness, the flood will come and end all life. It may surprise you to learn that the primary goal of the Servators is to prevent the premature onset of this prophecy."

"How can you hope to do that?"

"By opposing those who are trying to hasten that end."

"Are you suggesting that people with dark impulses have an agenda to end the world?"

"You've said yourself that you would prefer not to live like some of your peers who've made questionable life choices."

"They're just blindly following impulses. They could be accused of having bad habits, but that doesn't mean they have an evil agenda."

"Can't you think of agencies who cater to those impulses?"

"Yes, okay, there exist purveyors of indulgence and pleasure that are far from altruistic. I don't agree with their choices. I don't like that they profit from such things, but that still sounds to me like a selfish agenda more than an attempt to annihilate the world."

"Nico, selfish agendas always negatively impact the world around us. It may affect many or only a few, but it is destructive nonetheless. I believe you already understand this, but let me ask you — do you believe there are forces that encourage such things?"

"Are you referring to the wastrels mentioned in the scrolls? The beings who lead the world towards darkness?"

"The very same."

"I guess I always thought of them as disembodied spirits, tempting or tormenting individuals, not a coordinated agency with an agenda. Are you saying that you've encountered one?"

"What I'm telling you, Nico, is that wastrels exist. They do indeed tempt and torment, but not in so inefficient a manner as you have suggested. Wastrels offer promises of power. They hold sway over individuals and groups to serve their purpose on a much broader scale. They employ agencies to blackmail and manipulate powerful men and women to wreak havoc on as many as possible. It's these agencies whom we oppose. The majority of them are involved with an organization known as the Breachers. Our enemies work in the shadows and we fight them wherever they arise."

"You're telling me that a secret, evil organization, plans to destroy the world?"

Cello could tell that she was losing him. She was sharing too much, too quickly. He would need proof. She would give it to him but for now she just needed the benefit of the doubt.

"I know how it sounds. I can provide more concrete evidence than my word on the matter, but that will require time. Whether or not you can accept the idea of wastrel manipulation, it is sufficient for you to understand a simple truth. Criminal organizations deal in vice for their own gain. They're destroying lives with no concern for the suffering they cause. It's in direct opposition to the Maker's Way."

"That I can accept, and know to be true."

"Then you know who our enemy is. You know who we fight and those whom we seek to protect. Your parents understood this as well, and while we don't know precisely who killed them, we know that Breachers were involved."

Cello watched as Nico rose and began pacing the room. He looked both angry and confused. *Time to shift to another topic.* "I understand you're still considering whether you should accept control of your father's enterprises."

"How would you know about that?

"As I mentioned earlier, we have funded many of your father's ventures. We have a majority stake in most of them. People who worked with your father continue to monitor our interests. We're apprised of decisions that may affect our operations."

"Of course — that makes sense."

"I want to encourage you to accept that position, but I don't want to give you the impression that I'm applying pressure. Business has continued as usual since your parents passed. We have a say at the table in all business decisions and our resources are not at risk. I should acknowledge that it sometimes takes longer than when we could speak directly with your father about our needs, but we can usually find a way to get things done.

"I miss those days and long to have that kind of mutually beneficial working relationship again, but that's not my only reason for encouraging you. I have another selfish reason. We have gone as far as we can in tracking down those who murdered your parents. I already said we believe it was someone with whom he worked. While we have eyes and ears in Callan International, they do not have access to the same level of information as the head of the company would have. If we could gain that high-level access, we might find the missing pieces of the puzzle. I would dearly like to see justice done."

"Why haven't you approached Tenika Sheridan? As current head of the company, surely she could provide access?"

"As far as we know, Tenika believes that your parents died as the result of an accident. It would be necessary to take her into our confidence to request a search for a different cause. As for bringing Tenika into the fold — well, let's just say we've worked with her long enough to know that we don't trust her to see past her own ambitions.

"Having revealed my own selfish hopes, let me tell you the most important reason I believe you should fill your father's shoes. I see much of your father in you, Nico. I've watched you grow, and while you may have felt alone a lot of the time, you've had people looking out for you in subtle ways. I've followed your accomplishments and marvelled at your ability to draw people together. You're compassionate and slow to anger. You have a strong work ethic and you're a natural leader. People genuinely like to be around you because you make everyone feel important. Your parents shared those same attributes. I don't know whether it is a naturally occurring Callan trait or if it was the way your parents raised you, but you're a good person, Nico Callan. Your parents would be very proud of the man you've become. I know I am. The world lost much when your parents returned to the Maker. The world will regain some of what it lost if you pick up where they left off. If you're the man I think you are, you won't be content walking away from your legacy."

"Will you give me all of the information you've collected from your investigation into my parents' murder?"

"Of course."

"And you'll teach me everything you know about the Servators and their enemies? You won't only tell me what you think I need to know?"

"You would not be able to function properly in your role as a support to us if we kept secrets from you. So you know that I speak the truth, I'll do you one better. Your father left a great deal of documentation that he hoped would help you. We keep it secured at one of our safe houses. I can give you directions and security access to that location, but ask that you do not remove anything or produce copies. Security reasons, you understand."

Nico stopped pacing and blew out a heavy sigh. "I had already decided that I couldn't walk away from the business started by my grandfather and expanded by my father. It's all I have left of my family. To be honest, running a business never appealed to me. All I really ever wanted was a career where I could help others.

"Papa had such compassion for people. He was so spontaneous. His character seemed contrary to life as a businessman. I couldn't comprehend how he enjoyed it so much. I thought perhaps he was just carrying on the family business — you know, the obligation of a son to his father. I figured he was finding his joy in side ventures or hobbies. With these revelations about his life, I finally understand. He was living for something bigger than his greatest ambition. Nothing about his life was a compromise. No wonder he seemed so alive.

"I'm not sure if I was born this way, as you suggest, or rather raised to some ideal. However, knowing what I know now, I feel as if my arrival at this point was inevitable. I can tell you that I want this with every fibre of my being. I don't know what to think of everything you've told me. It's enough for now to learn the truth about my parents and to know that I can be part of something positive. Something they believed in."

Cello rose and stood before him. "Nico, your father's business isn't all you have left of your family. We're your family." She pulled him into a hug. He held back for a moment and then hugged her back fiercely.

Releasing her, he asked, "So where do we begin?"

Cello laughed. "Yes, you're definitely a Callan. I suggest you take a few days to let it all sink in. When you're ready, contact Tenika and inform her of your decision. She will arrange to have legal documents prepared. Meanwhile, I will introduce you to Brokar Luge. He's head of Servator operations, a secondary role within Callan Enterprises. Brokar can tell you everything you need to know about that side of the business and much more.

"I strongly suggest that you take those documents home to read before signing anything. Ask Brokar for help. He can arrange for a lawvocate to ensure the document is free from inconsistencies. In fact, lean heavily on Brokar. Do not hesitate to ask him for anything. If it is within his power to help you, he will. It's for this purpose that he serves in your company. I know he'll be very happy to be working with a Callan again.

"I think that's enough talk for now. We'll take our leave and allow you time to gather your thoughts. Take this secure tote-comm. Use it to contact me at any time. As I said, we're family. I'll call you tomorrow. Goodnight, Nico, and thank you. I will sleep very well tonight, knowing you will be at the helm of Callan International."

Chapter 40

It was a little-known tunnel. Normally an emergency escape route, it served now as Kayla's way in. View tokens were in place to monitor other entrances to the base so this was her only option.

This particular tunnel was a heavily guarded secret as it led directly to the chambers of the Chief Sentry. Only when a Chief Sentry retired was that information shared, passed on to their replacement. The only reason Kayla knew about it was because she grew up in her mother's living quarters.

It was rare for a Chief Sentry to house family on the base, but in the aftermath of her father's murder, her mother felt a need to keep her close. Kayla had been drilled repeatedly in the use of this tunnel — how to open and close the entrance, how to cover her tracks at the exit point, where to find the emergency food and water rations should she need to stay in hiding for any length of time.

The tunnel led to a small abandoned farmstead a league beyond Denmount City limits. It was at the end of a long-forgotten sheep path far from the main roads. Kayla had waited until dark to approach the farmstead and enter the tunnel. Two hours later, she was at the entrance to her mother's chambers.

Her first order of business was to gain access to the base security system. To do that, she'd need a high-level security token. Kayla didn't personally own one. She probably never would, now that she was an outcast. Fortunately, her mother, as the Chief Sentry, had the highest possible security clearance. A safe box was hidden within the tunnel and her mother kept a spare security token there for emergencies. Kayla wasn't supposed to know about it and she wouldn't have except for a bit of truancy. She'd been hiding in their chambers to avoid classes while her mother opened the tunnel entrance. Kayla had watched, terrified that she'd be discovered, as her mother accessed the safe box. Fortunately, she remained unnoticed, crouching in the shadows. The Chief Sentry never found out about that little security breach. Kayla held her breath as she quickly entered the code she'd seen her mother use all those years ago. Would it still work or had she changed it? The lid opened with a little tug. Kayla rolled her eyes at the failure to follow security protocol, even as she smiled in relief. "Seriously, Mother!"

Entering her mother's chambers, she strode straight to the study and turned on the desktop Q-view. She used the token to gain priority access and set herself up with full privileges as the token holder. Next she wrote a small program to override any security alerts triggered by her token's passage through the base. Then a second one to warn her of alerts triggered by anyone else. She hoped it would help her avoid any surprise visitors. Surely someone would come by eventually, if for no other reason than to perform some maintenance. As a final precaution, she set up a schedule for the system to auto-erase any recordings of the token holder's passage. As long as she carried the token with her, she was effectively invisible. Just in case, she dug around in her closet for an old hat and scarf to cover her features when moving about the base.

Kayla pushed away from the desk and leaned back in the chair, propping her legs up on the desktop. Her mother would have swatted her feet had she been there to see it. It reminded her how alone she was. Her mother thought she was still travelling. She had been allowed to retain her status as novice. It allowed her to visit Servator bases around the world — a perk available to trainees. Travelling exposed them to different languages, cultures and opportunities. Instructors encouraged novices to explore the full gamut of Servator operations. It helped build international cooperation and form well-rounded personalities.

Leaving had been the right choice. Everyone needed a degree of separation from her tragic failure. Tempers needed to cool. Wounds needed to heal before forgiveness could occur, but Kayla just couldn't stay away. She *had* travelled to the destinations discussed with her mother, but not for as long a time as she thought she would. She visited Jaihuwan and Arapanus, having always wanted to experience those two cultures, but found she couldn't enjoy her surroundings. The exotic sights, sounds, and smells were wasted on her. All she could think about was her burning need to fix the mess she'd made — to find absolution. Finally, she had given up and sailed home. The slow trip across the sea had given her a great deal of time to think and formulate plans.

The abandoned base was eerily quiet but it suited both her mood and strategy. The base was well stocked with supplies. She could live here for years, if necessary, without anyone noticing her presence. Kayla got up and prepared something to eat before bathing and heading to her room. Tomorrow, she would begin her research and start laying plans. She was moving forward at last. Tonight, she would crawl into her own bed. Having a plan allowed her the peace she required to drift into the first real night's sleep she'd had since this all began.

Chapter 41

Kade knew little about the mysterious Mr. Villecrest. He was at the top of the local food chain, but other than that, Kade had no idea what to expect. Decar wore a sour expression on his face during the entire trip to the administration building.

Should I be worried? He'd never seen Decar looking so nervous. Kade made a quick inventory of talking points. Most people didn't understand technology and often he could dazzle them with big words until their eyes glazed over.

The ground transport slowed to a stop in front of a utilitarian building. Was this the office for leadership? Kade expected something opulent, gaudy even. This looked more like a fortified bunker. He started to ask a question but Decar glared until he snapped his jaw shut. *Okay then.*

Kade had prepared himself to climb several flights of stairs to an office with a view as was typical for corporate heads. But the building rose only two stories. Decar walked right past the stairs heading up and started to descend instead. *How odd*, Kade thought. The whole affair was starting to creep him out.

At the bottom of the staircase, they turned left and started down a long hall. A door opened at the end and two men exited, turning down another hallway to the right. Were they carrying a body? Kade shook his head, *that can't be right. Probably just a shadow from the poor lighting.*

Decar stopped in front of the door and adjusted his appearance before knocking.

"Enter."

"Third Anarch! I have brought Mr. Brixton as you requested."

Third Anarch? What sort of title was that? "A pleasure to meet you, sir."

"Silence!"

The command struck Kade dumb.

"Leave us, Decar."

The man seemed positively eager to go. Kade had never seen this side of Decar. It made him nervous.

The Third Anarch was an imposing man. Tall with dark features. He had what looked like a scar from a burn near his right eye. His sharp angular features framed his eyes in a way that made them seem piercing. A shiver went down his spine. Kade was clearly out of his element here. He had no idea of the proper protocol in this culture, let alone this particular organization. This was the first time he had spoken with someone other than Decar in the chain of command. He tried again. "How shall I address you?" Kade never saw it coming. One moment he was standing, and the next he was lying on the floor with a huge welt on the side of his face.

"You don't address me. You answer my questions and nothing more. Do you understand?"

Kade nodded once. He started to rise and then thought better of it and remained on his knees.

"Perhaps you're not such a fool after all."

Kade noticed the dagger in Villecrest's hand for the first time. He was wiping it clean with a white square of linen. He placed the blade back in its sheath and licked some blood off his finger. Kade froze. He felt like prey, trapped by the stare of a predator considering its next morsel. He knew he was shaking, but couldn't compose himself.

"How close are you to completing your work on the facial recognition algorithm?"

Kade swallowed hard, trying to get his mouth to form words. "We've deployed the data directives for the feature identification nodes on the network..." He knew he'd made a mistake two seconds before a boot to his stomach had him doubled over gasping for air.

"I take it back. You *are* a fool. Dare to condescend at risk to your life. Answer the question I asked and nothing more."

Kade was terrified. The project was far from completion, but that was clearly not what the man wanted to hear. They needed him, didn't they? He considered the safest gamble. "We're perhaps three months from completion."

Villecrest's eyes flared and Kade prepared for another blow, but all the Anarch said was, "You have two weeks."

Kade didn't ask what would happen if he were unable to comply. All he wanted at that particular moment was to be far away.

"Leave! Tell Decar I wish to speak with him."

Kade sat in the hall, curled in on himself. He felt too shaky to stand. He didn't have to wait alone for long. Decar reappeared and quietly closed the door behind himself. Then he kicked Kade hard, in his already bruised ribs. The breath fled from his lungs at the pain and he was about to protest until he noticed Decar was sporting a black eye. Decar pointed up the hall, saying nothing. Kade was eager to leave. He half ran, half hobbled to the transport, despite his pain.

What had he gotten himself into? He couldn't finish the project in two weeks. It was an unreasonable demand. What would they do if he failed? They needed him didn't they? He suddenly remembered Decar's threat to force Selica into their employ. Then he remembered how many others had worked on the algorithm at Denmount. Third Anarch villecrest didn't really need him at all. Kade was a dead man.

Chapter 42

Tenika was fuming. "What happened, Halen?"

Halen Tu stood there, firm as always, not appearing the least bit ruffled in the face of her ire. "Nico took the contract to another lawvocate for review."

"I'm well aware of that fact! Why would he do that? *You* are the lawvocate for this company. What possible reason could he have to go to a third party?"

"I couldn't guess, but I would have done the same."

Tenika speared him with an exasperated look. "Whose side are you on?"

"I'm just saying, it's standard practice. I believe I warned you it might happen."

"I'm telling you, Halen, he practically ran out of my office when I last spoke with him. He confided that he didn't want to run a company. His eyes were virtually begging me to take this responsibility from him! I fully expected him to sign the contract and go back to whatever pampered lifestyle he's been living. Scrutinizing a legal contract is the action of someone who wants control and that is *not* the young man I met. Someone must have talked him into it."

"Be that as it may, the document was reviewed, revised, and signed."

Tenika sighed. "So, where do we stand?"

"The lawvocate was very thorough. He removed every clause that awarded you any degree of authority. As things stand, you remain employed in an advisory capacity, but all decisions fall under the authority of Nico Callan."

"How could you allow this to happen? Why did you let them add those changes? You should have pushed back!"

"I found nothing to contest. Nico owns the company. That was never going to change. This contract was only ever about how much authority he was willing to relinquish. He's fully within his rights to determine how he will run the family business and how much or little assistance he'd like. If I were him, I'd be wondering why the original document was written up the way it was. He may choose to interpret the language of the original clauses as a kind offer to shelter him from responsibility. I suggest you subtly reinforce that notion if he brings it up. Pushing the matter would signal that you don't want him in charge. That's not a perception you want him to have if you hope to retain employment with this company."

"This is unacceptable! I've invested the better part of my life building up this company! I'm not about to allow some pampered brat to prance into power and destroy everything I've worked so hard to accomplish! We need to find a way to stop this. Surely the contract contains a clause to protect the interests of the company — does it not?"

Halen allowed himself a small smile. Tenika was sharp, she always knew where to start looking for advantage and he had anticipated the question. "Yes, of course, standard clauses exist for protection of the company. Ownership will remain with Nico until his death and then passes to his next of kin. However, authority over the business dealings of Callan International would fall to someone else if Nico should prove to be of unsound mind. The same would occur if Nico found himself imprisoned due to involvement in criminal activity. He would be, effectively, out of the picture for the duration of his sentence."

"So, our options are to have him declared insane, or frame him for a crime?"

"Succinct as always, Ms. Sheridan."

"I want you to explore both options. Find an ironclad way to bring about one or the other and I'll see to it that you receive a very generous bonus."

Halen's smile grew into a wicked grin. "I've already begun."

"Oh, and Halen — dig around and see if you can discover who might have been whispering in Nico's ear."

Halen nodded as he turned to leave. Once the door had closed behind him, Tenika poured herself a drink and stood in front of the picture window. She stared out at the sea, willing herself to calm. *Why are you letting yourself get so worked up about this?* She chided herself. *You've fought worse battles on your way to the top.* She shook her head, realizing she knew why. It was because her opponent was a Callan.

She had secretly hated Nes Callan even while admiring his business acumen. Tenika had to admit that she had learned a great deal from the man. Even so, she did not mourn him, though she hid it well. Now she had to contend with his offspring. Bad enough he looked so much like his father, but if he had even half the talent, this would not be like other contests she had faced.

Her history with Nico's parents had dark undertones. Things she had buried along with them. It made her uncomfortable to be reminded. It hinted at a weakness that angered her. "Well, if the worst should come, I have contingencies." She quickly glanced around to see if anyone was in earshot. She hadn't meant to voice that thought. No one knew how far she was willing to go to get what she wanted. Not even Halen. The things she had already done — she would take them to her grave.

Chapter 43

Kade kept his mouth shut as Decar paced back and forth in front of him. The man had been venting nonstop for ten minutes. Finally, he stopped and turned to face Kade. The bruise under his left eye looked painful and he had a bandage on his arm. Blood seeped through, it needed changing.

"Didn't I tell you about the time restrictions on this project?"

"Yes, but I can't work twenty-four hours per day."

"You led me to believe you could easily complete this project!"

"That was before I knew the scope. The algorithm itself is near completion, but you never told me I would be integrating it into a customized memory stash archive for a global network!"

"You made me look like a fool in front of Third Anarch Villecrest!"

"Yeah, about that — what is all this Third Anarch business?"

Decar looked as if he wanted to scream, but instead he whispered, "watch your tone when referring to your betters. The walls have ears."

Kade looked around nervously while Decar continued.

"I will explain this to you once, and once only. You are in the employ of a vast underground organization known as the Breachers. They're global in scope and more powerful than you can possibly imagine. They operate in secret — outside of the law. All criminal elements answer to them, although most aren't aware of their true masters. The anarchs have authority over the Breacher organization, but they answer to a darker power. Toller Villecrest is Third in the regional hierarchy," Decar explained as though it should be obvious.

It wasn't a revelation to Kade that he was working for a criminal organization, but the magnitude of it was disturbing. "What do you want me to say? The task is impossible to complete in the given time frame."

"You still don't understand? One doesn't fail the Third Anarch. If you don't complete this task, we will both die! Villecrest has neither patience nor compassion. The man enjoys inflicting pain!"

Decar seemed to be reliving a memory. He paled and spoke with fervour. "I'll tell you this, if the Third Anarch loses control — and you'll know when it happens — then your best course of action is to infuriate him to the point that he immediately ends your life. If you survive long enough for him to regain composure, all that remains is terror. You will suffer a long and painful demise under his cruel ministrations."

Kade shied involuntarily at the intensity of Decar's warning.

"You begin to understand. This isn't your comfortable world of business contracts and legal obligations. If you disappoint Villecrest, you can't escape his wrath. No place you might run or hide is beyond his reach. No one will rescue you. Neither guardians nor watchmen, rulers or judges. Just as the Breachers own you and I, they own key personnel in every office of authority. You cannot escape their will."

"But it's an unobtainable goal! What should we do?"

"Anything is possible given enough resources!"

Kade was growing hysterical. "I can't do what you ask! It would take hundreds of writ weavers to finish in time!"

At that, Decar struck him across the face. "Are you telling me that we could have employed additional weavers this whole time? That this is work others could do as well? You fool! If you needed help, I would have had it here within a week! Do you need a hundred men? A thousand? Money is no object!"

Kade backpedalled from Decar's refuelled rage, waving placating arms. "Like I said, I didn't understand the extent of the task! I wasn't lying when I said that very few could help with the algorithm, but many could help us integrate it into the network."

Decar's expression shifted into something that might be hope. He thrust a pad of parchment into Kade's hand. "Compile a list of everything you need. People, necessary qualifications, equipment, space — everything! I want your recommendations within the hour." With that, Decar walked out, leaving Kade to begin his list with a shaking hand.

Chapter 44

Nico finished washing up and headed to the kitchen for a glass of juice to start his day. He was still drying his hair with a towel as he padded to the cooler and didn't notice the visitor sitting at his kitchen table.

He draped the towel around his neck, pulled the juice out of the cooler and leaned against the counter. Tilting his head back, he took a long draw from the flagon. As he placed the vessel back on the counter, he nearly choked when he spotted his unannounced guest. Not quite knowing what to expect, he froze.

A beautiful young woman sat at his table, equally frozen as she appraised his shirtless form. Almost as quickly, her cheeks coloured as she averted her gaze. Her self-conscious reaction was disarming and he relaxed enough to ask the obvious question. "Who are you, and how did you get into my home?"

"I came in through the study."

Nico had his guard up in an instant. As far as he knew, only the Servators had access to the secret tunnel leading to his father's study. Chief Sentry Vantos promised she'd inform him via encrypted tote-comm well in advance of any visit.

"I apologize. I couldn't very well walk up and knock on your front door. No one can know I'm here."

"I ask again. Who are you? What do you want?"

Instead of answering, she squirmed in her seat and avoided his eyes. "Ummm, could you put on a shirt?"

He almost laughed at that. It seemed unlikely that a potential assassin would invade his home only to become flustered by the sight of an exposed abdomen. He also doubted that a trained killer would sport such an animated face. The way her eyebrows danced — it had an endearing effect.

"You're not leaving my sight until you've explained yourself."

"My name is Kayla Vantos." She cocked her head to the side, one brow lifted as if waiting for an expected response.

"Am I to suppose you are somehow related to Cello Vantos?"

"Her daughter, in fact."

Now that he had a frame of reference, she did have a familial resemblance, but while Cello conveyed a regal and commanding presence, this young woman seemed lost.

"Cello never mentioned you or that you might be paying a visit." He pulled the encrypted tote-comm out of his pocket and began to punch in some numbers.

"Please, don't!" She begged, genuine panic filling her eyes.

Nico's soft spot for the vulnerable overrode his caution. He returned the tote-comm to his pocket.

"My mother believes I'm still in Arapanus. You can't tell her I was here."

"I work closely with your mother. If you're in some kind of trouble, I can't keep that from her."

"It's not that — it's complicated. I wouldn't know where to begin."

Nico offered her a comforting smile. "Listen, I assume you came to me for a reason. If you want my help with something, you're going to need to tell me what this is all about. Otherwise, I won't know what help I might offer."

She slumped her shoulders in defeat.

"Why don't you start by telling me how you know about me?" Nico prompted.

"Your father was a well-known supporter of the Servators, but aside from that, you were mentioned in the reports I read while preparing to bring in Leviticus."

"Wait a minute — Leviticus? As in, Leviticus Radix?"

"Yes, your friend, Leviticus. I was tasked with first contact for recruitment and had been keeping an eye on him — looking for an opportune moment to introduce myself. I watched you two interacting. You seemed close. I had the impression that he really trusted you. Right now, I can't contact anyone I trust in that way, and I thought...."

"Woah! Hang on! Recruit Lev? To the Servators?"

"Yes, that was our intent, but then everything went wrong."

Nico grabbed a chair from the table, spun it around and sat with his arms crossed over the backrest. He shook his head in disbelief. "I only just learned about the Servators, the Breachers and my father's role in this whole bizarre secret world. You're telling me that my best friend is now also a part of it?"

"He only learned about it himself a few months ago. We had to accelerate things when the Breachers tried to abduct him."

"The Breachers ... I can't believe what I'm hearing! What happened? Is he okay?"

Kayla gestured reassuringly. "It's okay, Nico. He's fine. He's training in Kemetica as we speak."

"Yes, I knew he was in Kemetica. His parents mentioned that he had accepted an incredible job offer, but the Servators — do his parents know?"

"I suspect not. Cover stories are standard procedure. A way to protect families."

"Tell me everything."

And she did. She shared how she saved Leviticus, about her mistakes and the unfortunate deaths of Servator friends. She explained how exposure caused by her actions had compromised the base. She recounted the angst of leaving her home, sparing the feelings of those suffering losses. She wept with guilt, until his heart ached so much that he gathered her into his arms to offer what little comfort he could.

"I'm sorry, Nico. I shouldn't be unloading on you like this. You don't even know me."

"Sometimes it's easier to talk to a stranger than those who know you best. Your presence isn't an imposition and you're helping me a great deal. I have been working with your mother on logistics — figuring out how to move people and supplies to the new base of operations, but I hadn't realized it was because they were abandoning the former base."

Kayla dropped her head in shame.

"No, please! I didn't intend that to come across as an accusation! Miss Vantos, look at me."

She lifted her eyes tentatively.

"None of this is your fault. You made some mistakes, but the Breachers are the true villains here. Everyone will understand that in time. You saved my friend — for that I am in your debt."

Her eyes welled up and her bottom lip trembled.

"Miss Vantos, I'm sorry, did I say something wrong?"

"No. It's just that you're the first person to acknowledge the one thing I did right. I didn't realize how much I needed to hear that. Thank you, and please, Call me Kayla."

They talked through the afternoon while sharing mid-meal. Nico answered questions she had about his life growing up as a child of the famous Callan family. Kayla hung on his every word, enthralled as he shared stories of his youthful adventures — a childhood so different from her own on the Servator base. She was particularly interested in his close relationship with Lev. She listened with longing in her eyes when he talked about their childhood adventures. Her sheltered youth had denied her such friendships.

Kayla told him about her father's death and her life spent on base as a result. She shared how difficult it was living up to the expectations placed on the daughter of the Chief Sentry.

Nico shared similar experiences as the son of the famous Nes Callan. They had much in common. Perhaps too much. The conversation suddenly turned sombre when they realized that both had parents who were murdered. Breachers had changed their lives forever and they both wanted justice.

As the day wore on, they finished off the last of the meal they had begun earlier. Nico stacked their empty plates and set them aside before finally broaching the subject of her purpose in coming. "Miss — I mean, Kayla. You still haven't told me why you're here."

"I want to make things right. It's something I need to do on my own. Well, not exactly on my own — how do I explain this? If I just let time pass and return to the Servator fold, no matter what I do to try and make amends, questions will remain. People will speculate whether it is remorse that drives me or the expectation of contrition as mandated by the Chief Sentry. To make matters worse, how will I ever know if I'm truly forgiven? I will always wonder if I'm granted a pass merely out of respect for my mother's position. Does that make sense?"

"I can only imagine how you must feel and while it's not the same thing, I do understand the need to prove oneself. I have to find a way to fill my father's shoes. I need to appear willing to learn in a company where I'm an unknown factor, while at the same time meeting the demands of the Servators who must remain a secret. I have two masters and no track record that would command the respect of either. I haven't a clue where to begin."

Kayla leaned forward. "That's it, exactly. I have something I need to accomplish, but I'm not sure how to do it or what that might look like."

"It sounds as if you have an inkling. What is it you'd *like* to achieve?" Nico prompted.

"The Servators are more than friends. I grew up knowing everyone on that base. They're my family. I can never replace the lives that were lost, but I'd like to give them back their home. I'd like to make it safe to return to the base in Denmount."

"From what you've told me, that could be a difficult task."

Kayla pounded her knee with a fist. "I know!"

"Hey now — difficult is a far cry from impossible. You're speaking to the new man in charge of Servator logistics. I'm sure I could help find a way. Actually, this may be just the kind of task I need to prove myself to the Servators. As for my employees, well...."

"Trouble in the ranks?"

"Perhaps. Your mother mentioned that the investigation into my parents' murder led to Callan International. They don't know who in the company might be responsible. She suspected that the company records might reveal further clues, records to which I now have access.

"As part of the legal process, the company needed to transfer its assets to my name. I signed an operational contract. It's basically a document that identifies the chain of command. I engaged someone to look over the contract. Strangely, it was riddled with clauses that would have limited my authority. It could be that they were just trying to spare me the burden of responsibility.

"Reflecting on how that could have prevented me from investigating my parents' deaths has made me suspicious. The thing is, I wouldn't know where to start looking for those clues. Leviticus is the one with an eye for discrepancies. He would be a real asset right about now."

"I might be able to help." Kayla offered.

"What do you mean?"

"The Servators expect every novice to train in all Servator skill sets. Towards the end of their studies, novices focus on two areas of strength. I was training to become a TokenWard."

"A TokenWard? I'm not following."

"A TokenWard must be competent at surveillance, able to assess a situation quickly, and ready to defend themselves. My first strength is combat skill."

Nico smiled at her attempt to draw out suspense but took the bait. "And your second strength?"

Now it was Kayla's turn to grin. "Analysis. If you can bring me those records, I can find what you're looking for."

Nico thought about it. Kayla was an unknown, but she'd opened up to him. He was surprised how much she shared, but as she'd said, she was alone and had no one to turn to. She was desperate, and taking risks. Could he take a risk on her as well? Everything she'd told him so far lined up with things he'd learned from her mother or Brokar. She couldn't know what she knew unless she was a Servator herself. He'd promised he wouldn't talk to Cello yet, but that remained an option if things became suspicious. Either way, it might be a good idea to keep an eye on her until he knew for sure. "I have a better idea. Why don't you come work for me? Then you can access the information directly."

"Come on, Nico, we only just met. Besides, I can't be seen in public. The Breachers have seen still-views of me."

Nico stalled her protests. "First of all, I've learned more about you today than I know about any person in my employ. The goals you've set out for yourself show a willingness to take on daunting tasks, and the persistence to see them through to the end. What more could a person ask for in an employee? If those credentials weren't enough..." Nico grinned, "you *are* the daughter of Cello Vantos, Chief Sentry of the Caralithican Host!"

That earned him a surprisingly hard punch in the shoulder.

"Owww! Seriously, Kayla, this could work. I can hire you as my personal assistant. We would arrive and leave together. Assistants often continue working beyond office hours. No one would find it peculiar. The senior management offices are only accessible to a few individuals. I can send you their files so you can determine if any of them pose a threat.

"I plan to take over my father's old office which has personal access to the garage. You can travel from the office to a ground transport without ever leaving the building. Once we get back to my house, you can leave through the study exit via the tunnels, back to the Servator base. I can set you up with a tri-wheel for transport in the tunnels. If that's not enough, we could also change your appearance — different clothes, hair style, and colour. I bet no one would recognize you."

Kayla seemed to mull it over. "It might be nice to escape the old me for a while."

"Sure, and it would mean we'd have plenty of opportunity to discuss options for reclaiming the base."

That piqued her interest.

"I don't have many people I can trust right now. You'd be doing me a huge favour." Nico paused for a moment realizing a potential flaw to his plan.

"What is it?" Kayla asked.

"I'd have to bring at least one other person into any plans regarding the Servators. Brokar Luge is my go-between for Servator operations within Callan International. His crew handles any projects related to Servator logistics. We need him onboard if we want to accomplish anything related to the Servator base. Kayla, he knows your mother." Nico watched her carefully to see how she would react.

"I've never heard that name before. He isn't from the base."

"No, he was my father's right-hand man. A big supporter of the Servator cause. I imagine your mother knows him by reputation more than personal contact, but I couldn't say for certain."

"My mother seldom took me off the base and if Brokar visited regularly, I'd know him. I suspect if he ever did meet me, it was only as a child."

"Let me run this by him first. He was very loyal to my parents. I can tell him that I want to start off on the right foot by upgrading the access tunnels and supply lines around the Servator base. I can ask your mother to approve the maintenance. Someone still needs to keep the base running, even if it's temporarily abandoned, right? What better time to consider upgrades? The work won't be interrupting Servator business. It's a perfect opportunity. We can incorporate additional modifications under the guise of maintenance. It's a plausible way to accomplish your goals without suspicion."

Nico was relieved that Kayla didn't object. If she came to work at Callan International, it would give him time to check out more of her backstory. He was getting excited thinking of the possibilities. "I was looking for a project to cut my teeth on. This would be perfect, and I'm sure Brokar will be eager for a significant Servator project after all these years. It will give me the opportunity to earn some respect from the Servator side of operations while I try to figure out the public face of Callan International."

Kayla was staring at him again.

"What?"

"You're cute when you're pacing and plotting." She reddened. "I didn't mean to say that out loud."

Nico affected a look of mock consternation. "I am *not* cute," he placed his palm against his chest, "I'm an internationally respected businessman."

That earned a snort and a giggle. Nico decided he liked the sound of her laughter.

"So then, partners?" He offered his hand.

She swatted it aside and pulled him into a grateful hug.

Chapter 45

Three more days to the deadline, Kade thought, *we're close.*

Decar had been true to his word. Within days, Kade had fifty people working under him. That number had grown to two hundred over the last week as more resources became available. He'd never seen so many writ weavers in the same place at the same time and they all answered to him. He might have enjoyed the power if it hadn't been for the sword waiting to take his head if he failed.

Kade wondered how Decar was finding all of this talent, but he wasn't surprised by how many jumped at the opportunity. A limited term project, for a great deal of money, proved an effective lure. Some of them were students eager to gain experience. Others found themselves drawn to the idea of visiting an exotic location — kind of like a work holiday.

What did surprise Kade was the sudden appearance of Selica Lor. His shock gave way to rage when he discovered that she was a long-time employee of the Breachers. He couldn't help but ponder what role she played in his current predicament. He planned to confront her, but that would have to wait. His life was on the line with no time to spare for personal drama. Selica had spent some time working on the algorithm at Denmount, and while she didn't have his depth of knowledge, she was more familiar with the writ weaves than anyone else Decar had provided. While Kade would have preferred to avoid her altogether, he had little choice but to rely heavily on her for help with work directly related to the facial recognition syntax.

For Kade, the most worrisome part of the whole exercise was the question of how to integrate with the Breacher viewcorder network. It was far from his area of expertise. He was massively relieved when Decar showed up with almost the entire team responsible for that network. Their intimate knowledge of its capabilities, shortcomings and infrastructure made an impossible task hopeful. He had since adapted the algorithm to take advantage of the network's strengths. He was also happily surprised to learn that the network engineers had used a common interface, similar to one he had worked with at school. Modifying the writ weave to mesh with the system turned out to be a simple matter.

A working model was currently running live and Kade had everyone busy with integration and performance testing. He had tasked himself with analyzing the accuracy of the results. In another room, workers busied themselves cataloguing still-view images. Every face found in the Breacher store of surveillance viewcordings was filed in a memory stash connected to the network.

As part of the testing, Decar had sent Breacher agents around the globe with orders to walk along predefined routes. Kade's job was to use the algorithm to identify those agents, then calculate their location and direction of travel. So far, the system had captured four out of twenty targets. Not great.

Kade was pretty sure he could gain a little more time to fine-tune as long as he could show a reasonable success rate. He hoped that he could increase efficiency to at least fifty percent before the deadline. That would make it somewhat useful. He prayed it would be enough to serve the Third Anarch's immediate needs, or at least tantalize him enough to keep Kade alive while he worked to improve the percentage.

At the moment Decar was leaning over Kade's shoulder, literally breathing down his neck. His breath reeked of the fish he'd eaten for mid-meal.

"How is it coming along?"

"Seriously, Decar! It's been five minutes since the last time you asked!"

Decar had been very accommodating lately, almost friendly considering their entwined fate, but he was growing increasingly agitated as the deadline drew near. He kept pestering people with requests for updates that were only serving to slow progress. Kade had pulled him aside at one point to tell him so, but found he didn't have the heart when he saw the desperation in Decar's eyes. Kade knew it wasn't fear for his own life that drove the man. It was worry about what could happen to his family that was filling him with dread. Kade had thought

Decar was exaggerating the cruelty of Toller Villecrest, but seeing Decar like this forced Kade to reassess. What if he had minimized the truth for sanity's sake?

"Don't worry, Decar. You've seen that the system works in a limited fashion. We have two days left and every hour sees improvement. We have proof of concept. It should be enough."

"You don't know our master!" Decar emphasized for the hundredth time.

Clearly Decar needed something to do. He had no skill to help the people over whom he hovered. *But he's very good at intrigue*, Kade realized. "Then why don't we tip the odds in our favour?" Kade whispered.

"What do you mean?"

"We have a higher rate of success in certain locations on the network, those with better lighting or newer viewcorders. If I were to plot those locations, could you calculate routes that offer high percentage results and arrange to have all of our test subjects travel those paths during our presentation to the Third Anarch?"

Decar's eyes lit with understanding. "Yes! Yes, I can make that happen. Get me the locations and I'll begin immediately!"

"We'll be okay, Decar, we're very close." Kade hoped it was true.

Decar straightened with new resolve and began shouting orders to his men.

Chapter 46

Kayla grinned as Nico paced his office. "You're acting like a nervous schoolboy."

"It's been months since I've seen Lev. I can't believe he's actually back in town. He's only here for a few days and I don't want to waste any time. Have you arranged his return flight and his local transportation as needed for the duration?"

"Yes, boss! Honestly, Nico, you've taken care of everything. You'll have plenty of time to reminisce about the good old days."

"Ha, ha. You know it's more than that. We need Lev's help on our project. I don't want to jump into talk about business too quickly. It's a delicate balance. I need enough time to visit, but not so much that we miss our opportunity to bring him up to speed. I don't know how soon we'll see him again, so we need to pick his brains before he leaves."

"Why can't you do both at the same time?"

"That's not the way Lev's mind works. If he agrees to help and sets his mind to the task, that will signal the end of any casual visiting. A lot has happened to both of us and I need to make sure he's okay before bringing up anything else."

"I already told you, he's fine."

"No, you told me he's safe. That's not the same thing at all. He was ripped from the life he knew, without a choice in the matter."

At Nico's statement, Kayla's face fell. He came to her side, placing a hand on each shoulder. "I'm sorry, Kayla. I didn't mean to imply that it was your fault. Don't think that way. The Breachers are to blame. You know that."

"I know, but that doesn't cover my shame about past decisions. I wasn't very kind to Leviticus during his rescue. I can't imagine what he must think of me."

"It'll be fine. Don't worry. What time did you say he was arriving?"

"Actually, he should be here any…" The door opened and two men entered, making a quick scan of the room. It seemed to Nico that Kayla recognized the men. She bowed her head, letting her hair hide her features. Nico knew she didn't want anyone to recognize her and stepped between her and their visitors. A moment later Leviticus entered the room. "Come on guys! Nico's on our side. Can't you lighten up a little?"

"We'll lighten up once we're on the LTA transport back to Kemetica."

Lev sighed. "Can we at least have a little privacy now that you've secured the room?" In answer, the rangers closed the door and left.

Lev shook his head. "I've taken those two to the mats on several occasions, yet they treat me like I'm some kind of delicate flower."

Kayla's brows furrowed, incredulous. "You've taken Tark and Yori to the mat?" She immediately reddened realizing she'd revealed more than intended.

Nico smiled. She looked so cute when she blushed. They had both been working hard to familiarize themselves with her new identity. They had decided on the name Seri Quin but one or the other slipped on occasion. *Now that I think of it, I called her Kayla twice, just before Lev arrived.*

"Lev! It's so great to see you!" Nico grabbed Lev in a bear hug.

Lev laughed. "It's good to see you, too! I've missed your sorry face!"

"Lev, I'd like you to meet my assistant, Seri Quin."

Lev's smile faded as he gently pushed Nico aside and settled into a defensive stance. "Nico, how is it that your assistant knows the names of two Servator rangers?"

"Whoah, settle down, Lev!" Nico jumped between the two. "We can explain!"

"You'd better explain quickly or she'll be answering to Tark and Yori." Lev started backing towards the door.

Kayla took a quick step forward. "You can't!"

"You think you could stop me?" Lev asked.

Kayla's face shifted from anger and pride to fear and uncertainty in three heartbeats. The display set Leviticus on his heels. Then he leaned forward and stared at her. "Do I know you?"

"You knew me as Kayla Vantos," she sighed.

Lev's eyes brightened in recognition. "Yes! I see it now. You've changed. When did you become a blonde? Actually, a better question would be, why are you avoiding your Servator friends?"

"Lev! What's with the interrogation?" Nico snapped.

"How long have you known this woman, Nico?" Lev didn't take his eyes off Kayla.

"You just said you recognized her!"

"When I saw her last, she had the whole Servator base in an uproar."

"That's not fair, Lev."

Kayla held up a hand to stall Nico. She faced Lev and gave a terse reply. "You're not the only one!"

"Excuse me?"

"I said, you're not the only one who lost something that day. My rank was stripped from me. I worked for that position my whole life, and now I have no future with the Servators. The people on that base were the only family I had and now none of them will speak to me. My mother sent me away because my presence is too painful for those who've lost someone. Until recently, I've been visiting Servator bases, travelling the world, keeping my head down. I can't walk in public anymore because the Breachers have a price on my head — the same as you. I may have messed up, but I put myself out there to save your life and I lost everything as a result."

Lev relaxed. "I'm sorry, I didn't know."

"I'm sorry for what you lost as well. I wish I could take back that day."

Nico snapped his fingers to get Lev's attention. "Do you no longer trust me, Lev?" He couldn't keep the anger out of his voice.

Lev looked chagrined. "You know I do — always."

"Then stow your suspicions and give us the opportunity to explain. This is my friend and the woman who saved you from the Breachers. She's been a big help to me in trying to find the people who murdered my parents. Show some respect."

"I heard about that, Nico. I'm so sorry."

Nico shook his head. He didn't want to talk about that now. It was a discussion for another time.

"Nico is correct. I owe you an apology — Seri. I'm grateful for your intervention. Nico is the best judge of character I know. If he vouches for you, then I have no reason to doubt your veracity. These last few months have been stressful and being back here where it all began is making me edgy. That's no excuse for my behaviour. Please forgive me."

"Nothing needs forgiving. I understand how hard this has been for you."

Nico clapped his hands together. "Well! I've ordered a feast delivered to the house. I made sure to request all of your favourites, Lev. What say we head to my place and continue this conversation in more familiar surroundings?"

"Lamb and garlic skewers?"

"That's just for starters."

"Lead on my friend. I've been dying for some Caralithican food. The fare in Kemetica gives me indigestion."

"I didn't think it possible for you to be further inflated than usual. Maybe we should eat outside."

Lev laughed. "I really missed you."

Chapter 47

It felt right to be here. He and Nico had spent a great deal of time in this house over the years. Lev almost felt more at home here than at his parents' place.

Yori and Tark had combed through the house and placed sight tokens around the perimeter. They set up a monitoring station in one of the bedrooms where they planned to spend the night, sleeping in shifts. Kayla had clearly been avoiding them under the guise of preparing food for the meal. Lev doubted she spent much time in kitchens. She hadn't gained knife skills to defend herself against a trencher of cooked meats. So far, neither of the rangers appeared to recognize her. Regardless, she clearly wasn't taking any chances.

Kayla joined them after Lev's shadows said their good nights. They carried away heaping plates from Nico's buffet, with pleased looks on their faces. It didn't take long before Lev, Nico, and Kayla were digging into their own selections. Nico had overdone it, but Lev wasn't complaining.

"I'm stuffed." Lev patted his belly with a satisfied exhalation.

"You should be. You ate enough for two. I don't remember you having quite so large an appetite."

"It's all the combat training." Lev graciously didn't comment on the fact that Nico had eaten nearly as much.

Kayla had no such reticence. "You're one to talk! You consumed no fewer than three platefuls — and you don't have training to blame your appetite on!"

"Says the girl who helped herself to two servings and three desserts!" Nico shot back.

"But the custard is soooo good and you need the pastries as a substrate to carry it on. Manners, you know. One does *not* eat custard with one's fingers."

"Unless those fingers are clutching a pastry." Nico ducked the playful backhand.

Lev watched the banter in amusement. He'd seen Nico smitten before. Yet it appeared to be more than that. He seemed — anchored. Ever since his parents' death, Lev had thought his friend seemed a little lost. Apparently, he'd found himself again after all these years. Words could not express how gratified he was at his friend's transformation. Kayla appeared to feel the same way about Nico, but he couldn't be certain. Lev was a very poor judge of such things. He sincerely hoped so, for Nico's sake.

"We could work some of that off later if you'd like. I could show you a few moves. A little sparring like the old days."

Nico seemed to consider it briefly before responding. "I don't think so. I've seen Kayla working out. If you've gained even a portion of her skill, it won't be anything like the old days. And now you've gained a serious weight advantage. You've really bulked up. I almost didn't recognize you when I first saw you."

"That's the truth," Kayla added. "When we met, you were a lanky middleweight at best, but you've gained some definition."

Lev noticed a dark look come across Nico's face.

"If you're serious about sparring later, I'd be game," Kayla offered. "I haven't had anyone to practise with in a while. I fear I'm getting rusty. Maybe you could demonstrate how you managed to take down Tark and Yori."

"On second thought, maybe I *will* join you." Nico wore a resigned look on his face as he said it.

"That would be fantastic, but perhaps tomorrow morning? I think we'd all be in danger of splitting open if we tried anything like that tonight." Lev eased himself from the table and made his way to the sitting room. "No, I'm more inclined to sit and listen to a good story. I believe you two promised me an interesting tale."

"Hey!" Nico exclaimed. Lev started laughing and picked up his pace. They shared an ongoing battle over who got the comfortable chair. Nico was at a disadvantage, Lev had too much of a head start.

"Some things never change," Nico grumbled, as he and Kayla found seats of their own.

The evening continued in amicable comfort. Kayla filled Lev in. She told him everything that had happened after bringing him to the Servator base. Lev reciprocated with his own adventure and then Nico shared his story. Lev insisted Nico show him the cornice moulding in his old room and elicited a promise to be shown the secret exit from Nes Callan's study. He also wanted to see the crypt where it all started. Oh, and the tunnelling machine. Lev definitely wanted to see the tunnelling machine.

As the chatter wound down, Lev shook his head in disbelief. "What a trio we are. Each of our lives have changed. Everything is upside down. I didn't expect to run into Kayla again. I wasn't certain I would get another chance to see Nico either. Now here we are, chatting as if this were the most natural thing in the world."

Lev felt a bond forming. Each understood how it felt to wake up to what seemed like a different world. Lev hadn't realized how much he needed to release his frustration and told them so. For the first time, he felt like he could move forward. Not because he had to, but because he wanted to. "You still haven't told me how you two met," Lev observed.

"That was my doing," Kayla began. "After all the damage I had done, I was determined to fix things. I had a thought of what I might do, but alone and without resources I wasn't sure where to begin. I couldn't turn to the Servators, but I thought I might find help among those who support the Servators. My mother had talked about how Nes Callan's son would soon be taking over Callan International and how eager she was to renew that relationship.

"As part of my operation to make contact with you, Lev, I had studied your files. So, I knew about Nico. It was only later that I made the connection with Callan International. It occurred to me that Nico might have contacts who could steer me in the right direction. I didn't know if he would be willing to help, but everything I had learned about him suggested that he would be approachable."

Lev looked at Nico fondly. "It's an apt appraisal. Nico couldn't turn away someone in need, even if he knew how."

Kayla was smiling at Nico, too. "I had nothing to lose by trying. He exceeded my expectations and hasn't stopped."

"Come on guys — anyone else would have done the same."

Lev interrupted. "No, Nico. I wouldn't have."

"Neither would I," Kayla admitted.

"Well," Nico replied, uncomfortable with the praise, "I guess that leads us to the part of the conversation where Kayla and I tell you what we've been planning and give you an opportunity to reciprocate."

"Yes," Lev asserted.

"Excuse me?"

"Yes, I'll help."

"You don't even know what we're asking yet!"

"It doesn't matter. Kayla saved me from the Breachers. I owe her my life. And you're the closest thing I have to a brother. Family sticks together. I'm here for you, whatever you need."

"Wow. Those philosophy and ethics courses really paid off," Nico deadpanned. His delivery was met with a pillow to the head.

"On second thought," Lev quipped, "you still owe me for those hours of my life I can never reclaim. I should be the one asking favours."

"I just fed you!"

Lev shook his head, stood, and smiled as he pulled Nico out of his chair and into a bear hug. He waved Kayla over and drew her in. "We'll do this together. Our worlds may have changed, but we can make a difference in this new one."

Chapter 48

The next morning Kade was scheduled to appear before the Third Anarch. The possibility remained that Villecrest might get called away on other business, but Kade held little hope for that reprieve. For some reason, the facial recognition algorithm remained a high priority for Villecrest.

Kade knew he wouldn't escape the spotlight. He was as prepared as he could be. Nothing he might add now would improve his presentation. Attempting any last-minute changes to the writ weaving would risk upsetting the slightly dramatized demonstration that he and Decar had arranged. Kade barely suppressed the terror he felt at the thought of someone discovering their subterfuge. He had to trust Decar. This was something the man did for a living. If he couldn't pull it off, they were both dead anyway.

The algorithm was working. It was integrated into the Breacher network and had a reasonable success rate, but Decar had made it clear that it wouldn't be enough. If their diversionary demonstration didn't go perfectly — if they encountered the slightest problem during the demonstration — Villecrest would consider it a total failure. This had to work. They needed time to perfect the system. They were very close.

Decar had said that Villecrest was planning to leave on a two-week business trip shortly after the demonstration. If they could just pass the Third Anarch's inspection, they would get the time they needed and he would never be the wiser. Dwelling on it was pointless. It only increased his level of anxiety. He needed a distraction and had decided it would be Selica.

They hadn't spoken about personal matters during this rush to complete the project, but if he was about to die, he wanted to know the truth. He had asked her to join him for dinner at his apartment under the pretext of going over some quant-axiom sets. She agreed, without suspicion. Why wouldn't she? Their interaction of late had been all business. It was good that it had been that way. There hadn't been time for distractions, but now it bothered him. She had never tried to bring up the subject of their time in Denmount. Did it really mean so little to her? Was she simply following orders? Was he nothing more than an uncomfortable task? If that were true, she was very good at her job.

He remembered the way she smiled at him during their time together. He was positive he'd seen joy in her eyes. She exhibited the enthusiastic abandon of someone seeing the sea for the first time. Wading in and then retreating with laughter as the waves came rushing towards the beach. *Yes, it was just like that. Teasing and then playfully retreating like a happy child.* Before he had asked her to dinner that night in Denmount, there had been a hint of the seductress, but when they finally got together, she proved enticing in an entirely different and innocent way. He tried to recall and analyze her words and actions from that evening. He attempted to guess at what her motivations might have been. The only impression he could muster was that she had seemed unguarded and genuine.

Perhaps he was the world's biggest fool, but he felt a connection. He was convinced that she had enjoyed her time with him. Selica had drawn him in and he was a little alarmed by his response. He couldn't stop thinking of the way she looked or the fragrance of her perfume. When Decar had threatened to abduct Selica, Kade's first instinct had been to protect her. Why? He barely knew her — apparently even less than he thought. Still, he wanted to give her the benefit of the doubt. He had to know the truth. Did Selica have feelings for him or had it all been an act? A knock sounded at the door. He glanced at the wall chrono. *Right on time.* One way or the other he would learn the truth in the next few hours.

"The door is unlocked, come on in."

Selica opened the door a crack and peered in before entering.

Habit of a spy's trade, Kade imagined, then mentally shook his head. *Benefit of the doubt, remember?*

"Selica, hello, glad you could make it," Kade called from the kitchen.

"Dinner is a simple affair — some noodles and grilled lamb. I hope that's okay."

"Sounds great."

"I'll be there with the food shortly. Make yourself comfortable."

Selica set a satchel of work parchments on the floor beside the small table and claimed a seat. A moment later, Kade entered with food and two mugs of mead. He set a plate in front of her and took a seat across the table. They ate in silence, occasionally broken by small talk about the project.

"I brought over the results of the latest stress testing. I can go over them with you."

Kade placed his hand over hers to stop her reaching for the satchel. "That won't be necessary. It's not the reason I asked you here."

Selica went rigid, averting her eyes and pulling her hand away. She said nothing, waiting for him to continue.

"You know that I'll be demonstrating our work to Villecrest tomorrow. I assume you also know that if it fails, things will not go well for me."

She nodded.

"I don't want my life to end without knowing the truth. I don't want to leave things unsaid. I think you owe me that much."

Again, a nod.

"When we were in Denmount, before I was dragged into all of this Breacher madness, I enjoyed our time together. Perhaps I'm a fool for thinking it, but I thought you did too."

A tear rolled down Selica's cheek. Kade hadn't expected that reaction at all. He thought she might become angry or maybe laugh at his pathetic infatuation. Instead she looked vulnerable, broken.

"I did enjoy our time together, Kade. You're the first man who ever treated me with such respect. It was the most wonderful night of my life. You made me remember what hope feels like. For a short time I was able to escape, to play at having a normal life. A life where I might meet someone and imagine a future together. For a little while you helped me forget that such a future isn't available to me."

"I'd like to believe that, but you were working for Decar. You're a part of all this," Kade swept his arm gesturing around the prison he called his suite. "You gave me hope too, but on reflection I can't help but think you were only bait for a trap."

"I *was* bait, but only part of it. The promise of money and a career was what lured you." A little sadness showed in her eyes.

Kade burst to his feet knocking his chair over. "Thanks for that, Selica!" His voice filled with heat. "Thanks for reminding me that betrayal is easy for a prideful, greedy, man! I guess I deserved this!" Kade inhaled slowly as he picked up his chair and sat back down. This wasn't getting him closer to the truth. Besides, he wasn't being entirely fair.

"I apologize. That was a tender subject. You're right, this is my own fault. My competition with Radix fuelled my pride, as did my desire to prove myself to my father. Greed drove me to steal the algorithm. Decar took advantage, but they were *my* shortcomings. I've been living with those regrets ever since."

"Kade — I didn't mean it like that. It's not your fault. This is how the Breachers operate. They take advantage of weaknesses. You're a victim. I'm no less of a casualty for being dangled as bait."

"You seemed a pretty willing partner in the *taking advantage department.*"

"No, Kade, it sickened me. Especially after you treated me so kindly, but I had no choice."

"Then why didn't you say anything to me? Warn me?"

Selica stood up and started pacing the room chewing on the nails of one hand while the other clutched the hair at her neck. "You've met Toller Villecrest." It was a statement more than a question but Kade nodded in response.

"Villecrest killed my father over some failed business deal. He took my mother and I as compensation. My mother was a beautiful woman and he sent her to his harem. She hated him for murdering her husband, but she knew that if she displeased him, he would send her to the brothels. She couldn't bear the thought that I might end up there, so she did what she needed to do, to protect me."

Kade was shocked. "That's horrible!"

"One day, I became violently ill. I could barely lift my arms. Sweat from the fever soaked my bedding. Toller chose that moment to come to our rooms. My mother asked him to come back another day. She told him she needed to care for me. He could easily have gone to one of his other women, but he insisted. My mother refused. Villecrest flew into a rage. He began to beat her mercilessly. While she lay motionless on the floor, he knelt over her and placed his hands on her throat. He killed my mother in front of me. I was nine years old."

"Selica, I'm so sorry! What did you do?"

"Nothing. I'm his property. He had me sent to the children's slave quarters and forgot all about me. I learned quickly that children without special skills end up in the mines or the brothels.

"I hung around the network room a lot. The viewcorder screens were like a window to the outside world. I used to imagine I was one of those people. A carefree citizen, walking home with a bag full of groceries. I began to pick up some things — listening to the workers. They tolerated me because I would run errands for them. One day I was looking over a technician's shoulder. Something looked odd about the writ weaving and I pointed it out. I didn't know what it meant, but I guess he saw some potential and began to teach me. Of course, he meant to use me to get out of doing his own work, but I didn't mind. It was a chance to forge another path even if it was still as a prisoner of the Breachers.

"It was my writ weaving knowledge that brought me back to Villecrest's attention. He wanted someone to pose as a student and try to steal the facial recognition algorithm from Denmount. He wanted me to seduce Leviticus Radix so they could find an opportune time to abduct him. When Radix disappeared, they turned to you."

Kade didn't know what to say. He felt anger at her admission that she tried to seduce him, but also deep sorrow for all that she had lost.

"Kade, Look at me."

He turned to face her.

"No, look into my eyes."

He lifted his head and looked up.

"I never wanted to hurt you. You know what Villecrest is capable of. I live in fear for my life. They've ordered me to do things I would never choose of my own volition. You know what that's like. They're forcing you in that same way. I hate Toller Villecrest. I would never willingly do anything for that evil man — believe me when I tell you this. What we shared was real to me. More real than anything else in my miserable life. I'm so very sorry that my actions played a role in bringing you here. It's one more thing I will add to my list of reasons to hate the Third Anarch."

"Why didn't you say something sooner?"

"When you realized that I was working for Decar, I saw the pain in your eyes. I thought you hated me. When you never brought it up, I was certain of it.

Can you forgive me, Kade Brixton?"

Kade took two quick steps to her side and drew her into his arms, "Can we start again, Selica Lor?"

"I'd like that, very much."

Kade sighed as he released her. At the start of this evening he was prepared for disappointment. Instead, Selica gave him hope on the eve before his possible execution. "I don't want you to leave," Kade said, "but I need to get some sleep before the demonstration tomorrow."

"You *must* succeed Kade. I can't bear the thought of Villecrest taking away another person I care about. I don't know what promises a slave girl can offer, but I can give you this." She placed a hand on either side of his face and gently kissed him. Then she gathered her things and slipped out while he stood there, staring at the door.

Thank you, Selica. That's a better promise than you know.

Chapter 49

The lab was clean and everything was initialized. Kade administered a final inspection of the search interface. It could use some improvement but would serve its purpose for the time being. Someone had erected a large screen so the Third Anarch could watch in real-time as Kade put the algorithm through its paces.

A few network operators stood at stations off to the side to handle any unforeseen issues with the network interface. Decar already had his operatives making predefined loops in the areas they had targeted. They were to repeat their laps every ten minutes. If everything went according to plan, the algorithm would identify all five of their chosen targets within a span of fifteen minutes or less.

A commotion sounded in the hallway. The time had come. Third Anarch, Toller Villecrest, entered the room without pomp or ceremony. Villecrest had little patience for such things. He merely stood in front of the large screen and commanded, "Begin!"

Kade quickly stepped forward to explain what was involved in the demonstration. He was careful not to embellish and stuck to the key points. "For this demonstration, we have entered still-view facial images of several Breacher operatives. We've placed those operatives in several cities around the world. We know which cities they're in, but not specifically where they are within those cities."

That last was a lie, but Decar was circumspect in how he worded his orders to the operatives. He wanted nothing to come back on them in the event they were ever questioned. He told them each to pick a random route and then to walk the same route repeatedly. Those instructions suited the conditions of the test as Kade had described. What those operatives hadn't known was that Decar had rented rooms for them in areas of peak camera efficiency and had them start making rounds days before the demonstration was due to begin.

He had each of them followed, noting their routes well in advance. Decar had chosen notoriously lazy operatives to walk the routes, warning them that the Third Anarch himself would monitor their movements. As for the operatives who were following their fellows; They were told that they were to observe whether their peers were completing their tasks.

The second group of operatives were not at all surprised that their lazy colleagues should be monitored and soon all operatives began to spread rumours of new performance measures. It served to put everyone on guard and was an elegant subterfuge. It made Decar's scheming appear as professional oversight. Villecrest would likely approve. Decar was frighteningly meticulous. Kade reminded himself, again, not to get on the man's bad side. Right now they were in the same boat and Decar's efforts would give them a much-needed advantage.

Kade handed a parchment to the Third Anarch with a list of the pre-chosen operative's names. It noted the cities where they were deployed alongside still-view images of their faces. "The algorithm scans facial features of anyone within range of the Breacher network's viewcorders," Kade explained. "When a possible match is flagged, the algorithm compares it against additional identifiers. Types and colours of clothing, hairstyles, and other details make it easier to track a flagged individual as they pass from one viewcorder's field of view to another. At that point, the algorithm will record facial features from multiple angles as afforded by viewcorder positions along the target's path. This continues until the system finds a potential match to one of the still-view images stored in the database. I've modified the algorithm to gather and store multiple facial angles of matched targets to improve positive identification speed over time."

Kade hoped that last tidbit would plant the idea that any current shortcomings weren't a result of his own failings, but rather a limitation of the number of cameras available. If he was fortunate, it would appear that his algorithm was helping to overcome that weakness. The truth was he had not finished work on that feature. Another gamble with his life.

"Adding more cameras will help?" It sounded more like a statement from Villecrest than a question. Inwardly Kade was elated with that little triumph. Outwardly he replied in a carefully modulated voice. "I hadn't thought of that, Third Anarch. Yes, that would help a great deal."

Toller made a derisive snort as if it should have been obvious.

"I've already entered the operative's images and need only start the initiation sequence at your command."

"Yes, yes, begin already!" Villecrest waved his fingers impatiently.

Kade felt more like he was throwing dice than pressing a button. The only thing left to do was pray. The first two minutes passed in silence. The Third Anarch began tapping his foot.

"I, um, forgot to mention that it could take up to fifteen minutes for the algorithm to locate targets depending on when they happen to be in view...." Kade tapered off as Villecrest glared at him.

Another minute passed. It felt like an eternity. Kade was sweating. Decar appeared equally concerned and stared at him like a drowning man asking for a rope. A chime broke the silence, quickly followed by a second. Two faces appeared on the viewscreen. The Third Anarch held up the parchment in his hand and compared it to the screen.

Two matches! Kade allowed himself to breathe. *Three to go.* Another two minutes passed, and then five more as a third and fourth image appeared on the screen. The Third Anarch seemed to be leaning forward in anticipation. No more images were forthcoming. Villecrest checked his wrist chrono. "Fifteen minutes have passed, Brixton. Where is the fifth target?"

What happened? This was pre-arranged! Kade worked to speak past the lump in his throat. "Sometimes network transmission delays occur." That earned him some angry stares from the network operators on the sidelines. He quickly added, "another possibility is that the target never entered within range of any viewcorders."

Decar took advantage of the insinuation. "If any of our operatives have been spending time in the gambling houses instead of tending to their duties, I'll see to their immediate discipline!"

Villecrest looked at Decar and nodded.

Decar's interruption bought them another minute and the system chimed as the final target appeared on screen.

We did it. Kade almost collapsed from the nervous tension. Decar's cheeks puffed as he blew out a breath in relief. Kade wasn't sure what to expect next. Was Villecrest satisfied? Would he leave now? *Oh, please leave.* The Third Anarch remained where he was. He reached into his coat, pulled out a slip of parchment, and handed it to Kade. "Enter these targets." Kade accepted the parchment with shaking hands. His face blanched. The demonstration wasn't over. Villecrest had added four new targets.

"We need still-view images," Kade offered lamely. He hated how whiny his voice sounded.

"I hope for your sake that you had enough intelligence to include the Breacher archive in your implementation of the algorithm. The targets are well known."

"Right! Yes, of course!" Kade searched the archive and called up the requested information. It filled him with both relief and dismay when still-views of the new targets appeared alongside the names he'd entered. Without really thinking, he started the new search before asking permission. The original results disappeared and the screen went blank once more as the new search proceeded. Villecrest's eyes remained glued to the screen.

The second search took much longer. The first result didn't come in until the eighth minute. The second at the twelfth minute. Kade was amazed to see any results at all. They weren't prepared for this kind of test. At the fifteen-minute mark, they still had only two results. Toller said nothing. Another minute passed and a third face appeared. They waited an additional five minutes. Villecrest looked at his wrist chrono and turned in displeasure to face Kade. Before he opened his mouth to speak, a chime announced the appearance of a fourth target on the screen. Kade couldn't believe his luck.

"Can you tell me the location of these targets?"

"Yes sir! Well, their last known location at least, plus their direction of travel."

"Do it now and send the details to this tote-comm." Toller handed him a number and Kade quickly sent the requested details. Toller pulled out his own tote-comm and barked orders. "I want teams searching the locations I've just provided for the identified targets. Call me immediately when they're in your custody."

"I should get out of your way and leave you to your business," Kade offered.

"Brixton!" Villecrest roared, "what did I tell you about speaking out of turn?"

Kade involuntarily threw up his arms to defend himself.

"You will remain where you are until I dismiss you!"

Ten minutes passed... Twenty... Villecrest's intensity filled the room with tension. Kade thought his heart might stop if it continued much longer. He was breathing too quickly. It took a moment before Kade realized someone's tote-comm was buzzing. Toller answered. "You have them? All of them? Excellent! Kill them."

Kade's mind went numb. "Wait. What?"

The Third Anarch sported an ugly smile on his face.

"You... You... You're using the algorithm to find targets for assassination?"

"Yes, Brixton." He seemed to find Kade's discomfort amusing. Villecrest walked over and leaned in until their noses almost touched. "And I have you to thank for it!"

Kade was hyperventilating.

"I expect you to improve the search speed."

Kade crumpled to the floor. The last thing he heard before everything went black was, "I have a lot of people to find."

Chapter 50

The Second Anarch was livid. "What was that fool Villecrest thinking?"

No reply was forthcoming, it was Kenric's habit to think aloud when he was alone.

He paced his gilded chambers imagining his palm was Villecrest's face as he pounded it with a fist.

It took decades to lull the Servators into complacency while the Breachers slowly advanced their technical capabilities. "Now that fool has alerted them!"

For too long the Breachers had been at a disadvantage. It drove him to distraction trying to discover how the Servators had gained their technological edge. He'd tried planting moles within their organization but they never got past the front door. That too was a mystery. *How did they always know?*

The Breachers never succeeded in capturing a piece of Servator technology. They had witnessed the tech and could guess its purpose, but whenever they touched one of the devices, it would disintegrate. It didn't seem to matter whether it was weaponry or a recording device. It was like magic. At one time he had been so intimidated that he thought his goal was hopeless. Over the decades those seemingly magical Servator devices had become less effective against his own equipment and he became bolder.

Kenric was a patient man. Sooner or later he would gain the upper hand. He had invested heavily in the sciences, hiding his efforts in plain sight. The magnanimous efforts of his botanical researchers brought healing balms to the masses while secretly supplying the Breachers with addictive hallucinogens and potent toxins. Likewise, the viewcorder network was his brainchild. Coupled with his security forces, a much-valued impression of safety entered the public perception, despite the fact that the security force was comprised of the very thugs they feared. He couldn't fathom how the obvious eluded them. People believed what they wanted to.

The wealth of ammunition for blackmail those viewcorders collected was astonishing. Public administrators, military commanders, peacekeepers and adjudicators, he owned so many of them, he had lost count.

Kenric had many high-tech projects operating around the globe. And every few years he would hire the top talent from those ventures and set them up in research facilities developing new products — preferably with military and intelligence gathering applications. His penultimate investment, the piece that would usher in his final play, was the facial recognition program at Denmount. It was discreetly funded and intentionally progressing slowly so as not to draw attention. No one would imagine it was a Breacher initiative. As far as anyone could tell, it was a pet project of the Computational Engineering Program. Something to use as a teaching aid. Bringing the technology to market wasn't a priority of the program. At least until Kenric was ready to put it to use. Once everything fell into place, he would be able to coordinate his final strategy with such speed and flexibility, his enemies wouldn't stand a chance.

He planned to hire talent from Denmount to complete the facial recognition algorithm at one of his facilities when the time came. Toller had ruined that with his clumsy attempt at abducting the very talent he would have wooed. The man had added insult to injury, stealing what the Breachers already owned! Now the Servators were on alert, looking at everything with suspicion. It would take years to calm that mess. "That ignorant buffoon!"

Kenric had meticulously set everything into play. A world-spanning Jumkano game board. Every game piece placed to greatest advantage until the day came when the trap he prepared was impossible to escape. But his plans relied on lulling his opponent. It was the very reason for the Trantor uprising in the first place. He wanted his opponents to see Breacher actions as brutish blunt force affairs. He wanted to be underestimated while he grew in strength. He needed his enemies to feel safe until it was too late. "But now that fool is killing them!" Kenric wanted to scream in frustration. Things had quickly gone from bad to worse.

Villecrest's ambitions were no surprise. Kenric planted spies within the man's retinue on the day he was elevated to Third Anarch. Toller was entirely clueless, proving his incompetence. At the beginning, Villecrest's dreams of grandeur had been all bluster of little consequence. Kenric was content to let the man's tiny mind fester in his inconsequential corner of the Breacher hierarchy. But now, recent events brought to light his own complacency. *One should never ignore a potential rival, no matter how unlikely.*

He had underestimated Villecrest's impetuousness. Kenric's own caution had led him to believe others in the chain of command would be equally circumspect. That a man of ambition would risk his own life so carelessly was difficult to comprehend. Rumours that Toller was insane would explain much. The man was full of himself. He actually believed the Sicari were working for him. Those devils worked for no man. As if on cue, a knock echoed through his chamber. "Come."

A black-clad Sicari strolled in, his leathers bristling with the hidden tools of an assassin.

"What have you to report?"

"The Third Anarch has increased the number of targets for his kill squads. He plans to continue exponentially — hunting all Servators 'until they are eradicated' as he puts it."

The messenger issued his report as though he couldn't care one way or the other. *He's likely a willing participant of Toller's kill squad.* Kenric mused. "This is intolerable. The Third Anarch has gone too far. He's ruining years of carefully orchestrated plans and must be stopped."

"As you say, Second Anarch." The Sicari deftly caught and pocketed the bag of coins Kenric tossed his way.

"Bring him to me by nightfall and I'll double your usual fee."

"It will be done, Second Anarch."

Chapter 51

"Get lost! This is my spot!"

"You don't own this spot! The street belongs to everyone!"

"Is that so? I'm bigger than you and I say this is my spot, so you and all your little friends had better leave!" Kade gave the kid a shove. The shopkeeper often handed out sweets to the kids outside his storefront at the end of the day. Kade didn't feel like sharing.

"Don't push me!" The boy said as he attempted a retaliatory shove. Kade threw him to the ground and turned towards the others.

"We're going to tell your mom!" a girl threatened.

Kade didn't recognize her. He doubted she knew who his mom was. "Leave now, or you'll get the same!"

"You leave my friends alone!" The one on the ground demanded, with tear-filled eyes.

The world shifted.

Suddenly, Kade was on the ground, and it was his voice that was yelling. "No! Leave them alone!" A dark beast loomed over him. It blocked out the sun along with any hope of escape. Kade was terrified. "No. Please, don't."

"Kade."

"No... No!"

"Kade, wake up!"

"What? Who?"

"Kade, It's Selica. Wake up!"

Kade squinted. Everything was still a little fuzzy. "Where am I?"

"You're in your bed."

"How did I get here? I don't remember coming home."

Selica brushed the hair out of Kade's eyes. "You fainted. Decar had you brought to your rooms. I spoke to one of the network engineers helping you with the demonstration. He told me you passed out. I slipped away to check on you. I don't have much time, but I wanted to make sure you were okay."

It all came rushing back. A moan escaped his throat as he relived the moment. "No, no, no."

"Kade, what happened?"

"Villecrest! After we completed our demonstration, he had me enter some new targets to track. I thought he had discovered our ruse and was testing us. I thought I was a dead man."

"Kade? What ruse? What are you talking about?"

"Somehow the algorithm worked. It found the targets. I couldn't believe the dumb luck. But they weren't Breacher operatives. They were some other people. I didn't realize..."

"What are you saying?" The confusion on Selica's face was mixed with concern.

"Selica! He killed them!"

"Who?"

Kade grabbed her arms. "I just told you! Villecrest! He used the algorithm to track those people down and then he sent operatives to kill them!"

Selica looked sad, but not surprised.

"Didn't you hear me? He killed all of those people — and then he smiled! How can you be so calm?"

Selica sighed. "Toller Villecrest is a twisted monster. He values people only so long as they benefit his plans. You told me you once saw some men hauling one of his victims away. I watched him kill my mother. That's the kind of devil he is. This is the life we live now."

"No, you don't understand. He thanked me. I helped him do this. I killed those people!"

Selica pulled him into her arms. "You can't believe that, Kade. You didn't know. You didn't give the kill order."

"But I enabled him. I stole the algorithm, I integrated it into the Breacher network. He couldn't have accomplished it on his own. I've given him a terrible weapon, Selica. It's been difficult enough to accept that I'm an unwilling thief. I can't be a killer's accomplice. I always imagined I would repay what I stole someday, but it's impossible to provide recompense for murder! I can't live with that!"

Selica looked uncomfortable.

"What is it? You're holding something back. Tell me."

"After the demonstration, I was told you were taking the afternoon off and they gave me some targets to add as well. I was told to set them for long-term monitoring. I assumed they were looking for recruits. After what you've told me, I'm beginning to suspect something more sinister."

Kade held her eyes, waiting for more.

"Kade, they're monitoring our classmates. Others who took part in the project at Denmount."

"You don't think he's going to kill them, do you?"

"You and I belong to him. He doesn't need anyone else. If he gets rid of everyone familiar with the algorithm and destroys the original copy, then he maintains full control of the technology. It would take years before anyone could begin to understand the writ weaving well enough to interfere with his plans."

Kade felt ill. "He's going to kill them."

"We don't know that for certain. Even if that's his plan, he won't do anything right away. He asked for long-term monitoring."

"That's right! Why would he do that?"

Selica covered her face with her hands and slowly drew her fingers down to her chin. "I hate it that I can even imagine such things, but I've been with the Breachers so long...."

"What? What would they do?"

"They wouldn't want to draw too much attention. They would probably wait for people to graduate and gain employment, maybe move to other continents. After several months pass, they would begin slowly eliminating people over a period of time — unfortunate accidents that don't form a pattern. If they did it right, no one would intuit a connection to the algorithm. I've heard of things like this before. The anarchs like to play a long game."

Kade was breathing fast again. "We can't let this happen. We have to stop them!"

"What can we do? We're helpless to intervene."

"Maybe we can warn our classmates somehow."

"All of our communications are monitored. When was the last time they let you leave this building alone?"

She was right. He had been so consumed with meeting Villecrest's deadline that he hardly noticed his surroundings. Now that he thought about it, some thug always shadowed him. "We have to escape — get back to Denmount."

"Kade, it's not possible to hide from the Breachers. Even if we could somehow slip past our keepers and travel all the way to Caralithica, without being discovered, what would you do when you got there? Turn yourself over to the authorities and confess your crimes?"

"Why not? I'm the one who deserves punishment. They can throw me in prison. If it means saving innocent people, I'll do it. Besides, then Villecrest couldn't get to me."

"Are you listening to yourself? Prisons house criminals. Criminals work with Breachers. Do I need to spell it out? And where am I in all of this? Do you want me to flee with you, only so you can abandon me?"

"That's not what I meant."

"Kade. There is nothing — we — can — do."

"There has to be something," he whispered. "Wait! What if I hid a message in the algorithm? No one here would understand what I was doing, but someone from Denmount might notice. Leviticus would notice for sure, that guy is some kind of savant. He was constantly picking out little flaws in my work — so annoying."

"How is anyone from Denmount supposed to see anything? Your modified algorithm is on the secure Breacher network."

Kade deflated. *Stupid. What was I thinking?*

"Listen, Kade. If I knew for certain that I could escape this place and no one would find me, I'd seize the opportunity in a heartbeat. Believe me, I've considered it from every angle. I just don't see a way out."

Conviction filled him then. "You were alone before. Now you have me. I swear to you, we'll find a way. We will stop Villecrest and we'll escape — together."

"Okay, Kade." She gave him a half-hearted smile.

He knew she didn't believe him, but he *would* find a solution. If he could finish the algorithm with an impossible deadline, then he could find a way to *destroy* the algorithm, given enough time. That hope would have to be enough for now.

Chapter 52

I can't believe I agreed to this. Nico lay on the mat fuming. This was the third time Leviticus had thrown him. His bruised body didn't hurt as much as his ego. It would probably be a good idea to call it quits, but he had no intention of leaving Kayla alone with Lev.

It was foolish, he knew. Lev wouldn't be interested. Kayla wasn't his type. Truthfully, it wasn't Lev he was worried about. The admission filled him with shame. Kayla was his friend. He should trust her. Besides, it's not like he had told her how he really felt about her. He had no true claim on her affections.

Still, Leviticus Radix didn't realize the effect he had on people. His 'lone wolf' aloofness drew people's attention. Lev's indifference was actually just preoccupation, but it made an impression. Blend that with his intelligence, add his infallible memory, and he seemed superior to everyone around him. It didn't hurt that he was also reasonably attractive.

The combination evoked disdain in some while drawing others like moths to a lantern. Most of the latter were of the female persuasion. Nico suspected Kayla would be immune to Lev's unwitting charms, but he wasn't taking any chances.

You're being ridiculous. Nico had never felt threatened by Lev's presence before, but Kayla was special and he felt both protective and possessive at the same time.

Facing off again, Nico took a swing. He missed and lost his balance. Lev tripped him up and caught his arm before he hit the mat.

Lev offered a few pointers. It wouldn't have bothered him had it just been the two of them, but with Kayla watching, it just made him feel inferior. Having Kayla offer tips as well was pretty crushing to his already battered pride.

"Take a break for a few minutes, Nico." Lev nodded towards Kayla. "Kayla looks ready to burst. I think she needs to work off some pent-up energy."

Nico didn't want to admit how exhausted he was. Speaking would have given it away, so he looked at Kayla and gestured as if to say, he's all yours. Making his way to the sidelines, Nico checked to make sure they weren't watching and gratefully sank to the floor.

"Okay, Mr. Radix, let's see if the combat instructors in Kemetica have been teaching you properly."

Lev watched warily as Kayla circled. Each assessing the other, looking for openings. Nico thought they looked like two panthers. *When did lanky Lev gain such poise?*

Kayla sprung forward with two quick jabs followed by a side thrust kick as Lev leaned out of reach. "Not bad. Now *you* come at *me*. Let's see what you've got," Kayla taunted.

Lev threw a scissor kick. Kayla darted underneath with a leg sweep but Lev lifted into a back flip and landed untouched. Nico stared slack-jawed. He'd watched Kayla practising forms, but seeing her in action was amazing. His admiration for her grew. Looking back at his childhood friend, on the other hand, filled him with confusion. How could Lev possibly do what he just did? *He's only been away for a few months.*

"Okay, pretty boy. You've shown that you can defend yourself — mind if I let loose?"

"I thought you just did," Lev taunted.

That drew a scowl from Kayla. *Uh, oh*, Nico thought. *I know that determined look. Lev may have bitten off more than he can chew.* Nico grinned in anticipation. It would be good for Lev to end up on his back. *Good for me, too*, he admitted.

Kayla let loose. It was inspiring. She was all fluid grace and force. One moment she was striking, the next blocking. She bobbed and weaved in intricate patterns. Nico thought he spotted some of her practice forms in practical application. Nico would have collapsed in exhaustion by now, but Kayla was moving even faster, if possible, until suddenly she wasn't. The change was so abrupt that Nico straightened, despite his aching back. He was trying to figure out what had just occurred. Kayla was standing stock still, staring at Leviticus. Her chest was heaving and her eyes were wide. "That's impossible!"

Nico took a second look and noticed that Lev was still standing in more or less the same spot as when they began. It looked as if he hadn't moved. Playing it back through his mind, he realized that he had been so enthralled with Kayla, that he hadn't been paying attention to Lev. Kayla had moved around the mat, circling and advancing from every direction. Lev had remained within four cubits of his starting point the entire time. Lev had effortlessly redirected every blow as Kayla moved around him.

Great. First he was merely a gifted savant, now he'd become an apex warrior. *Just what I needed.* Nico became angry with himself. Lev couldn't help who he was. Still, how was this possible? Kayla beat him to the question. "I didn't believe you before when you said you had taken Yori and Tark to the mat. I apologize. How long have you been training?"

"About seven months."

"No — that's impossible. You fight like someone who has been training for decades. You anticipate like a master. I was able to connect only once!" Kayla looked to Nico for confirmation.

"I'm as mystified as you. Lev and I took some basic boxing in school, but before he left, we were evenly matched."

"I may have picked up a few things from Akhen," Lev offered.

Kayla's head whipped up. "Akhen? As in Akhen Hor, undefeated Warkata World Champion?"

"He's the world champion?" Lev asked. "Huh. He never told me that."

"He never... Wait, this makes no sense. Akhen doesn't fight anymore. He found no challenge in it. Many have asked for his help with training but he flat out refuses. Why would he decide to train someone with only a few boxing lessons under his belt?"

"Oh, he's not my combat instructor, we just spar sometimes."

Kayla was laughing now. "You say that as if it were the most ordinary thing in the world."

Leviticus shrugged.

"Okay, I'll bite. How does one go about becoming best buddies with

Akhen Hor? I wouldn't mind getting a few pointers from him myself."

Now, Lev was laughing. "Best buddies with Akhen Hor? Have you never met the man? Akhen is nobody's buddy. He *is* my mentor, however."

"But Akhen Hor only mentors analysts and he hasn't taken on a novice since before I was born." Kayla's eyes grew even wider.

Nico was getting uncomfortable being out of the loop. "Kayla? What's going on?"

"Lev's mentor is Akhen Hor."

"I heard that. So?"

"Akhen Hor doesn't train novices."

"Obviously, he does."

"No. He seldom trains senior analysts, for that matter, because he can't teach them."

"What kind of mentor can't teach his students?"

"What I mean is, they can't learn from him. They can't reach his level of ability." She shook her head trying to clear the clutter of questions. "Lev?" She hesitated. "How many tokens did you identify in your analyst exam?"

"Eight at last testing, though Akhen insists I can do better. Hey! Are you telling me other analysts only have to take that test once?"

Kayla looked lightheaded. She dropped to her knees. Nico rushed to her side. "Kayla, what's wrong?"

"No wonder my mother sent him to Kemetica. Of course he can fight... Nico, he's an *eight* and maybe more!"

Lev was shaking his head. "I need to stop sharing that tidbit with people. They always get weird."

Nico shot Lev a look of annoyance and tried to lighten the mood. "Come on, Kayla, no woman has ever rated Leviticus higher than six out of ten. Eight is stretching things."

"Hey!" Lev protested.

"You don't understand, Nico." Kayla gripped his forearm. "There hasn't been an analyst apart from Akhen Hor, to score higher than five in decades."

Leviticus sighed. "I'm guessing we're done sparring. I'm going to go wash up." He picked up his towel from the bench where he had left it neatly folded, and draped it around his neck as he walked off.

Nico sat across from Kayla, eyes glued to the mat. "So, Lev is an eight?"

"Isn't it incredible?"

Nico rolled his eyes. "Yep. Lev is incredible — always has been."

Kayla looked at him, confused.

"So how would I rate, a two?" Nico asked.

Kayla laughed. Nico's expression grew even more sullen.

Kayla's face shifted from confused — to comprehending — to angry, in the blink of an eye. "He's not my type."

"Oh! Um, what is your type?"

Kayla punched him in the shoulder. Hard.

"Oww! What was that for?"

"Nico Callan! I know I'm not a typical girl, but seriously — are you saying you couldn't tell I was flirting with you this whole time we've been together? Some field operative I'd make!" Her bottom lip stuck out in a pout that made Nico want to kiss her. He started to lean in, but froze with uncertainty.

"I can't believe this!" Kayla threw her arms in the air. "You're my type, you thick-skulled oaf!" She stood up in a huff and stormed out of the room.

Nico just sat there with an idiotic grin on his face, as he watched her leave.

Chapter 53

The weeks weighed heavily on Kade's soul. It was difficult to balance his attempts to delay progress on the algorithm with the Third Anarch's impatience. He needed to retain both his autonomy and his life if he hoped to stop Villecrest's madness. The cost was too high. With every increase in network performance, more innocent lives were lost. At times he feared the anguish would drive him mad.

"It's not your fault, Kade. You didn't ask for any of this. Villecrest is to blame." Selica was his anchor. Time and again she reminded him who the true villain was. It did little to assuage his guilt, but it reminded him of the only route he could imagine for his redemption. It fuelled his determination and instilled in him just enough courage to carry on.

A new-found sobriety took hold. He no longer craved the oblivion alcohol offered. The thought of losing his focus was repulsive. That, and his growing relationship with Selica, helped him to see how much more life could be when one's thoughts were not primarily for oneself.

He watched her with admiration as she worked on a calculation. She was the one good thing about this whole mess. They had built up a carefully crafted facade for their relationship. When they wished to spend time together outside of work, a convenient quanta structure issue would arise in the writ weaves necessitating several late nights of 'brainstorming' after work. The result of these sessions was always a serendipitous resolution to the problem.

The pattern became a familiar one to their co-workers and keepers. As long as progress ensued, their supplementary efforts were encouraged.

Their extra support for the cause had the side effect of earning Villecrest's trust. At least to the extent such a thing was possible. It was a very necessary footing to cultivate if they ever hoped to be free of their handlers long enough to accomplish anything of worth.

To that end, whenever Villecrest was in the lab, Kade displayed great enthusiasm over each successful kill of a target. Afterwards, when he was alone in his suite, he would empty his stomach in revulsion.

He and Selica had spent months considering opportunities to sabotage the network or corrupt the writs in the weaving and escape. Every plan so far had hit a dead end.

Their plotting usually occurred in his suite. The one place they could be alone without his keepers. Even so, they needed to be careful. He had no doubt that listening devices riddled the walls. They had worked out some simple hand signals for rudimentary conversation. Things like yes, no, danger, or keep silent. For numerical expressions, they used coins of differing values, stacked to denote multipliers.

"Would you like some more kofa?" Selica asked, as she pointed to the coins she had been arranging. She was working on a new avenue for a contagion writ. She slid over a tablet with some accompanying notes as he went over her numbers.

They had reverted to using a stylus on some old wax tablets Selica discovered at the bazaar. It provided them a medium for more complex conversations. It was a simple matter to press down on the wax and erase anything written there.

"Yes please," Kade answered. "Selica, do you think we could slow down an attack on the network from this vector if we added an automatic shut down sequence here?" Having offered food to the ears of eavesdroppers, he shifted the coins to correct a small error in Selica's calculation. It was a good idea and he gestured his approval from across the room. Selica finished reading from a second tablet that he handed to her on the way to the kitchen. It offered yet another one of his ideas for escape. She tugged on her ear indicating that he should accept her next words at face value. "I don't think that will work."

Kade sighed. He had learned not to waste time questioning her when she was this direct. It meant she had already unsuccessfully investigated something similar in the past. Kade was grateful for Selica's knowledge of Breacher ways, but saddened that she had gained it at the cost of her innocence and freedom. He marvelled that she could still hope.

One of their considerations involved Selica returning to Denmount for a visit as an alumnus. Selica was opposed to that option, because it meant only she would have an immediate chance to escape. Kade argued for it, because it would allow her to leave a message on the original network for his ultimate escape as well. It would also provide an opportunity to warn their former classmates. Kade felt that Villecrest might be open to an attempt to corrupt the original algorithm. It would leave him with sole ownership of the technology. However, they couldn't suggest the idea unless they gained both Villecrest's trust and his comfort in her writ weaving skill. Selica worked hard to gain the necessary fluency. She was a fast learner and Kade wondered if Villecrest even needed him anymore. He hoped the man never realized or Kade would lose what small leverage he had.

Most of their efforts involved subtle attempts to nudge people in a fortuitous direction. Much of the time it failed, but sometimes they moved one step closer to the goal. One of those successfully planted seeds was the suggestion that it would be wise to create a contagion writ. They could use it to test vulnerabilities of the Breacher network and then develop ways to counter attempts at a malicious attack. Kade had rightly surmised that Villecrest's suspicious nature would not let him ignore the possibility. He felt vindicated when Toller provided a small isolated network in another building and ordered him to develop defensive structures and counter-attacks.

Those exercises gave the Third Anarch a dangerous overconfidence in his preparations. It would be his downfall when the time came, but that was not Kade's primary goal in putting forward the suggestion. What he hoped was that Villecrest would ultimately choose to use the contagion writ on the original algorithm at Denmount. The man was too intelligent not to recognize the opportunity placed before him. He also had to know that Kade and Selica were the only two who could implement such an operation. The fact that Villecrest had not approached them worried Kade. He feared they would never gain his trust enough for that door to open.

Kade was growing impatient. Restlessness drove him to try his original idea of embedding a message into the Breacher algorithm. He knew it was a long shot. Few people would notice such a message and none had reason to look for it. As far as Kade knew, no one was aware of the algorithm running in the background on the Breacher viewcorder network. For his plan to work, a very resourceful person would need to notice something peculiar about the viewcorders — someone who could also find a way to access the writ weaves that flowed through the network. It pained him to acknowledge, but he could only think of one person who fit the bill. Leviticus Radix.

Kade didn't have an inkling where Radix might be these days, but his profile was in the Breacher archive along with the rest of his Denmount peers. That meant he would learn Leviticus's whereabouts soon enough.

A growing number of the viewcorders on the Breacher network were replaced with a newer model that could rotate. Kade had demonstrated to Villecrest how such cameras would improve efficiency. The twisted monster, eager for more prey, immediately ordered upgrades. It would take time, of course, but Kade had been able to direct the first replacements to popular thoroughfares in major cities. It would increase the chance that Leviticus might walk past.

His plan was simple enough. He provided data directives that would cause those newer cameras to jerk back and forth whenever they identified Radix. They would do that for no one else. It would be easy enough to write those motions off as an occasional glitch as far as his co-workers were concerned. Leviticus, on the other hand, would not be able to ignore the sudden motion in his vicinity. On closer inspection, he would notice viewcorders following his movements. "The man is obsessive about anything out of place," he mumbled.

"What did you say, Kade?"

"Oh, nothing. It's getting late. Maybe we should call it a night."

Selica gave him a hug and a silent kiss. He clung to her, longing for a day when they didn't have to hide their affection.

"One day," he whispered in her ear.

"One day soon," she whispered back, in their customary parting. Then, she was gone.

He needed this to work. *If you come through for me Radix, I'll forgive you for every indignity of the past.*

Chapter 54

The week went by quickly. Nico had contacted Cello Vantos to give his recommendation regarding the scheduling of maintenance repairs on the access tunnels for the abandoned Servator base. The Chief Sentry had agreed that it would be a good time for servicing and gave her blessing. She had actually been quite pleased with the suggestion, noting that it was just the sort of thing his father would have done. She made no effort to hide how grateful she was that a Callan was once again at the helm of the family business.

Nico had also spoken with Brokar Luge, the head of Servator operations for Callan International. The man was fairly dancing, despite his age, at the thought of several large new projects. Nico directed him to begin assessment of needed repairs for the tunnels. In addition, he was to get the tunnelling machine near his estate, in running order. Using a map of the larger tunnels provided by Kayla, Brokar would move the machine into position, close to the Servator base. It would serve as the starting point for several new tunnels.

Nico had explained to Brokar that the new tunnels and terminals were a personal initiative at Nico's expense, intended to improve Servator transportation logistics. It was to be a surprise gift to the Chief Sentry. Brokar assured him that he had a large staff of Servator supporters who were used to working in secrecy.

Leviticus and Kayla had spent a few days alone at the vacant base going through Servator archives. They poured over local topography, population densities, popular travel routes, geology and other details to search for inaccessible locations that might work as hidden transportation hubs. Once they had settled on the best candidates, they mapped potential paths for tunnelling to those locations. Lev's unique abilities had proven invaluable in spotting obscure formations and map discrepancies that revealed long forgotten discoveries. By the fourth day, all agreed on three promising options.

The first was nestled in the mountain range fifty leagues south of Denmount. Lev had identified a long abandoned mine in the heart of the mountains. The second was Sola Canyon, eighty leagues to the east, and the third was a series of underwater caves beneath Callan family land. Three teams had been sent out to investigate the locations and they were all gathering now to hear the reports and make a decision. Once everyone had arrived, Nico cleared his throat to get their attention. "I know we're all excited to hear what the exploratory teams have found, so why don't we get straight to it. Cal, why don't you begin."

"Thank you, sir. Our team was sent to investigate the abandoned mine site in the Tellur mountain range south of Denmount. Our LTA traversed a wide circle around the coordinates at low altitude and found no signs of roads or paths in the area. Any ancient method of ingress has long since been erased. There are no mountain passes into the area. It would be difficult to access by any form of ground transport. We couldn't see any sign of mining activity from the air, so we decided to land on a narrow plateau we had sighted and explore on foot.

"As we descended, we were surprised to find that the plateau extended quite far back into the mountain face. An outcropping of rock obscures it. When we exited the craft, the wildlife in the area seemed abundant and curious, suggesting they weren't familiar with the possible threat of hunters. On one side of the plateau we found a natural cave and at the very back we discovered the mine shaft. A crude, narrow affair. Any efforts at mining were short-lived by the looks of it. The cave and plateau are large enough to hold several craft and remain invisible from the air. Also in favour of the site is a nearby river.

"As for travelling through passes by air while remaining out of sight; we found no deep passes into this particular valley. Once over the western ridge, a number of passes open up and lead toward the sea. It may be possible, over time, to excavate a depression. We'd only need to carve it deep enough to pass through to the next valley while avoiding line-of-sight to any nearby settlements. For the time being, we would need to rely on night flights with beacons to avoid detection. We feel the pros for this location far outweigh the cons." Cal sat down following his summation.

Velena Poh immediately stood. "We were tasked with investigating the Sola Canyon east of Denmount. Unlike the Tellur Range, the canyon ridge is easily accessible by ground transport. Still, it would be relatively easy for LTA to remain out of sight of Denmount by following the river to the sea, down between the canyon walls. Water transport could also travel downriver. Unfortunately, a number of nomadic tribes live in the area making it unlikely that our operations would go unnoticed. While visiting some of the tribesmen, we learned that flooding is frequent in the area. We also learned that parts of the canyon walls collapse on occasion. The type of rock in the area does not seem stable for the kind of development necessary. In summary, we do not recommend this as a viable option."

"Thank you, Velena. I believe that leaves the report from the sea caverns. Janoff?"

Janoff seemed eager to share. "Thank you, Mr. Callan. It was my first time aboard a sub-aqua transport and it proved quite the adventure, I'll tell you! The base of the sea cliffs hide the wreckage of quite a few vessels. The fear of travel along that route is well founded. It may be worth considering salvage operations. Who knows what treasures await on the sea floor?" His eyes held a sparkle of excitement. Janoff had a tendency to get sidetracked and Nico raised an eyebrow reminding him to return to the topic at hand.

"Yes, well, the undersea caves do indeed exist. We noted several of them. The first three we entered terminated quickly, but the fourth was larger and progressed much deeper into the rock. Imagine our excitement when the passage began to rise and we surfaced in a huge cavern with a natural beach above sea level! We tentatively exited and discovered fresh air and a slight breeze, signifying natural ventilation. Along the strand are several adjoining caverns and tunnels too numerous to explore during our brief visit.

"Mr. Callan, It's perfect! Completely hidden, inaccessible except by a feared and treacherous part of the sea. Yet beneath the surface, it was smooth sailing for our transport, at least at the lower depths where the caves are located. We enthusiastically endorse this location as a viable option!"

Nico smiled. "That does indeed sound very promising."

Janoff took his seat looking quite pleased with himself.

"Well my friends, we were hoping for two possible options, and it appears we've found them. We still need to complete a great deal more work before we'll know for certain, but I suggest we move forward under the assumption that these two options are viable. All in favour?"

The ayes were unanimous.

This is quite the group of optimists I'm working with Nico chuckled to himself. The excitement was infectious and he smiled as his eyes took in the roomful of pleased faces.

The mountain location would be the destination for their first tunnel. The sea cavern would be the target for their second tunnel. Nico had hoped the sea caverns would turn out to be a viable option. If they could successfully finish that tunnel, it would allow them to return the tunnelling machine back to its original resting place behind the family crypt.

"Okay everyone, that concludes our business for today. Brokar will be in touch with each of you regarding next steps. Thank you for your efforts!" Nico, Lev and Kayla remained behind. They had additional business to discuss.

"So? What do you think?" Nico asked as the door closed, affording them some privacy.

"The geology of those two locations shouldn't pose any difficulty for the tunnelling machine," Lev offered.

Kayla was nodding. "They're both well hidden. I have a good feeling about this."

"But we still need to figure out a way to tie this all into the Servator base while keeping its existence hidden." Nico shrugged. "I haven't come up with anything on my own. I'm open to suggestions."

Kayla glanced at Lev who nodded encouragement. "I had a thought, and Lev has been helping flesh it out."

"I'm all ears." Nico leaned forward.

"Okay," Kayla began, "we had to abandon the base because my actions lead the Breachers to suspect Servator activity in the area. The disappearance of Lev and myself from a room below the archive building suggests a hidden room or a tunnel. The Breachers don't know the extent of Servator operations because of my mother's quick action. They haven't seen or heard of a Servator in the area since. Unfortunately, the site is now actively monitored, which means we can't increase activity anytime soon. That got me thinking. What if we were to expose some tunnels to the public? Make it so that those tunnels aren't a secret?"

"I'm confused. Isn't that exactly what we're trying to prevent?"

"We have a tunnelling machine, Nico."

"Oh, forgive me. Somewhere between discussing its use a few minutes ago, and now, I must have forgotten." That earned a raised eyebrow. Kayla didn't find humour in the sarcasm.

Nico held up a hand forestalling a tongue-lashing. "Sorry, continue."

"We have a tunnelling machine, and a means to make artificial tunnels appear completely natural using token technology. I propose we create a labyrinth of caves and tunnels and open it to the public as a tourist attraction. The tunnels can wend their way below the city, never coming near the Servator base.

"Tour guides could share a history of how the cave system was discovered — something about it appearing in a historical parchment found within the city archives. They could spin a tale about past use of the tunnels for illicit activities. Perhaps suggest that in recent years a few students had discovered a way into the tunnels through the archive building basement, a popular place for young couples to retreat.

"It serves several purposes. One, it offers a plausible explanation for how Lev and I could escape from the archive building basement. Two, it acknowledges a network of tunnels that will be extensively mapped and open for public exploration — tunnels that will never reveal a Servator base. Three, it creates a busy public attraction filled with visiting strangers. Busy public places make it easier for Servators to move about without drawing attention to themselves. Four, a labyrinth provides a natural choke point as a security feature for the base."

Kayla held her hand palm up, gesturing toward Lev, a cue for him to continue.

"I've spent a little time studying the token technology during my time in Kemetica. I'm confident that I can use the Denmount equipment to do what Kayla is suggesting, but I propose taking it further. The Servators already use the technology to hide base entrances. I propose we connect the labyrinth by spokes to an outer ring. From there we would create a single point of access to the base. The quantum positioning network would continuously open and close random portions of the outer ring, effectively creating loops that return to the labyrinth. There would be only one way to traverse the outer ring without ending up back in the labyrinth. It would require coordination with the quantum positioning network. That can't happen without a Servator Q-view."

Lev and Kayla waited silently as Nico absorbed it all. It was elegant and absolutely brilliant. He stared off into space as a huge grin spread over his face. "That — is — incredible! It's genius! This is perfect. How did you think of it?"

"It was all Kayla's idea," Lev said.

Kayla shook her head in disagreement. "I've had a lot of time to think about it, but I wasn't sure it could work until Lev parsed it through that brain of his and picked it apart."

"It doesn't matter. I love it! I love you both for thinking of it. This can work. It's all coming together. We can do this!"

The three of them sat there smiling at each other, Enjoying the moment.

"Then my work here is done!" Lev rose. "For the time being at least. I have to return to Kemetica tomorrow to continue my training."

They shared hugs of congratulation and farewell.

"You'll keep Nico in line?"

"Someone has to." Kayla quipped.

"If I could stay...."

"We know, Lev, we feel the same."

"If you find yourself in Kemetica, look me up."

"We'll see each other again before you know it," Nico promised, "it turns out I have a few transportation options at my disposal."

"Did you purchase them with discount scrips?" Lev teased.

"It's how I got where I am today." Nico smiled.

"Time to go!" Yori barked, within inches of Nico.

Nico jumped. "Stop doing that! Where did you come from anyway? Be gone!"

"Yes, sir!" Yori and Tark snapped to attention, then spun on their heels laughing as they dragged Lev out of the room.

"What is it with those two?"

"Ranger humour — you'll get used to it."

"I'm not sure I will, unless I can sharpen my reflexes. As it is, I'm in panic mode every time they catch me off guard."

"Nico, are you asking me to teach you warkata?"

"What if I am?"

"Oh, no ifs. You're committed now buddy. I need to get back to work, but I'll see you on the mats tomorrow morning at first light!" She left with a little bounce in her step.

Nico knew he was in for a world of pain, but he'd do anything for that girl. *And next time Yori sneaks up on me, he's gonna pay!*

Chapter 55

Lev leaned behind the pillar and took another sip of kofa. It was his favourite Kemetica blend — so much better than what they served back home. Or was this home now? It was hard to believe how quickly a person could find the familiar in a new place. His life had changed so quickly. A year ago he wouldn't have been able to afford a flight on one of the new Lighter Than Air transports. Now he had flown on them several times.

As a child, he had admired the sleek lines of the craft when they first came off the assembly lines. Some people joked that they looked like balloon birds, but he admired the smooth aerodynamic lines. The thick body and wings housed stores of helium that gave the thin hard shell its near zero weight. On-board compressors and tanks stored and released gas as needed to increase or reduce buoyancy. They also provided emergency compensation in the event of a leak. Swept back wings provided lift and control surfaces to navigate. It was an efficient design.

It was also the only way to travel, Lev decided. Thanks to the powerful thrust fans, the craft moved quickly through the air. Travelling by sea took weeks, the same trip only took hours on an LTA transport.

They had landed two hours ago and should have proceeded directly to the Kemetica base, but something had caught Lev's eye. He had first noticed the pattern disruption back in Caralithica, but at the time he thought it random. Akhen had told him repeatedly that he should trust his senses and never dismiss an irregularity until he understood the cause. Lev would heed that advice now.

When they had disembarked at the air field, Lev noticed a security viewcorder slowly moving over the crowd. Whenever the viewcorder pointed in his vicinity, the device made an odd jerking motion and stopped as if focused on him. He had noticed that same odd motion on a viewcorder in Caralithica. It was too much of a coincidence to witness that same glitch, in a different model viewcorder, on an entirely different continent. Lev had turned to move against the crowd pushing back toward the LTA, startling Yori and Tark. The viewcorder swung to follow him. He held up a hand signalling them to remain where they were as he returned. The viewcorder moved with him. Lev felt a chill move down his spine.

He shared his observations with Tark and Yori. They were immediately on alert, not questioning his suspicion. Lev supposed that was part of being a ranger. Suspect everything and trust no one until that trust was earned. It struck Leviticus that their response indicated trust in him. He hoped that he wasn't being paranoid. They had continued toward the market square where Tark spotted another viewcorder that appeared to be following them. Lev found a kofa vendor near the edge of the square. The viewcorder field of view fell just at the edge of the table they chose. They ordered mugs and sat for a while to see if the viewcorder would continue with regular sweeps of the crowd. They would learn the truth soon enough. *At least the kofa is good.* The viewcorder remained frozen on their little group until Lev leaned behind the pillar beside their table. As soon as he disappeared, the viewcorder began to move away but then returned. *Odd.* Lev leaned back into view and the device made a shaking motion. *Even stranger.* "Did you see that?" Lev asked.

"Yes," Yori nodded, "it seems interested in our party but very excited about Radix."

"It appears that your love for machines is requited!" Tark quipped.

Lev rolled his eyes. "I like women just fine. I don't understand them is all."

Yori snorted. "I don't advise encouraging this device's affection. I'm going to try something. Lev, lean behind that pillar again."

Lev did as instructed while Yori stood and strode from their table. The viewcorder followed as he wove his way through the crowd and returned. Yori joined Lev behind the pillar. "Your turn, Tark." Tark repeated Yori's journey but was ignored. The viewcorder returned to a regular scan of the crowd. Yori leaned back into view. Lev remained behind the pillar. When the sweep of the viewcorder passed the table, it froze on Yori. He motioned to Lev who leaned back into view. The viewcorder began to shake.

"I saw that," Tark said, as he returned to the table.

"This is new. We need to get back to the base and report. If these viewcorders are monitoring some of our operatives, we risk compromising the base's location. I know of a tunnel entrance near here — in the warehouse district. Last time I checked, no viewcorders were installed in that area. We'll need to avoid any that we come across on our way there."

"Once we're away from the public I'll contact base on my Q-view and recommend a temporary lock down," Tark offered.

"Good idea. Let's get moving. We're too exposed here."

Lev dreaded the thought that he might soon be responsible for a second Servator base closing down. He kept silent on their way to the base while guilt nibbled at his conscience.

Chapter 56

Kayla replaced the stack of parchments on the shelf and removed the next pile. Over the last few weeks, she'd spent the majority of her time in the file room. It was part of her role as *Seri Quin*, assistant to Nico Callan, head of Callan International. She smiled at the honorific. Nico was so far from the stuffy stereotype implied, that it was a surprise anyone took him seriously. Most seemed to like him, though. He had a way with people.

Nico had arranged for a desk in the corner and brought in some plants and a couch to make it comfortable. At least as comfortable as the confined space would allow. Nico was constantly apologizing for the lack of windows and had tried to convince her to take a nicer office down the hall. She'd insisted that an assistant would not get a window office and it was necessary to keep up the facade for her own safety. He had reluctantly agreed.

Kayla set the new stack on her desk and sat down. "And I thought the Servator archives had a lot of parchment," she groaned. *Callan International is a global enterprise*, she reminded herself for the hundredth time.

So far, she hadn't uncovered anything pertinent to their investigation into the death of Nico's parents, but her efforts provided valuable insight regarding company operations. Nico had been able to use that information on several occasions to improve his credibility with staff.

It was boring work parsing memos and ledgers. Kayla found her mind drifting to the recent conversation she'd had with her mother. Kayla figured that her mother would begin to worry if she continued the pretense that she was travelling. It wasn't possible for the daughter of the Chief Sentry of Caralithica to go unnoticed while visiting an international Servator base. No doubt every base on the planet had already been asked to keep an eye out for her. Prolonged silence would have been suspicious, so she had decided it was time to contact her mother and let her know how she fared. Cello had appeared greatly relieved when she learned that Kayla had landed on her feet and was working for Nico under an assumed name. Always security conscious, Cello understood the need for an alias and approved. "It's going to take me some time to get used to the hair colour," she had said.

As for living arrangements, she was staying in the guest house on the Callan estate for the time being. Kayla had explained their arrangement and how it allowed them to travel without being seen publicly. It relieved her mother up until the point that she learned Nico and Kayla were seeing each other.

"An unmarried couple should not be living in such close proximity," her mother admonished.

Kayla had been quick to shut down that line of reasoning. "I'm not a child, Mother. It hardly matters whether I live on the same estate or across the city. If we choose to do something inappropriate, location isn't going to be the deciding factor." She thought the concern misplaced considering she had been more at risk of that sort of danger while travelling alone on the other side of the world.

Overall, it was much as she expected from her mother. The normalcy of the exchange almost had her weeping with gratitude. Kayla wasn't sure what she had anticipated, but after the events of recent months, she had begun to despair that anything would ever be the same again.

Even so, her mother had been overly dramatic as far as Kayla was concerned. Nico was a gentleman. That didn't stop her mother from going full on commanding officer as she grilled Nico about his intentions. Poor Nico flushed red in mortification. Kayla had never before heard "Yes, Ma'am." repeated so often in a twenty-minute stretch. The encounter finally ended with the Chief Sentry dismissing Nico — from his own office! He couldn't leave fast enough. Kayla laughed remembering how he had hidden in the staff lunchroom until Cello left the building. Kayla knew her mother, though. She was very pleased that Nico was courting her daughter. Of course the Chief Sentry wasn't about to let Nico know that. She wouldn't dream of giving up leverage for future negotiations.

Aside from putting her mother at ease, the meeting had worked to her advantage in other ways. Since Kayla was remaining in Denmount, her mother tasked her with the role of Servator representative to the maintenance crews while work proceeded on the tunnels around the base. It saved her having to send someone every time it was necessary to allow access to a particular tunnel or temporarily shut down security safeguards. Her mother had increased the security access permissions on Kayla's Q-view so she could function in that capacity.

Kayla couldn't believe her luck. Now she could access the base freely without fear of being caught and asked a lot of uncomfortable questions. It made their plans so much easier. Now they could move forward with an extra veneer of legitimacy. Their plans were coming together. Kayla was so grateful for all of the help Nico and Leviticus had provided. She was getting her chance to make things right and that had never been a certainty. It filled her with hope for the future.

I'm happy, she realized. She had a purpose that challenged her. She had friends, allies and most of all, she had Nico. Things were going so well between them. She never imagined herself in a relationship. She had always pictured herself as a field agent. A professional loner. She'd spent so much time honing her craft in an attempt to prove herself, that she hadn't allowed herself a chance to feel. Considering it now, she realized how angry and lonely she would have been, if she had continued along that path. For the first time in far too long, she sent a quick prayer of thanks to the Maker.

Getting back on task, Kayla continued scanning the ledger she had lain out on the desk. It was filled with typical financial transactions of the kind she had begun to recognize over the last few weeks. She scanned the last column and reached for the next sheet, but something made her hesitate. It was the analyst habit her mentors had drilled into her. She drew her finger down the middle column, slowly this time. *There!* She stabbed the entry with her finger. It was a large payment without explanation, payable to a name she had not seen before. Kayla knew better than to let excitement get the better of her. An analyst required evidence of repeating patterns before any further investigation was warranted. Over the next two hours, she discovered similar entries on four other occasions within a two-month period. It revealed a clear pattern. *Finally! something to work with!* The rest of the day passed in a blur.

Chapter 57

Nico sat at his desk going over their plans for the mountain and sea cliff terminals. Sub-aqua transports were ferrying material to the sea terminal. Work crews were reinforcing the caves and tunnels. Construction was well under way for docking facilities in the cavern harbour. They hoped to reinforce as much of the cavern as possible before the tunnelling machine arrived. They didn't want to risk a collapse in front of the machine at its arrival.

The mountain location required less engineering. Workers focused on creating a work camp and levelling the plateau for aircraft landings. They had also decided to take a long, subdued approach to carving a channel into the adjacent valley. The plan was to excavate small areas at a time in a staggered pattern and then replant trees. It would help to obscure any obvious clearing. Secrecy was paramount.

EP Reactors were already in place at both locations providing power for the work crews. Paths for the tunnels were plotted and surface beacons were in place for guidance. The tunnelling machine had been serviced and was even now beginning its first journey toward the mountains. Everything was proceeding on schedule. Nico felt alive. *This must be the fire that burned in my father.* He chuckled remembering how he thought his father had lived a boring life. His parents would have loved this. Sadly, they were no longer around to see it. His reverie was interrupted as the door to his office burst open. Kayla stood there breathing hard. *Has she been running?*

"Hi, Kayla — I mean, Seri. Uh, what's up?"

Seri's expression morphed from a look of anger to one of horror and back again.

"Seri? Is something wrong?"

"I found something," She blurted, as she closed and locked the door behind her. She dragged a chair to his desk and sat down beside him. "Look at these ledger entries." She spread several parchments across his desk and pointed to each in turn. "Each of these entries shows a large payment made to an individual by the name of Ain Rujgar over a two-month period. I've found no records of Callan International having conducted business with this person before or after these dates."

It took Nico a few heartbeats to understand what she was showing him. "Wait. Isn't this around the time my parents were killed?"

"Yes! The first two payments before and the second two after."

"That can't be a coincidence."

"I thought so too, but I wanted to make sure. The Vault of Denmount distributes all expenditures for Callan International, drawing from the company accounts. I figured if I could find out who collected those payments, it would give us a lead. The Servators have substantial holdings at the vault. We have sources working there who provide copies of security viewcorderings for exactly this sort of situation. I went through those viewcordings for the days noted in the ledger. The same individual showed up each time. Here, look!" Seri held her arm in front of him as it began to bubble. Nico leaped from his chair, eyes wide.

"Woah! Kayla, your arm!" When he looked again, there was a gauntlet on her forearm replacing the leather bracelet of a moment before. Kayla had her arms crossed and one eyebrow raised, "Seriously, Nico? You're supposed to call me Seri and you've seen tokens at work on several occasions. I've told you that every Servator carries a Q-view."

"Yes, but the tokens I saw were always on an inanimate object, like a wall. I didn't know a token could mimic flesh! You nearly gave me a heart attack. That's really creepy — can I see it again?"

Seri rolled her eyes, but obliged as the Q-view reverted to the appearance of a simple leather band with an embossed symbol.

Nico touched her forearm. The texture felt right but the warmth of flesh was absent. "How did I never notice this before?" Nico shook his head in wonder as he took a closer look at the symbol on the band.

"It's the symbol of the Servators," Seri explained, "if you ever find yourself in trouble, search for it. Where this symbol is displayed an escape or a friend is always nearby. In this case the symbol is a token trigger for the Q-view. Now, can we get back to business?"

Nico sat back down as the Q-view reappeared on Seri's forearm. She tapped on the display and brought up an image captured by the vault's viewcorder. "Do you recognize this man?"

"No."

"Well, I do. I can assure you, his name is *not* Ain Rujgar."

"Who is he?"

Seri's face filled with rage. "His name is Qas Drugarish, a highly skilled Sicari assassin who works for the Breachers."

"Are you certain?"

"I recognize his face. This is the man who killed my father! Now we know he killed your parents as well. The only unanswered question is, who hired him?"

"There has to be a record of the person who approved the payment."

Seri kept looking at him strangely. "There is."

"Well, don't keep me in suspense! Who was it?"

"You, Nico."

"Excuse me?"

"The approving name on record for those transactions is Nico Callan."

"Ha, ha, very funny."

Seri's expression didn't change. An anxious feeling twisted in Nico's stomach as a thought occurred to him. "Seri, tell me you don't think I was working with your father's killer?"

Seri was digging through the parchments she had brought to his office.

"Seri, I was ten years old when my parents died. I loved them! I had never set foot in a vault at that age. I wouldn't have known how to arrange a business payment!"

"No, Nico. Of course not. I was just looking for this."

Nico slumped in his chair. "You've almost given me a heart attack, twice now!"

Seri rolled her eyes and gave him a pat on the cheek. "Someone has altered the record of approval. It's very professional work, but under magnification you can see that the perpetrator bleached and re-tinted the parchment. The tones don't quite match." Kayla watched him with a bemused expression. "Were you really less worried about being framed, than what I thought of you? Nico, anyone who knows you would never believe you'd be in league with an assassin. Besides, my father was murdered when you were six years old. I suppose if you had been seven, I might have wondered." She nudged him with her elbow and gave him kiss.

Nico blew out a breath. "So I have nothing to worry about."

"I didn't say that. Someone with high-level access at Callan International altered these files. If anyone ties these documents to the murder of your parents, you'll likely end up in prison. I think it's fair to assume that the authorities will conveniently discover this information at some point in the future."

"No one is going to believe that a ten-year-old boy hired an assassin to kill his own parents!"

"Nico, listen to me. It doesn't matter what the average person thinks. You will have to defend yourself in the courts. The Breachers own half of the magistrates. You can bet that the verdict of a trial will not be in your favour. This ledger will provide hard evidence. It won't matter to a crooked court whether the evidence is fabricated, only that they have something to point to."

"So, we get rid of the ledger, or change it back."

"Each ledger has a duplicate. One is missing. Anything we do now will make it appear as though you're the one responsible for tampering. When that missing copy surfaces, the absence or modification of this particular ledger would be incriminating."

Nico ran fingers through his hair and knotted his hands at the back of his head. "What do I do now?"

"The good news is that we discovered this before they made their move. That gives us a little time. We'll think of something."

Chapter 58

Beniti Abrax surveyed the control room. As Chief Sentry of the Kemetica Host, he spent much of his time here, directing operations. Located at the centre of the base, several levels down, the control room sat immediately above the Quantum Positioning Network on the lowest level.

The iron rich soil surrounding the lowest two levels had undergone a slagging process, heated through a matrix of boreholes ten cubits deep creating a first line of defence against potential tunnelling. One cubit of forged iron lined the interior walls. It was the most secure place on the base, accessible via a single entrance. Even so, Beniti was unsettled. The discovery that viewcorders were tracking some of his people meant that the Breachers had identified more of his operatives than he would have guessed. There was a very real risk that they could locate those operatives and send kill squads. None of his people were safe until they could figure out how the Breachers were doing it. He harboured a suspicion. It was why the Servators had been monitoring Denmount in the first place, but he didn't want to believe it.

Servators had always been years ahead of the Breachers in technology, but their sources for new tech had dwindled over the years. Meanwhile, Breacher technology had been playing catch up. He pounded his fist on his chair in frustration. Several heads turned his way. *Steady Beniti, they need your confidence right now.* As Chief Sentry of the Kemetica Host, he had voted against sharing technology when the council last gathered. Many in the Host felt it a Servator duty to share advancements with the world to reduce unnecessary suffering.

It wasn't that he was inherently selfish or wanted others to suffer, but if they lost their advantage to the Breachers, they risked everything. A great deal more suffering would occur if the Breacher plague wasn't restrained. So here they were, just as he feared. One Servator base shut down — his base possibly next in line. Reports of Servator deaths were coming in from bases around the world. They were under attack and no one wanted to be first to admit the dreaded cause. Facial recognition. No one spoke it because only those in command knew it was a harbinger of something far worse. If they didn't act quickly and decisively, it would be the end of them all. *Don't go there yet. First we need confirmation.*

He had sent Yori and Leviticus out with a team. It was a tested fact that those two could be tracked and they'd already volunteered. He wasn't happy about it, but they were the obvious choice. Leviticus's safety was of particular concern. He needed the young Mr. Radix to remain safe, so he could analyze whatever was recovered. Cello Vantos had filled Beniti in on the young man's work at Denmount and the Breacher's interest in him. Leviticus was the only one who would recognize facial recognition at play if it were possible to identify from what they could glean. Some of his men thought him overly cautious when he ordered two full compliments of rangers to accompany them, but Beniti wasn't taking any chances with their lives.

They still had some advantages over the Breachers. One of those was the ability to intercept writ weaves over a network. They couldn't directly access a secured memory stash archive, but the analysts always surprised him with how much information they could glean from a string of commands sent over a network.

Yori and Leviticus had spent the morning in the market near the viewcorder they had previously identified. They passed in and out of its field of view, moving at different speeds. They changed clothes, wore hats and made faces. They tried anything that might elicit a different string of commands while they captured every combination for later review. In this case they hoped to compare the captured viewcordings with any responding commands. It would confirm that a system was recognizing individuals. They also needed to understand the reaction to Leviticus. Why did the viewcorders shake whenever he entered the field of view?

Thankfully, the team had returned safely and now they were waiting for the analysts to compile what had been gathered. The Chief Sentry held on to hope that there were Breachers sitting at a desk somewhere viewing a live feed and manually entering commands to re-position the viewcorders. They could deal with the inefficiency of a manual system, but if it were automated....

"Sir? We've downloaded the captured viewcordings and writs. They're ready to view on your screen."

Beniti searched the faces in the room. "Mr. Radix?" Movement off to his left caught his attention and he saw a hand in the air.

"Here, sir!"

"Please, join me. The rest of you, go back to your regular monitoring duties."

"What do you need, sir?"

"I understand you were part of a team working on a facial recognition algorithm at Denmount."

"Yes, sir. Is that what you think this is? I have my doubts. The work at Denmount was the first of its kind. No one else I'm aware of is working on anything similar."

"But if it were something of the sort, would you be able to tell?"

"I believe so. The concepts are unique, but the approaches for this type of work are limited. If someone else is involved in similar research, I should be able to recognize it."

"Akhen tells me you're a promising student. I'll need you to apply what you've learned to identify anything peculiar, no matter how insignificant."

"I'll do my best."

Beniti adjusted the screen to give Leviticus a better view. He was amazed at how quickly the young man was able to scan through the content. Leviticus worked with a split viewscreen. The left side displaying an ongoing viewcording while the right displayed the corresponding writs. He slowed playback each time the viewcording began tracking a target.

"I don't understand how this is possible sir, but these writs do appear to be near instantaneous responses to an identification trigger. It's not something that a human operator could sustain. I would suspect that a memory stash archive is involved. Do you see this trigger point here? It..." He trailed off as his eyes widened.

"What is it?"

"That's not possible."

"What do you see?"

"Sir, every writ weaver has their own style of weaving. I recognize this command string. This is *my* weaving!"

"You wrote this?"

"During my tenure at Denmount, yes, but I swear to you I never had any dealings with Breachers! I signed a confidentiality covenant and by my honour, I upheld it, sir! All work was performed onsite. No weaving ever left the campus."

"Keep your voice down! No one is accusing you of anything."

Leviticus scrutinized him. Beniti had received that look from Akhen and he didn't like it at all. It made him feel exposed.

"You know something. Is this why the Breachers tried to abduct me?"

Beniti nodded once in affirmation. "Listen to me son, you need to keep that to yourself. A great deal is at stake and it needs to remain a secret for the time being."

"Understood, sir."

Beniti was certain Leviticus would have follow-up questions. If he were half as skilled as Akhen suggested, the boy would find his answers. He sighed. That was a problem for another day.

"Do you see anything else?"

Leviticus began scanning again. This time he spent more time on the sequences where the viewcorder was tracking him. His eyes had taken on that look Beniti had sometimes seen with Akhen. It was as if he was focused on something beyond the content he was scanning.

"There — that doesn't belong."

"What did you find?"

"It's a string of characters typical for a text message. It doesn't belong in this kind of instruction set. Someone has added text as if it were part of a command, but it can't actually do anything in this format."

"Explain."

Lev pointed at the screen. "Here, you can see some numbers, then an alert writ followed by a request for a helper writ. More numbers are appended at the end. That's it, nothing more."

"Do the numbers have any significance?"

"Hmmm. It looks a bit like a very basic cipher. Just give me a second."

Leviticus grabbed some parchment from the desk and looked askance.

Beniti handed him a writing instrument and Leviticus immediately began scribbling. "The cipher does produce words, but they don't make any sense. The first says *sage pet* and the final says *bricks*."

"So the whole text would essentially be — sage — pet — alert — helper — bricks." Beniti prompted.

"That's what it amounts to, yes."

A look of recognition and stunned disbelief fixed on the young man's face. "No! I can't believe he would stoop so low!"

"Mr. Radix, I'm not a mind reader."

"I had what I guess you could call a nemesis at Denmount. He was always giving me grief. He referred to me as the sage's pet. His name is Kade Brixton."

"Ah. Bricks. I see. So your friend found a way to get your attention and send a message addressed specifically to you, in a way that only you would understand. Very clever."

"He is *not* my friend! He's clearly a thief working with the Breachers."

"I don't think it's quite so simple as that. He has gone to great lengths to ensure that only you could find and understand his message. Why would he try to hide it from the Breachers if he were willingly working with them? Why would he try to contact you at all?"

"I don't know what his motivations are. I do know he's untrustworthy."

"Be that as it may, your ... least favourite acquaintance has put out a call for help. Knowing the way Breachers operate, I am inclined to believe he's under duress. Perhaps they abducted him just as they attempted with you."

That gave Lev pause, although he looked as if he were eating sour grapes during his contemplation. "I suppose it's possible, sir."

"Would it also be correct to assume that Mr. Brixton had a hand in implementing a facial recognition algorithm for the Breachers and would have knowledge on how to stop it?"

"That would be my conclusion, sir."

"Then it seems to me we have little choice, but to see where this leads."

Chapter 59

Chief Sentry Abrax had summoned Leviticus to his office.

Lev sat quietly in front of the desk waiting for him to finish reading a report. Like most Servators, the Chief Sentry was a fit man. Lev estimated his age to be around fifty-three. He was about Lev's height with dark skin and hair, greying at the temples.

His office wasn't as spartan as that of Chief Sentry Vantos back in Caralithica. It was orderly, however. The polished granite desk matched an ancient-looking statue standing in the corner of the room. The sculpture looked old, but he wasn't sure what it represented. *Some kind of cherub?* A leather couch along one wall looked like someone spent many nights on it, judging by the permanent indentation. Lev wondered when the Chief Sentry had been home last. Or maybe this was home. *I wonder if he has a family.*

Lev came back to attention as a throat was cleared. The Chief Sentry was watching him. *How long has he been waiting?* "Sorry, sir."

"It's fine son, you remind me of Akhen, and I'm used to dealing with him."

What's that supposed to mean? Lev wondered.

"I wanted to discuss our options regarding Kade Brixton."

"I think you should ignore him, sir."

The Chief Sentry smiled. "Perhaps you'd care to elaborate on your purely objective assessment?"

Lev felt his face heating. "I know how it sounds, but Kade has always been a manipulative bully.”

“You’ve never made a mistake?”

“Of course, but I’m not talking about mistakes. I don’t like the man, it’s true, but it’s not because our personalities clash. It’s because he has an untrustworthy character.”

“His message seemed a cry for help. Difficult experiences can be humbling. He may not be the same person you once knew. It’s the Maker’s Way to offer forgiveness and a second chance.”

Lev bit his tongue.

“You’ve made your objections clear, however it’s not your decision to make. We need more information and we need to determine whether Mr. Brixton can, or will, provide it. As for your concern about his honesty, it’s possible to lead a conversation in a way that exposes falsehood. I suspect Akhen has taught you something of how to use your talents in this regard?”

Lev nodded, considering the possibilities.

“First things first. I need to know if it’s feasible to subvert the information sent from the viewcorders. It would be helpful if we could give the appearance that everything is functioning normally while returning false information.”

“Are you hoping to have the viewcorders ignore identification writs specifically associated with Servators?”

“Is that possible?”

“Using the information we’ve collected so far, we could probably figure out which writs are in play for Yori and myself and weave something like you describe. The problem is that we don’t know the writs of any other Servators. We would need to monitor a viewcorder like we did before, and parade every Servator across its field of view to collect information whenever the device reacts.”

The Chief Sentry scratched his chin. “That sounds like a logistical nightmare.”

“We could probably automate it somewhat, but the bigger problem is sending false information back through the Breacher network. Our only point of access is through a very limited interface. We would need to install a device within every viewcorder on the network, assuming we even know where they all are. As part of that effort, we would need to have each viewcorder tied into the Servator memory stash to access the growing list of Servator identifiers the Breachers are collecting. Otherwise, we would need to update each camera manually every time we added a new identifier to the list. That's assuming the Breachers don't notice our tampering when a viewcorder inevitably requires repair by a network engineer."

The Chief Sentry interrupted. "You forget our token technology. It would be a simple matter to disguise our intrusion. The quantum positioning network could also come into play as far as creating a hidden connection to our own network. Communication through the ether is one area where we're still decades ahead of the Breachers."

Lev hadn't been thinking along those lines. Much of the Servator technology was still new to him. His mind was buzzing with possibilities. "To be honest, sir, if we're seriously considering putting in the effort to hijack every camera and tie them all to the Servator network, then we may as well go all the way. We could just create our own facial recognition algorithm. It would automate the whole process. By collecting our own identifiers of the general public, we could more easily compare responses against Servator identifiers from the Breacher network. It would give us more flexibility when responding to changes in the Breacher algorithm."

"Do you retain enough knowledge of your work at Denmount to recreate the algorithm from scratch?"

"I could do better than that. During my time at Denmount, I conceived numerous improvements, but it would have involved rebuilding from the ground up and the project lead had little interest in *going backwards*, as he put it."

The Chief Sentry looked thoughtful. "Let's leave this line of thinking for the moment. Perhaps we'll return to it if other options don't present themselves. What I'd really like to do is blow up the Breacher archive and be done with it. Far more satisfying!"

Lev let out a short bark of laughter. He hadn't expected a comment like that from an exalted commander. He needed to remember that Servators considered themselves servants. Titles didn't seem to puff them up like most leaders.

"Unfortunately, we don't have the resources or the location to consider such an endeavour. Which brings us back to Mr. Brixton and the chance, however unlikely, that he might be willing to help. So the question then becomes a simpler one. Can you communicate with Brixton through the Breacher network using a viewcorder interface?"

"That shouldn't be difficult. If Kade is expecting a response, then it would be logical to use the same method he employed. We could insert a message using false instructions and ciphers. If we can create a token disguised interface as you suggest, then it would make most sense to have it insert a response to the Leviticus Radix identification writ. If Kade is monitoring anything, it will be my location.

"If you want to make sure that he notices, then I'd suggest modifying a viewcorder close to a known Breacher stronghold. Once that's in place, I could appear within its field of view. Not only would it respond to me and send our message, but I suspect it would set off a proximity alert he couldn't ignore."

The Chief Sentry was frowning. "Mr. Radix, do you have a death wish? I wasn't comfortable with you parading in front of the viewcorders last time. That was in a relatively safe part of the city. Now you're suggesting I put you within arm's reach of a hotbed of Breacher activity? How exactly do you propose to follow up on your other suggestions should they become necessary? Kind of difficult to do from a Breacher cell."

"I don't know what to tell you, sir. I didn't ask for any of this, but the fact remains that the Breachers have an interest in me, as does Kade. That puts me in the thick of things whether I like it or not." Leviticus pressed the argument. "I don't enjoy feeling like a helpless victim. It's one of the reasons I agreed to join the Servator cause. When my efforts frustrate a Breacher, I feel like I've reclaimed some of what they've stolen from me. It gives me hope for a future."

"I suspect many Servators feel the same. Very well, talk with the analysts and see what you can come up with, something along the lines of a token derived viewcorder interface. I'd like you to weave an appropriate writ, one using your identifier and another using Yori's. You're not to be involved in the installation or testing of a Breacher viewcorder. I'll assemble a team under Yori's supervision who will be responsible for that. Let me know when it's ready. As for the rest — I need time to think."

Chapter 60

"So, how did I do this time?"

"Give me a minute." Akhen was busy resetting the testing stage and cataloguing results.

Lev released an overly loud sigh of frustration. "Every day we do this and every day it's the same result. I don't understand the point in continuing. Shouldn't we just focus on honing the abilities I currently have? How much longer are we going to continue with this exercise?"

"Yes! Twelve!"

"Twelve more times? That seems pretty arbitrary and not anywhere near as exciting as you make it sound."

"Leviticus, you identified twelve tokens in ten seconds. That's two more than my best! This is fantastic!" Akhen hugged him and danced around the room pumping his fists into the air.

"Um, has anyone ever told you that you're weird? Why are you so happy to be bested?"

"Because now I can finally teach you. Now I can finally learn again!"

"Like I said, weird."

"For all of these years, people have expected me to teach something that is beyond most of my students to learn. Believe me when I tell you, without progress, satisfaction wanes. From the first day we met, I knew you were different. Your natural abilities are far beyond any novice I've ever encountered, and I've seen many over the years. You see things in the way that I see things. I've managed to teach a few students to see dimly, but you see with clarity. More than that, in our time together it's become clear that you possess an extraordinary capacity I lack."

"What do you mean?"

"When we play a game of Jumkano, you never stop to think about your next move. You instantly react to mine. Do you know how you do that?"

"We're both playing to win, so when you move along the path toward victory, I block or counter with an advance of a higher threat, forcing you to block in your next turn."

"Yes, yes, of course," Akhen waved away Lev's explanation. "I'm not asking you how the game is played. I'm asking how Leviticus Radix can move without thinking and still win the game."

"You can only move so many ways if you intend to win."

"And how is it you know that my turn is the beginning of an inevitable path? I could be attempting to misdirect you."

"It doesn't matter. I would just compare any move you made with potential moves and countermoves."

"Exactly! You've memorized all possible permutations of the game."

"Plenty of Jumkano masters can do that. I don't always win."

"So, you're a Jumkano master now?" Akhen teased.

"That's not what I meant."

"I know, and therein lies the difference. I'd like to try something. Please return to your position in front of the testing stage."

Lev groaned, but complied.

Akhen made some adjustments on his Q-view and the stage populated with the familiar tokens. "Okay, I want you to rearrange the tokens to the positions they were in fifteen days ago, during your first attempt of the day."

Lev was incredulous. "What? That's impossible. I can't do that. No one can!"

"I believe *you* can."

"You can believe the sun is purple if you'd like, but that doesn't make it so."

"Humour me, Leviticus. It won't hurt to make the attempt. Don't overthink it. Just imagine you are playing Jumkano and make what you know is the correct move."

Lev shook his head and turned to face the stage. *This is insane.*

"Begin," Akhen persisted.

Not knowing what else to do, Lev imagined himself on that day and was astounded to realize he remembered a great deal about that particular morning. The clothes that Akhen wore and the smell of kofa with a hint of cinnamon as was Akhen's preference. He remembered hearing an argument in the hallway and feeling the beginnings of a headache. He remembered seeing the date and time at the top of the Q-view screen as he looked over Akhen's shoulder at the previous day's results. Then he remembered standing in front of the stage and realized he did know where everything belonged.

Lev followed his impulse, quickly moving each token to the position he felt was correct. He didn't need to first identify where tokens had moved because he had done this before. He executed the task and held up his hand indicating completion.

Akhen stopped the timer. "Seven seconds. Let's see how you did." Akhen split the screen. The original placement from first attempt fifteen days ago was on the left, Lev's attempt at recreating it was on the right. Akhen carefully compared the two before casting a look of consternation at Lev. "We've been wasting time!"

"I told you it wouldn't work." Lev countered defensively.

"Your recall is one hundred percent accurate. It's as I suspected. When you play Jumkano, you draw from the memory of every game you have ever played. If you played often enough with a variety of people, at some point you would be unbeatable."

Lev wasn't sure if he should be enthusiastic or horrified. *I'm some kind of freak after all.*

"How precisely do you access these memories? How do you catalogue them? Is it a component of your observational acuity or something else? Is it a process others could learn? I have so many questions and so many tests in mind."

Lev shrank back involuntarily. He knew that look in Akhen's eye. Training would redouble.

"Starting tomorrow, we will cut back on all your other areas of study. You will be spending the majority of your time with me. We have a great deal of ground to cover and much more still to discover."

Akhen suddenly became uncharacteristically silent. He fixed Lev with a look mixed with longing and uncertainty as though he needed to express something for which he lacked words.

"Leviticus, I-I want to thank you. I never thought this day would come, but here you are. All I ever wanted was to explore the limits of my abilities. Far too soon, I found no one left to teach me. Every time I'm tasked with tutoring others, I'm reminded that I may never learn more about my own gift. But, now? Now, I finally have a student to whom I can impart absolutely everything I know. More importantly, I can begin to learn again! Together we will discover new things about this gift we share. Your unique perspective will reveal avenues I would never have considered on my own. Even if I'm unable to achieve the same results, I will know what is possible. I will have new challenges to overcome. You cannot comprehend the value I place on this gift. I pray that you will not deny me this opportunity to pursue something I thought I could only dream about."

The fervent plea ignited something in Lev. Hadn't he always been searching to understand his gift? Here standing before him was the one man in all the world who could help more than any other. This celebrated instructor was begging Lev to let him make the attempt. He could feel that same earnestness growing within and realized he too lacked the words. Instead, he held out his hand.

Akhen grasped the offered hand with both of his. The gratitude in his eyes would carry Lev through the inevitable frustrations of future training sessions.

No longer will I play the role of victim forced into training. Lev realized. *I want this. I choose this*. He saw that Akhen understood. A silent agreement passed between them. Tomorrow was a new beginning and the start of a different relationship. Now they were peers. Neither knew where it would lead.

Chapter 61

It had taken a great deal of convincing. In the end, the Chief Sentry reluctantly agreed to include Lev in the operation. Yori had led a team through the city of Ebot to locate viewcorders that reacted to his presence. *It must be unnerving to know someone is watching your every move.* The thought made Lev shudder. Yori's efforts revealed several remote locations that were suitable for phase one. At least three of those options were near known Breacher facilities, suitable for the second phase of their plans.

In preparation, the team had removed one of the viewcorders, bringing it to the base for study. Lev was able to prepare a writ weave for the interface they had developed. Once the viewcorder was in the lab, they were able to establish communication with the device and locate the best place to hide an intercept token within. The analysts had mapped the coordinates of the viewcorder's interior in proximity to the lens on the exterior of its housing. When the time came, an operative would only need to place their Q-view in position over the lens and submit those coordinates. From there, the Quantum Positioning Network could materialize the token in the correct location within the casing of their target viewcorder. As long as it was the same model, the integration was seamless.

The procedure had been tested on a few remote cameras with a high success rate. That efficiency and speed of placement would be critical once they were in Breacher territory. Anyone climbing up to a viewcorder would be highly visible and extremely vulnerable.

With all groundwork prepared in advance, Yori's team completed phase one during the night. The team remained undetected as they inserted an intercept token into the target viewcorder. Now that the sun had risen, it was time for the bait. Yori gathered the team for final instructions before they returned to the scene of the previous night's activities to attempt phase two of the operation.

"I don't need to remind you of the danger. Leviticus is untrained and will be exposed. Due to Breacher proximity, we'll have very little time to respond. The Chief Sentry wanted to make clear that under no circumstance is Leviticus to take unnecessary risks. If the Breachers target Leviticus, and their numbers are overwhelming, we will retreat immediately without exception. Is everyone equipped with stun batons?" The team sounded off in affirmation.

"You are not to use that ordinance in public view. Wait until you're at one of the designated muster points. Let's go over the details once more.

"Leviticus?"

Leviticus repeated his part. "Yori will give a brief appearance within the viewcorder's field of view. I will test our connection to the token and determine if it's receiving Yori's identification string. Then, I will perform a second test to see if we can insert our own instructions. Once I've confirmed that both are working, Yori will immediately move to his coordinating position on the rooftop across the street and I will wait for Tark to initiate the next phase."

Tark picked up where Lev left off. "When Yori confirms that all teams are in position, Leviticus will begin his walk down the middle of the street. Dav, Lindar, Previt and I will be following at a distance of twenty cubits. The analysts have set our Q-views to chime when the viewcorder identifies Lev and begins tracking him. Things will begin moving quickly by that point. Our hope is to enter the destination alley unimpeded, but we need to make sure Lev is detectable long enough for the Breachers to respond. In the event Breachers appear before we reach the safe zone, we're to scatter. Each of us will head toward our assigned route. I will remain with Leviticus. The rest of the team will be waiting in groups of four at each of the designated muster points."

Yori took over for final instructions. "You are authorized to engage with any Breachers that pursue along those routes. Once you have disabled a threat, or if you see no pursuit along your route, you are to proceed to the closest remaining muster point to provide backup. Keep your ears open to your Q-view prompts. I will be coordinating from my vantage point as much as possible. When all of us have gathered at the final muster point, we will leave immediately in the waiting ground transport. Any questions?"

No one responded, so Yori simply said, "Whenever you're ready, Radix."

Over the last few days, Lev had kept his mind occupied with writ weaving and other preparations. He hadn't given much thought to his role in this part of the plan. Now that the time had come, his stomach was in knots. *What was I thinking? Why not wear a lambskin and walk into the lion's den while I'm at it?* "I'm ready."

"Gentlemen, take your positions and wait for my mark."

Far too quickly, everyone was in place and the time for thinking was past.

"I'm making myself visible to the viewcorder now." Yori's voice came over the Q-view as Lev checked the token for the expected response. "The Breacher network has transmitted an identity. The token has successfully returned a false writ to mask Yori's identity," Lev announced.

"I can confirm that the viewcorder has moved on and is ignoring my presence." That was good news. The team waited as Yori moved to the rooftop.

"I'm in position." Yori was barely visible behind the parapet on the rooftop. "Proceed."

"Go!" Lev felt a shove from Tark.

Lev inhaled deeply and walked briskly to the middle of the street. *Slow down Lev, you need to give them time to react.* That was easier said than done. His flight response was screaming. Lev was about halfway to his destination when a door flew open to the sound of shouted commands.

"Run, Lev!" Tark shouted.

Dav, Lindar and Previt scattered. The Breachers were confused for a moment until someone ordered them to split up and give chase.

Lev heard Tark yelp in pain. He risked a quick glance over his shoulder. Someone had thrown a knife and Tark was on his knees, "No! Tark!"

"Don't stop!" Tark screamed. "Go, go, go!"

Two of Lev's pursuers were overweight and out of shape. Lev left them far behind, but one pursuer persisted. He was young and Lev couldn't shake him. *I just need to get to the muster point — backup is waiting.* Lev turned into his designated alley and prepared for his next turn into a secondary alley. In his panic, he turned left instead of right and was confronted with a dead end. Chest heaving, Lev spun to face his pursuer. The brute outweighed him and he had an ugly sneer on his face. The Breacher closed the remaining distance quickly and attacked without hesitation. Lev didn't react quickly enough and knuckles grazed his chin. A wave of fear washed over him and then he heard a voice. *Remember your training.* His body fell into the stance his warkata instructor had drilled into him. Akhen's training kicked in right after that.

The details of his environment came into sharp focus. The smell of rotting waste, a fly moving leisurely past his face. Everything slowed from his perspective as he catalogued his surroundings. The Breacher's left hip turned slightly, right heel lifting off the ground, shoulder dipping. It was like a child moving a Jumkano piece clumsily across the board. *Left jab incoming* — Lev's hand moved past his face, the fly spun, buffeted by the air disturbed in its passing. Lev blocked and redirected the attack as his fingers curled around his opponent's wrist. Twisting at the waist, Lev leaned back and pulled the Breacher over his extended leg and to the ground. Suddenly, Lev was on top of him. Striking — first in panic and then in rage. *They hurt Tark! They tried to hurt me!* His mind went grey as he struck again and again.

"Lev, stop! You'll kill him!" A hand grabbed his wrist before it could descend. It was Tark, he had a bloody wound on his shoulder.

"Tark?"

"He's not a threat anymore! Stop!"

Lev came to his senses and looked down. The man's face was a mess. He felt nauseous, but stood up prepared to run. "We have to go, more are coming!"

"No, Leviticus. We stunned them when they entered the alleys. The rest of the team will be here shortly and we aren't leaving without *him*." Tark pointed at the fallen Breacher and then knelt to feel for a pulse. "Why didn't you just stun him?"

"I — I don't know. I panicked."

"You nearly ended his life is what you did. We don't kill, Lev. Not if we can possibly avoid it."

"He would have killed *me*! How can you defend him? He's a Breacher!"

Tark threw him a dark look and stalked off as the others arrived. Yori tried to assess Tark's shoulder, but Tark shrugged him off and kept walking. Taking in the scene, Yori ordered the men to carry the Breacher to their transport.

"What will happen to him?" Lev asked.

"We'll care for his wounds and then he'll spend a year or two on one of our rehabilitation islands. He deserves a chance to see what life can be like — away from Breacher influence. A lot of these young men have never had a caring family. They don't know any other way. Once his obligatory time is complete, he'll have the option to leave. Many choose to stay. If a Breacher returns to their former activities, we imprison them for life if they're caught again."

"I don't understand. Why would you accept that risk? Tark took a Breacher knife to the shoulder and then got angry with me for retaliating! It makes no sense."

"Lev, Tark was one of those who received grace on a rehabilitation island. When you threatened to take away a Breacher's hope for redemption, you were attacking Tark, and he's one of the most loyal men I know. All of us deserve a second chance. Remember that the next time you have the urge to judge someone. Come, we can't remain in this area. We've accomplished our goal and the others are waiting. Once we're back at the base, you have a message to send to someone else who needs a second chance."

Chapter 62

Kade rubbed his eyes. It had been a sleepless night. He and Selica had argued when Kade vented at their lack of progress in finding an escape. He had suggested an admittedly risky plan and she'd shot it down. In a moment of frustration, he'd lost his temper. "Do you even *want* to leave?" The hurt in her eyes spoke volumes and he'd immediately regretted his outburst. Unfortunately, the words were already out and it was too late to take them back. She hadn't responded, she didn't need to. She just grabbed her bag and left.

He looked across the lab at Selica for the tenth time in as many minutes. She was ignoring him. *You deserve it, you jerk*. Kade sighed. It wasn't the first time he'd let his temper get him into trouble. Time weighed heavily on the scales that were Kade's shoulders, balanced by an equal weight of guilt. Every day, people died because of the algorithm he had woven for the Breachers. Nightmares plagued him. He wasn't sure how long he would have lasted on his own. Selica was the one good thing in his life and now he'd messed that up. *Maybe she just needs a little time*.

Decar was pacing behind him. The Third Anarch had been pressuring him for greater results. That grief rolled downhill and fell into Kade's lap.

"Status?"

"Nothing new to report, Decar. You'll know when I know."

"It's not your family the Third Anarch is threatening. Can't you make this thing work faster?"

Kade felt a twinge of guilt. He wasn't particularly fond of Decar, but he would hate to see the man's children suffer at Villecrest's hand. He thought of Selica's childhood — victim to Toller's cruelty. Kade glanced at Selica again. He wouldn't wish that on anyone. How could he have questioned her desire to leave? *Stupid! Stupid!*

"We need to round up at least four more Servators before the week's end or the man will have my hide!"

Villecrest's bloodlust was unquenchable. Kade didn't know how many more excuses he could give for the lack of progress. Something had to give. His station chimed and he returned his attention to the screen. A proximity alert was blinking. Decar was there in a flash.

"What is it?" He demanded.

"A proximity alert in Kemetica."

"Show me!"

Kade pulled up a map. The coordinates were for the city of Ebot near the warehouse district.

Decar pointed at the display. "That's a Breacher distribution facility. What fool Servator would risk coming so close? This could be what we're waiting for! If we foil a Servator attack on one of our assets, we can take out several of them simultaneously. We would meet our quota while proving the value of this system for something other than finding targets for the kill squad."

Kade eyed Decar curiously. Could it be that the murders were weighing on him as well? Regardless, it was a good thought and a possible new avenue of delay. Maybe they could play on Villecrest's paranoia to convince him that it was in his best interest to spend time monitoring Breacher assets with the viewcorders instead of spending all of their time hunting Servators.

"What are you staring at me for? Eyes front! Give us access to the viewcorder. I want to see what's going on."

Kade pulled up feeds for several viewcorders in the area. It was early morning in Kemetica and the streets were still empty. All, that is, except for one. Four individuals were casually walking past the Breacher facility. One was slightly ahead of the others, but they were obviously together. What were they doing? The pace looked forced, almost as if they were hoping someone would notice them.

"Can you make it bigger?" Decar was uncomfortably close as he pushed his face nearer to the screen.

Kade zoomed in on the lead individual and jerked in surprise, catching Decar on the chin with his shoulder.

"What's the matter with you, Brixton?" Decar exclaimed.

"Sorry, not enough sleep."

It looked like Leviticus. It couldn't be. What would he be doing in Ebot?

Decar yelled across the lab at Selica. "Lor! Contact the head of this facility. I need to speak with him!"

Kade cut the feed and called up the algorithm results.

"What are you doing? Bring it back!"

"Don't you want to see if the algorithm recognizes these people as Servators before you contact the facility? What if it's just some revellers finding their way home after a late night?"

"Then do that split screen thing! I need to see what's happening."

Kade complied and a second later wished he hadn't as two names appeared on the screen. One of them was indeed a Servator. The other was an impossibility.

"Of all the dumb luck!" Decar breathed, "It's Leviticus Radix! We've been scouring Caralithica for him. What's he doing in Kemetica? Never mind, it doesn't matter. If we can catch Radix, we'll score serious points with the Third Anarch. It will validate our efforts."

Selica appeared behind Decar with a worried look on her face, "You should be connected with the facility now."

Decar pulled out his tote-comm. "Who am I speaking with? Who's in charge? Well, go get him! Tell him the assistant to the Third Anarch of Caralithica has orders!" Decar tapped his foot impatiently as he waited. "I don't care if you were sleeping, you incompetent fool! Servator operatives are standing outside of your facility. You need to act — now. The youngest one is important to the Third Anarch. We need him alive. If you accomplish this, I will see to it that you receive a handsome reward. If you fail, I will be reporting your incompetence to the Anarchs of Kemetica. You can explain to *them* how Servators went unnoticed at the doorstep of a major Breacher asset! Contact me immediately when you've succeeded." Decar closed the connection and returned his attention to events unfolding in Ebot. It didn't take long before Breachers were streaming into the viewcorder's field of view. A squat man appeared to be passing orders.

Kade went rigid. *Radix, you idiot, what are you doing? Run!* A moment later the four men on screen scattered with Breachers in pursuit. His attention was fixed on Leviticus. Two of the three that were giving chase dropped behind, but one was hot on his heels. Then they were out of range. Decar slammed his hand on the table. "Get them up on another viewcorder!"

Kade did a quick check for resources, but no other viewcorders were in the vicinity. "Nothing else is available. We'll need to wait to hear back from your contact." Kade felt like one big bundle of anxiety. He had known contacting Radix was a long shot, but all hope would be lost if the Breachers captured him. He hadn't realized how tenaciously he clung to that small chance. Dread filled him. It was the worst possible outcome. Another escape plan would be dashed, and if Radix wound up in Breacher clutches, they wouldn't need Kade Brixton anymore. That scenario ended one way for him and that wasn't the escape he was after. *I need Radix to live*, he realized. It was bad enough watching strangers die. *I can't bear it happening to someone I know. Not even Leviticus.*

Nothing was happening onscreen, but a Breacher might reappear with a victim in tow at any moment. Kade moved the viewcorder feed to a large screen in the middle of the lab, luring Decar away. He needed to be alone to think. Could he do anything from here that might help? Who was he kidding? He couldn't even see what was happening. Decar's tote-comm chimed. Kade held his breath.

"You lost all of them? How is that even possible?" Decar was raging now. Kade released his breath and tuned him out. He'd heard Decar's diatribes before. It was enough that Radix had escaped. Kade could still hope that Leviticus would get his message one day. Turning back to his screen, he noticed an error code in the bottom left corner. He had missed it in all the excitement. *Now what?* He opened an editor to check the writ weave. *That's odd. I don't recall inserting that instruction set.* He'd have to ask Selica if she had made some modifications.

It looked oddly familiar. Maybe something they had been working on together after hours? Then he saw it. A false instruction set. It contained a familiar cipher along with a message in the form of commands. He highlighted the section with shaking hands.

-Brick-initiating-helper-sequence-sage-pet-

Chapter 63

Akhen felt like he had a new lease on life. Working with Leviticus the last few weeks had been invigorating! He'd known for years that he wasn't happy with his current role. He hadn't realized until now the degree to which it had been crushing his spirit. No one else could fill his shoes, so he continued on. It was necessary. But now he woke excited to see what each new day would bring. He was eager to advance and to test himself again. It had been so long since he felt challenged. It was a precious gift from the Maker and he intended to take full advantage of this providence.

Akhen reminded himself not to push Leviticus too hard in his own eagerness. *Let the revelations come as they will, Akhen. You have time.* He considered the list of things he still needed to teach the boy. Standard analyst training would prove a trifle for Leviticus. The boy could absorb like a sponge and retain what he learned indefinitely. Akhen had decided to get the basics out of the way first so they could move on to more interesting endeavours. Leviticus was already familiar with the use of his wrist Q-view for communication, but all analysts needed to master token formation.

"What am I doing wrong?" Lev asked. A malformed lump sat on the stage.

"Did you memorize the directory for basic token templates?"

"I memorized the directory for *all* of the token templates in the archive."

Could he really have memorized the entire directory? Of course, he could. Akhen knew better than to question Leviticus's ability in this regard. So, why was he having difficulty? As long as an analyst knew the general location of a template, they could quickly find what was needed. Invoking a token was a relatively simple matter of providing coordinates and a template to the quantum positioning network. The QPN would handle the rest, following a blueprint provided by the template to materialize the requested token at the appropriate location. Most novices understood the concept immediately. Where they struggled was memorizing the directory, so they could quickly find what they were looking for. Memorizing was painless for Leviticus, and he was clearly using proper coordinates, so why couldn't he correctly materialize a template? The process should be foolproof.

"Akhen? Can I ask you a question?"

"Of course, that *is* why we're here."

"It's a personal question."

"I see. I'm not just your instructor, Leviticus — I'm your mentor as well. I hope you feel comfortable discussing anything that's on your mind." Akhen was pleased. Leviticus had started to open up since they had become peers of a sort.

"When I was still in Caralithica, Chief Sentry Vantos told me that not all Servators held the same views on the Maker's Way. She seemed to suggest that some supported the Servator cause and agreed with its principles, but not necessarily its beliefs."

"Following Servator principals is the same as following the Maker's Way. They are one," Akhen responded.

"So why don't those who adhere to the principles hold the same beliefs?" Lev countered.

Akhen rubbed his chin as he considered the question. "Ah. You're not asking about statutes or lifestyle choices. You wonder about articles of faith?"

Leviticus remained uncertain. "Perhaps. I understand that regulations are necessary to function in a large organization like the Servator Host. I also understand that guiding principles help define goals. Yet it seems to me the two aren't quite as singular as you suggest. Servator hierarchy provides structure while the Maker's Way provides an ideal for ethical and moral behaviour."

"Yes, I suppose you could divide them in that way, but what I meant was, they have a united purpose."

"But what is that purpose? Increasing good while diminishing evil is a worthy goal, if it's possible to delineate the difference. However, that alone does not seem to be a consistent driver."

"Can you provide an example?"

"You've heard about my recent altercation with a Breacher?"

Akhen frowned. The violent encounter had indeed been reported to him.

"There, you see! You disapprove. "It's not the Maker's Way," Tark told me. I couldn't understand his reasoning at the time. I later learned that he was once a Breacher. That revelation provided some context, but clearly I'm missing something. I can accept that I failed a moral imperative, but it felt like Tark was focussed on something entirely different."

"And what do you think he was focussed on?

"Redemption."

Lev's astute observation impressed Akhen, but he remained silent, sensing more to come.

"Life here feels like an unfinished puzzle, and I'm the only one who notices the missing pieces. It's as if some unspoken fear is about to reveal itself — something only a few know and hold close. The Chief Sentry himself swore me to secrecy on a matter, with no explanation. I could tell he was afraid. Moral codes and organizational statutes are *not* driving these men, they are moved alternately by fear and gratitude."

Akhen had his arms across his chest, one hand lifted to pinch the bridge of his nose. He hadn't expected to have this conversation so soon. He wasn't certain it was his place to speak of such things. The boy's abilities were ranked high enough that he would learn sooner or later. Lev interrupted his thoughts.

"From the look on your face, I suspect you're one of those who is familiar with the unspoken?"

"What do you wish to know, Leviticus?"

"Do you believe in the prophecy of a coming flood?"

Akhen peered into Leviticus's eyes. *Could he have figured it out on his own? No. Impossible.*

"We have come full circle. You are indeed asking about faith. It is what drives the Chief Sentry, Tark and yes, myself. Sometimes truth is undeniable. We may not fully comprehend it but neither can we ignore it. I believe in the Maker's Way as I believe in the Maker Himself. And in answer to your question, Yes, I believe in the prophecy of the coming flood. It is truth."

"How do you know?"

Akhen made a decision. "Come with me. You need to see something."

Chapter 64

Toller struggled between the two Sicari, attempting to free himself, "Let go of me! I'll have your heads for this! Release me! Obey your Anarch! Where have you brought me?"

"Welcome, subject Villecrest."

Toller was practically frothing. "I'm no subject! I am Third Anarch!" Raising his eyes to see Kenric smiling at him did nothing to reduce his ire. "Trantor! What is the meaning of this?"

Careful Kenric, calculate each move. Perhaps a dig at his position? "I wished to receive a report." *He seems affronted. Excellent.*

"A report? You had me abducted to demand a report? You could have used approved channels! This is unacceptable! You arrogate authority beyond your right. Who do you think you are?"

"I am Second Anarch and you are beneath me."

Toller lunged, but the two Sicari held fast.

Careful now. We can't have him flying into a rage. "Pardon me, I meant to say you are below me in the chain of command. A slip of the tongue, nothing more."

Toller was glaring at him with raw hatred. "I'm an anarch! I demand the respect of my rank!"

Shift to contrition. Appeal to his sense of superiority. "Of course. My apologies. I merely wished to discuss your recent achievements." He waved for the Sicari to release their charge and dismissed them. "The Sicari were to escort you. Surely you don't hold me accountable for their actions. You know how brutish they can be." Kenric raised an eyebrow. *Two equals sharing their disdain for the servants.*

Toller snorted in derision and nodded. "Unthinking animals."

"Exactly so. Necessary at times, but near impossible to control." *Stroke his ego.* "You are the only anarch I have ever invited here. Did those two oafs honestly believe I would allow any but an honoured guest into my personal chambers?"

Toller looked around for the first time, perplexed.

"Please, take a seat. Can I offer you a drink? I have a very fine seventeen-year-old wine from Arapanus."

Toller accepted the offer as he reclined, clearly caught off guard.

That's right, you misread the situation. I'm the docile lounger you've always imagined, not the least bit threatening. Kenric poured them each a mug from the same bottle as Toller watched. Then he sipped from one before handing it to his guest. Proper precautionary etiquette among Breacher elite. *You see? I treat you as an equal.*

Toller visibly relaxed as he accepted the mug and took a draft. Kenric hadn't tainted the wine with toxins, but he did have it fortified to increase the alcohol content. Kenric mimicked his guest's pulls on the mug but was merely sipping. He topped off both of their mugs and returned to their conversation. "I understand you have developed a way to track the Servators."

"More of them die at my command every day. Soon we will be rid of them all."

"Then I suppose I must congratulate you on your success. Will you be ramping up to spread your program among Breacher factions around the world?"

"I haven't yet decided how I will deploy *my* operation."

Ah, there we go. Heavy emphasis on the word 'my'. "I have many contacts among the Breacher leadership around the world. Perhaps I can offer assistance?"

"*You* want to offer *me* assistance?"

"I do have a great deal of experience in large operations."

Toller scoffed. "Surely you're not referring to that pathetic little uprising all those long years ago?"

Good, the wine is having its intended effect. Kenric put on an indignant air.

"That was a very successful operation involving hundreds of operatives!"

"You're living in the past. What have you done since?"

Brazen, this one. I wonder how he lasted this long? "I have many irons in the fire. As it happens, your little project has been interfering with my own operations. It would seem you could use a little oversight." *Careful...*

"Oversight! You don't fool me, Trantor. You still cling to the tattered glory of your pitiful uprising. No one cares anymore! My work threatens to overshadow that ancient achievement. Your performance has been lacklustre ever since."

A little pleading... "I can help you. You need me."

"I don't need anyone — least of all, *you*. Look around old man. You've surrounded yourself with indulgence. You've gone soft."

Now, set the trap. "You answer to me! I am Second Anarch! You will submit to my leadership in this matter or suffer the consequences."

Toller didn't so much as flinch. The lack of response astonished Kenric. An angry anarch was not one to be trifled with among the Breachers. Yet Toller showed no fear. Kenric had hoped that would be the case, but he wondered again how the man had made it this far. A part of him worried that he may have overplayed his hand.

Toller interrupted his train of thought, "I do not recognize your authority!"

"You have no choice."

"I do. I appeal to the overlords."

Of course, you do. "I don't think that would be wise."

"No surprise you'd think so, and yet I demand an audience, as is my right." Toller stood, his smug sneer dripped with arrogance as he looked down his nose.

"I can present your objection to the overlords."

"You're afraid! Has no one challenged your competence before?" Toller's eyes widened with the look of someone who had just grasped a hidden truth. A cruel smile of triumph followed. "You *will* grant me an audience, now, and preserve what little dignity you have left. If you refuse, I will take the key from you by force."

Kenric did not speak, or look Toller in the eye, as he retrieved the key and moved to unlock the door of the overlords. Then he spoke truthfully. "Only a fool would go through that door."

"We'll see who's the fool. Enough delay. Open the door — now!"

Kenric obliged. *So predictable.*

Toller strode in. Kenric closed the door and locked it.

It took longer than he expected, but soon he heard the anticipated pounding on the door. Then a desperate scrabbling near the floor. Kenric turned on some music just in time to drown out the screams.

Chapter 65

Lev had never been to this part of the base. He was surprised when they began descending. In his limited experience, the concept of being below the surface was a one level affair. Getting used to living on the base had meant ignoring the weight of earth above his head. One layer's worth was more than enough to contemplate. The assumption was silly, he realized. An underground complex could expand lower in the same way an above-ground structure could rise higher.

It seemed that they had descended several levels before reaching their destination. Security was tight. Several guards held the familiar stun batons and a sonic cannon was mounted above a heavily reinforced door. Akhen approached one of the guards and said something Lev couldn't quite hear. A password, perhaps. The guard held his Q-view to a panel and then stepped aside. The second guard did the same.

The door squealed in protest as it slowly rolled aside. It was so massive that the threshold felt more like a tunnel than an entryway. What could possibly require such protection? Lev felt he had comported himself well, considering all he had seen so far. Even so, the gravitas of this place unnerved him.

The room was circular. About eighteen cubits in diameter. Viewscreens covered the walls, and people sat at workstations busy with unknown tasks. In the centre of the room, one viewscreen dominated. Or at least Lev thought of it as some kind of viewscreen. It seemed to him more like an open window. That was, of course, impossible — they were deep underground. One more technological wonder to add to his list of new discoveries.

An analyst, senior ranked in appearance, spotted Lev and protested. "Akhen! What is the meaning of this? Novices are not allowed in this room without proper clearance!" Akhen lifted calming hands. "He exceeds me, Hemish. You understand our need better than most. Would you deny him? It's inevitable that he will be shown this place."

Hemish nodded, a glint of hope in his eyes. "I defer to your judgment in this, Akhen."

All activity ceased as everyone turned to look at them. Akhen walked to the centre of the room and waved Lev forward. He advanced, mesmerized by the tableau. "It looks so real." He shifted unconsciously to that way of seeing which set him apart. "It's the same, but different. Like I know this place, but it doesn't belong here."

The view before him was of a grassy slope. At what seemed a little less than arm's length away, stood a single flower in full bloom. It was too vivid, somehow. Unnatural. It drew the eye away from everything else. "Akhen, what am I looking at?"

"You might think of it as a portal to a kin world."

Kin world? Lev wanted to turn and ask Akhen for a better explanation, but he couldn't seem to avert his gaze. His entire being was focused on the... *What did Akhen call it? Portal?* Without knowing why, he reached through and plucked the flower. *Definitely not a viewscreen.* He marvelled at the flower in his hand, transfixed. His stupor evaporated when someone from across the room gasped, "It can't be!" He looked around. Every face was staring at him with a mixture of awe and fear.

"Um, what's going on? Akhen? Why is everyone staring at me like I just grew horns?"

They were gathering around him. Some were touching him, checking to see if he was real or perhaps an apparition.

"What's happening?" Lev was frantically pushing away hands, moving away from the pressing bodies.

Akhen appeared at his side. "Forgive them, Leviticus. Something of this magnitude hasn't occurred for a very long time. The last instance was over seventeen hundred years ago. Most thought it would never happen again.

Certainly not in their lifetime. Leviticus, you may have just become the most important person in the world."

Chapter 66

I can't believe it actually worked! The message of the previous day lingered in his mind's eye. Kade didn't quite know how to feel. He was elated, of course, but the part of him that had hated Radix for so long was displeased. If anyone might notice his desperate attempt, he suspected it would be Leviticus. Having that suspicion proven only served as a reminder that Radix really was superior to other people. Oh, how desperately he wanted that to be untrue.

Old feelings of rivalry surfaced, but he was also profoundly grateful to have contact with someone from his former life. It galled that his nemesis might become his rescuer, but the far greater discomfort of his current circumstances offset any reservations. *Stop it, Kade. You are not that man anymore!*

What was Radix doing in Kemetica? And why was he in the company of Servators? It made no sense. As far as he knew, Leviticus had never travelled beyond the borders of Denmount. The how didn't matter, he realized. It addressed a far bigger concern. When he originally concocted this plan, he had spent many sleepless nights wondering what Radix could do to help if he found the message. Would he go to the City Sentinels? That seemed the only reasonable expectation, but first Kade would need to find a way to let Radix know where he was and what kind of trouble he was in.

Supposing he could somehow explain his plight, it seemed unlikely the Caralithican authorities could act on the information. Would they believe him? Would they have any jurisdiction in Sumakad? And why would the local authorities of Denmount even bother? Yes, they would like to question him about his role in the possible theft of intellectual property, but would they actually consider confronting a foreign power for a suspicion? Their efforts wouldn't gain a commensurate reward.

Kade had heard too many of Selica's stories and spent enough time with the Breachers himself to know that contacting Denmount authorities might make things worse. The Anarch's reach was long. Even if Leviticus were to stumble upon a trustworthy person, any attempt at rescue would require a force. What were the odds that word of Kade's predicament would reach uncorrupted ears? If word got back to Villecrest, Kade would be dead before anyone could even consider an investigation. The prospects of success for a martial intervention were poor and the chance that Radix could do anything of value on his own was depressingly low.

Yesterday's revelations had given him new hope. If Radix had a connection to the Servators, it was an entirely different matter. Servators had reason to intervene in Breacher affairs. Servators had the operatives and resources. In fact, the more he thought about it, Servators were the only ones who actually stood a chance of performing a rescue.

It was pointless to overthink. He had this opportunity and he had to find a way to make it work. Kade hadn't known how Leviticus might acknowledge the receipt of his message. He hadn't figured that far ahead. The only thought he'd given the matter was that he would run the first message for a week, then send a new message with his location the following week. He would repeat that process until something happened.

It had astonished Kade when Radix's message appeared on his screen. The network was protected from external writs that might try to send a command. Radix had been very clever. He'd found a way to insert a message into his own identifier. The algorithm considered it to be the expected response, at the expected time, to the expected conditions. The parsing writ had ignored extra characters. *Leviticus would never have left a security gap like that.* Kade scolded himself.

"What's wrong with you, man?" Kade shook his head. *It was never your goal to protect Breacher assets. You've been developing a writ contagion, for crying out loud.* Kade chuckled at himself and composed a response to Leviticus's message. He used the same method, but decided to obscure his identity further by shortening it to a few characters. Radix knew what to look for now.

He started a few times and finally entered -sp-query-initiate-exit-br- and inserted the new writ into the algorithm. The system flagged a new sighting for Leviticus almost immediately. "That's odd," he muttered. "It shows his location as still in Kemetica, but in an entirely different City."

Kade didn't expect a reply so soon, but checked the writ weaves anyway. Radix must have been waiting because a fresh message had appeared in response to his own.

-br-variables-exceed-environment-query-new-input-sp-

Radix wants better access. Kade had always known it might become necessary, but he couldn't think of a way to let someone from outside into the system without alerting anyone or incriminating himself. He and Selica may be the facial recognition experts, but plenty of network engineers knew enough to watch for intrusions.

Selica rushed into the lab. He waved her over to his station unnecessarily as she was already making a beeline. "Selica! I did it!"

She looked confused.

"Radix!" He whispered. "He found my message. He responded."

"Kade! Shhhh!"

Did she just shush me? "Didn't you hear what I said?"

"We don't have time for that!"

What was her problem? Something was finally going their way. Sure, he'd presented some dumb ideas in the past and this hidden message thing had been a long shot, but it was a long shot that was paying off and he wanted a little credit. "That's it? You're just going to dismiss the option? We have to make this work!"

Selica pressed her lips into a firm line. She issued the hand signal that meant keep silent. Kade became instantly alert, scanning the room for threats. Two guards entered the lab followed by someone whom Kade had never met. That in itself was unusual. Villecrest permitted very few people near his pet project.

"May I have your attention, please?"

All eyes turned to the speaker.

"I am Second Anarch Kenric Trantor."

Kade glanced at Selica. She looked ill.

"It is my sad duty to inform you the Third Anarch is no longer among the living."

Kade couldn't believe his ears. Was it true? Could that monster really be dead? Or perhaps this was some new form of torment. A way to test loyalty. He was afraid to let himself hope. Selica's eyes locked onto his. They conveyed wonder, mixed with relief and possibly a little fear of what this change might mean. How would this affect their plans? Would it bring new opportunities for escape?

"I will be overseeing this operation until we can find an appropriate replacement."

Uh-oh, direct oversight from an anarch in higher authority than Villecrest? That doesn't bode well.

"Which one of you is Kade Brixton?"

Oh, no! Kade lifted his hand.

"Mr. Brixton, I understand we have you to thank for the facial recognition algorithm?"

"It was a team effort, sir."

"Oh, don't be so modest. I am aware that you cut your teeth on the technology while attending Denmount. You will make a fine instructor."

"Instructor, sir?"

"Unlike the Third Anarch, I am a prudent man, meticulous in my ways. I prefer contingency plans and redundant resources. This project offers nothing of the kind. That shortcoming will be rectified. I have a very experienced team of computational engineers on staff. You will teach them everything you know about the algorithm. You will show them every writ weave and explain each in detail. You will continue until I am satisfied that each and every person on my team is fluent."

Kade's eyes grew wider with each proclamation. He would become irrelevant very soon. The true purpose of his writ contagion would come to light. They would discover his messages to Leviticus.

The window of opportunity for receiving outside help was rapidly closing. They needed to escape, *now*, or they would find themselves in the same condition as Villecrest. An old poem drifted through his mind. *Twas only but a brief respite, we'll see you on the morrow.* Kade scowled at the grim turn of phrase. All he could say was, "As you wish, Second Anarch."

Chapter 67

Leviticus sat across from Beniti Abrax in his office. Recent events had him rattled and he was staring at nothing, as he tried to process the seemingly endless revelations. The world was nothing like he had thought. How does one move forward when nothing from the past seems relevant to the future?

"Leviticus, are you okay? I know this is a lot to take in." The Chief Sentry looked concerned.

Say something, Lev. "Chief Sentry, I — "

"Please, call me Beniti. I'm no longer your superior."

"Excuse me? I'm still a novice! Has the whole world gone mad? What am I saying? I don't even know what the real world is anymore! For all I know, that other place I saw in the bowels of this base is the real world and I'm a madman living out some deluded fantasy."

"You're as sane as anyone in this room, Leviticus."

"Then I don't know how to proceed. I have no context. What point of reference can I use to begin asking questions? Tell me what I need to know, so I can understand — anything."

Beniti exhaled loudly and rubbed his temples. "I don't suppose it would surprise you at this point to learn that the history you know is somewhat inaccurate."

"Somewhat? Oh, please, do go on. Recent events have already stripped away my sense of reality, what more do I have to lose?"

"Recorded history always portrays a bias to justify those who are in power. As a result, it is difficult to preserve a true record over time. Servators don't aspire to power. As a global, multi-national organization, we have a well-rounded view of events from many perspectives to provide checks and balances. We focus on identifying the failings of man. We stand apart, not glorifying any nation, but humbling all. For these reasons, our historical record is closer to the truth than any other. We're the keepers of truth from the days of the beginning."

"Oookay — so why are you telling me this?"

"You need to understand that what I am about to tell you is recorded truth, not a mythical tale. From your current perspective, you will likely find it difficult to take seriously."

"Let me be the judge of that."

"Very well. Sporadically, throughout history, individuals arise in times of great need. The Maker sends these arbiters to accomplish something that will bring about change. We call them the Levigators. For over seventeen hundred years, we have been waiting for the next Levigator. Now, here you are."

A nervous laugh escaped from Lev. "Okay, you got me! This is another test, right? A way to weed megalomaniacs out of the recruitment pool? I gotta say, I'm kind of relieved." *Why isn't he smiling?*

"I'm sorry, Levigator, but this isn't a joke."

"Yeah, don't call me that. My name is Leviticus, or better yet, just call me Lev."

Beniti cocked his head. "The similarity in name and title does seem like too much of a coincidence."

"Let's just take a few steps back, okay? I'm still trying to understand this whole Maker's Way thing. If recent events are any indicator, I'm failing miserably. If these Levigators even exist, or rather existed, I'm the last person the Maker would choose."

"Lev, No one knows what the Levigator will bring. Sometimes it's a sea change and other times it's a drop in the ocean. The scope of the change doesn't matter, only that it occurs."

"Fine, believe what you want. For now, can we just deal with some practical matters? Something I can wrap my head around? Like, where do we go from here? What does everyone expect from me?"

"All I know," Beniti began, "is that this changes everything.

To be continued in **Levigator – Dictates of the Servators Book: 2**

I hope you enjoyed reading Leviticus.

Visit my website https://www.kallensamuels.com and subscribe to the mailing list for information about new releases and exclusive content.

Don't miss the rest of the series:

Levigator – Dictates of the Servators: Book 2

Betrayals and shifting alliances among the Breachers incites the Second Anarch to accelerate his plans. A sudden increase in aggression places the Servators at a disadvantage as they struggle to address their growing vulnerability.

Separated by distance and circumstance, Leviticus's friends work in the background, proving themselves invaluable as they develop inventive new defensive measures that they hope will counter the looming threat.

As Leviticus masters his own unique abilities, he discovers a closely held secret. History is repeating itself on countless other worlds and one of them may provide a solution to the Breacher menace. Bearing a roadmap from the Chief Archivist, Leviticus sets out to find answers, but time is running out.

Leavening - Dictates of the Servators: Book 3

Chaos threatens the world as the Breachers gain ascendancy. Extermination of the Servators is well under way and the remnant gathers at their final refuge, prepared to make a last stand.

A small hope remains as Leviticus searches the journals of the Levigators. If he can reclaim the knowledge of his predecessors he might prevent disaster — his power means nothing if he can't find the answers he seeks.

Read on for a preview of the first chapter in the next book.

Levigator

Dictates of the Servators: Book 2

Chapter 1

Leviticus strode atop the rampart surrounding the old quarter of Ebot. He liked to come here to think. He needed time away from the expectant stares that followed him wherever he went. Since his encounter with that mysterious gateway, everyone at the base was acting strangely, fawning in his presence. The ancient buildings of Ebot's old quarter reminded him how insignificant he was, in the grand scheme of things. It grounded him.

Lev held no illusions of privacy. He could count several rangers keeping pace. They maintained a respectful distance while remaining close enough to come running to his aid if necessary. They moved with the practised ease of men familiar with such duty. It was the closest thing to privacy he could hope for.

The rampart widened in spots to create muster points. Over the years these had become food courts or rest areas. The city's architects transformed this particular spot into the famous hanging gardens of Ebot. This was was Lev's destination. As he approached, he veered in the direction of his favourite bench. Lev smiled at the irony. Another bench in a different part of the world had precipitated a dramatic change in his life. Now, he was heading toward his new favourite bench, to reflect on an even bigger life change. *What is it with me and benches anyway?* This particular bench faced an archway of flowering vines. It framed the view of an oasis some distance from the city wall and created the impression of a green path carving through arid dunes. Lev was disappointed to discover that someone had already claimed the bench. As he drew closer, his disappointment turned to surprise. A familiar voice answered his unspoken question.

"Beniti said I might find you here."

"Chief Sentry Vantos! What are you doing here?"

Cello motioned him to join her on the bench. "It's a mesmerizing view, I can see why you like to visit this spot. The whole world seems to fall away."

"It's my little escape," Lev admitted. "It's good to see you, Chief Sentry. Are you here on business?"

"Please, call me Cello."

Lev curled his lip. "You, too?"

Cello Shrugged. "It is the way of things. Actually, I'm here for *you*. Beniti thought you might appreciate a familiar face from home."

Lev wondered if he could call any place home these days. "I'm fine, you really didn't need to travel all this way."

"I wanted to come, Leviticus. Nico and Kayla had hoped to join me, but they have a possible lead on the person responsible for the murder of Nico's parents. They didn't want the trail to get cold."

"That's good." Lev nodded. "Nico needs closure."

"Nico is coming into his own. He's very much like his father." Cello smiled fondly. "He's good for Kayla. I don't think I've ever seen her so happy."

"I could say the same about Kayla's influence," Lev added. "Nico seems whole now, and it's because of her presence in his life. Kayla makes him very happy."

Cello patted Lev's arm. "And they would say you've been a very good friend to them both. It's important to have friends you can rely on."

"I wish I could see them more often, but..." Lev shrugged. "You'll give them my well wishes when you see them again?"

"Of course. They send their greetings as well. I want to assure you that they're doing fine. I hope it will relieve you of any concern for their welfare. You have more than enough on your plate without having to worry about friends or family."

That's an understatement, Lev thought. He had been proclaimed 'Levigator', a title that came with authority he wasn't comfortable wielding. Lev considered the many people he'd already placed in danger. Kayla had lost her career as a result of saving him from a Breacher planned abduction. That action led to the abandonment of the Servator base beneath Denmount. Tark, a ranger and friend, had been stabbed in the shoulder trying to protect him. Even Kade

Brixton, his school nemesis, found himself a captive of the Breachers. Their original plan was to abduct him, but they grabbed Kade as an alternative. *Disaster follows me and still, I'm asked to lead.* Like everything in his life these days, he hadn't been offered a choice in the matter.

"Speaking of family," Cello continued, "your parents are also doing well. I have rangers checking in on them regularly. The agents pose as employees of InnovaMech, the company providing your cover story. A weekly payment is delivered to your parents' home. The company subsidizes families of employees who work abroad. I'm sure your family would appreciate the inclusion of a personal note, on occasion. It helps to keep up appearances. If you have anything you'd like to send home, just bring it to the InnovaMech office here in Ebot. They'll see to its delivery."

"That's very generous. Thank you for keeping an eye on them. I do have a copy of a Kemetican recipe that I think my mother would enjoy. I'll pen a note to include with it and have it delivered to InnovaMech."

"That would be perfect. Your parents will be happy to hear from you." Cello leaned forward tilting her head and looking up into his face. When she caught his attention, she asked, "And how are *you* holding up, Leviticus?"

Lev grunted. "In a few short months, I've discovered that an ancient, clandestine organization lives in an underground base below my home town. I've seen technology that shouldn't exist. I've learned that my abnormal brain is actually a gift more powerful than I could imagine. I've been drafted into the Servator cause and I can't tell anyone from my past or go back to my former existence. My life has been in constant upheaval. I hoped by now I'd have a better grasp of my situation. I thought I could settle into this new life, but I have no idea what I'm doing. In truth, I have even less of an idea now, than when this all began. For a short time, at least, I had instructors teaching me things. People would explain what my role might be, but now...."

"You still have access to those resources Leviticus."

"Sure, but those relationships have all changed. Now, I'm this so-called *Levigator*, whatever that means. I'm treated like a commander when I don't even know what it means to be a Servator. My instructors, and those of higher rank, tiptoe in my presence. They preface every answer with hesitant caution. My *mentors* worry they'll limit my potential by inserting a personal bias. That, I'm told, might interfere with the will of the Maker. They refuse to help me understand what the Maker's *will* might be. I ask for more guidance and I'm offered less. They give me freedom to do or say *anything*, without the context to make such decisions."

"They don't know what you should, or will do Leviticus. There hasn't been a Levigator for..."

"Seventeen hundred years, yes I know. Surely someone as familiar with the histories as you, could venture a guess. I have spent less than a year with the Servators, but have been granted keys to the kingdom. If I told rangers to turn themselves over to Breachers, would they do it?"

"They might," Cello admitted.

"That's insane. That's — that's terrifying!"

"Leviticus, I can't begin to guess what you're going through."

"No. Don't do that! It's not helpful. This isn't the same as when someone loses a loved one. There are no feelings to consider here. I need practical knowledge, if I'm to be of any value. I'm not the type of person who can blithely make uninformed decisions. I agonize over detail. It's part of my *gift*, or call it a curse if you prefer."

"Sometimes, you're asked to make a decision that has no obvious solution," Cello noted. "Perhaps it simply requires faith."

"Then I need to know *that*!" Lev insisted. "I need to know what former Levigators have done and what we've learned from those actions. I need to know what events preceded the arrival of previous Levigators. I need to know the outcomes — I need to analyze the..."

Lev stiffened. *The patterns. It's my gift. I need to analyze the patterns.*

"Leviticus? Are you alright?"

"Yes — yes, I think so. Do you mind answering a few questions without worrying about how it may influence me?"

"I'll try."

"What does *Levigator* mean?"

"A Levigator is something or someone that alleviates burden and smooths the way. In your case, someone."

Lev cocked his head. "In order to do that, a Levigator would need to know what the burden is, wouldn't they? Surely pointing me in the general direction of the problem won't create a bias will it?"

Cello smiled. "I suppose not."

"I need you to explain that to Chief Sentry Abrax."

Leviticus was overcome with a wave of relief. He'd felt adrift and didn't know how to express his concern. Cello had helped him to frame his thoughts. Now, he saw a way to get what he needed from his mentors. It was a start.

"Thank you, Chief Sentry Van — I mean, Cello. I'm glad you came. You've already helped more than you know. I hope you can stay a little while longer. I have a few more questions."

The story continues in **Levigator** - Dictates of the Servators: Book 2